BY ANNA QUINDLEN

FICTION

*Miller's Valley*
*Still Life with Bread Crumbs*
*Every Last One*
*Rise and Shine*
*Blessings*
*Black and Blue*
*One True Thing*
*Object Lessons*

NONFICTION

*Lots of Candles, Plenty of Cake*
*Good Dog, Stay*
*Being Perfect*
*Loud and Clear*
*A Short Guide to a Happy Life*
*How Reading Changed My Life*
*Thinking Out Loud*
*Living Out Loud*

BOOKS FOR CHILDREN

*Happily Ever After*
*The Tree That Came to Stay*

# Miller's
# Valley

# Miller's Valley

A NOVEL

*Anna Quindlen*

RANDOM HOUSE
NEW YORK

Published in the United States by Random House, an imprint and division of Penguin Random House LLC, New York.

RANDOM HOUSE and the HOUSE colophon are registered trademarks of Penguin Random House LLC.

LIBRARY OF CONGRESS CATALOGING-IN-PUBLICATION DATA
Quindlen, Anna.
Miller's Valley / Anna Quindlen.
pages ; cm
ISBN 978-0-8129-9608-1
ebook ISBN 978-0-8129-9609-8
1. Girls—Fiction.   2. Farm life—Fiction.
3. Domestic fiction.   I. Title.
PS3567.U336M55 2016
813'.54—dc23
2015025157

Printed in the United States of America on acid-free paper

randomhousebooks.com

9  8  7  6  5  4  3  2  1

First Edition

Book design by Caroline Cunningham

Illustration by Gustavo Garcia

*For my mother and father*

*Blessed forever in both*

Perhaps home is not a place but simply an irrevocable condition.

—JAMES BALDWIN

# Miller's
# Valley

# Prologue

It was a put-up job, and we all knew it by then. The government people had hearings all spring to solicit the views of residents on their plans. That's what they called it, soliciting views, but every last person in Miller's Valley knew that that just meant standing behind the microphones set up in the aisle of the middle school, and then finding out afterward that the government people would do what they planned to do anyhow. Everybody was just going through the motions. That's what people do. They decide what they want and then they try to make you believe you want it, too.

Donald's grandfather was at every meeting, his hands shaking as he held some sheets of loose-leaf he'd been reading from so long that they were furred along the edges. He carried a big file with him everywhere, even when he went to the diner for breakfast. Early on he'd switched out the original file for the accordion kind because the first one got too full. But it was full of the kind of stuff old guys pull together, newspaper clippings with uneven edges, carbon copies of letters ten years old, even the occasional sales receipt for a sump pump or a new well, as though someone was going to be inclined to pay him for all the years he'd spent fighting the water. I always wondered if they wrote him off because his name was Elmer. The government people talked a lot about the future. Elmer was such an old guy's name, a piece of the past.

"The best we can do is make sure we get as much as we can out of the bastards," Donald's grandfather said at what turned out to be the next-to-last meeting.

"There's no need for that, Elmer," my mother said. She meant the profanity. She was as interested as the next person in milking the government for money. A lifetime working in hospitals had shown her the wisdom, and the ease, of that. She was upright but not stupid.

My mother was a person of stature in Miller's Valley. She'd lived there all her life. Her mother had raised her and her younger sister, Ruth, in a one-story three-room house at the edge of the valley with a pitted asphalt roof and a falling-down porch, and when she'd married my father and become a Miller she'd moved to his family's farm, right at the center of the valley, in its lowest place, where the fog lay thick as cotton candy on damp mornings. She was a Miller of Miller's Valley, and so was I. People thought my mother could take care of just about anything. So did I, then.

The government people were all job titles instead of proper names. They dealt out thick business cards with embossed seals; we found them in our pockets and purses long after there was any point to it. There were geologists and engineers and a heavyset woman with a sweet smile who was there to help people relocate after the government took their houses. A resettlement counselor, they called her. She had the softest hands I'd ever felt, pink and moist, and when she'd come toward my mother, her hands like little starfish in the air, my mother would move in the opposite direction. It's hard to explain to kids today, with everybody touching each other all the time, kissing people who are more or less strangers, hugging the family doctor at the end of a visit, but my mother wasn't a huggie person, and neither were most of her friends and neighbors. "She can just forget about patting me, that one" is what she always said about the resettlement counselor.

I felt kind of sorry for the woman. It was her job to make it sound as though one place to live was just as good as another, just as good as the place you'd brought your babies home to from the hospital fifty years before, just as good as the place where your parents had died and, in a few cases that you could tell made the government people really uncomfortable, were buried. They could make moving to a new house with a nice dry basement sound like a good deal, but there was no way they could put a pretty face on digging up a coffin that went into the ground before the First World War.

When people would talk about the government's plans, at the hospital, in the market, someone would always say, "Can they really do that?" The answer was yes. "They can do what they want," my mother said, and when she did, Donald's grandfather held his file in front of him like a shield and said, "Miriam, I don't think you understand the situation." But that wasn't true. My mother always understood the situation. Any situation.

"I figure by my breathing I'll be gone by Sunday," she said years later when she was dying, and she was right on schedule.

At all the meetings they handed out little pamphlets with a drawing on the front of people walking around the edge of what looked like a big lake. There were sailboats, too, and a woman behind a motorboat on water skis with one arm held up in the air. Inside the pamphlet said, "Flood control, water supply, hydroelectric power, and recreation: these are the advantages of water management in your area!" On the back it said, "A bright future through progress." It's a wiggly word, *progress:* a two-lane gravel road turned into four lanes paved that makes life a noisy misery for the people with houses there, a cornfield turned into a strip mall with a hair salon, a supermarket, and a car wash. Corn's better than a car wash. We washed our own cars with a garden hose until our kids got old enough to do it for us.

My eldest nephew, the smart one, did a project once about Miller's Valley, and he interviewed me one afternoon. "Why didn't you fight?" he said.

I understand. He's young. Things seem simple when you're young. I remember. I'm not like some older people who forget.

There were people who fought, although there were fewer and fewer of them as the years went by. Donald's grandfather had printed up bumper stickers and buttons and tried to get people riled up, but there weren't that many people to begin with in the valley, and by the time it was all over there were hardly any at all.

I may have been the only person living in Miller's Valley who had read all the geologists' reports, looked over all the maps, knew what was really going on. Somewhere there's an aerial photograph taken before I was even born, and if any reasonable person looked at it, at the dam and the course of the river and the unused land and the number of houses involved, they'd conclude that there was a big low area just begging to be filled in with water. I'd seen that photograph when I was seventeen, sitting in a government office with gray walls and metal furniture, looking at the center point of that big low area, at the roof of our house. I knew better than anyone what the deal was. When I was a kid I'd play in the creek, stack up stones and sticks and watch the water back up behind them, until finally it filled a place that had been dry before. The difference is that with a real dam, sometimes the place that fills up with water has houses and churches and farms. I saw a picture once of a big reservoir behind a dam in Europe that had a church steeple sticking up on one side during a dry spell.

That's what they meant when they talked about water management, the government people, except that we didn't have a steeple high enough in the valley to stick up and remind people that there had once been a place where the water would be. A bright future through progress. There was just a handful of us in the way.

Everyone was waiting for my mother to fight, although no one ever said that. Everyone was waiting for her to say that they couldn't do this, take 6,400 acres of old family farms and small ramshackle homes and turn it into a reservoir by using the dam to divert the river. Everyone was waiting for her to say that they couldn't just disappear our lives, put a smooth dark ceiling of water over everything as though we had never plowed, played, married, died, lived in Miller's Valley. It wasn't just that my mother had lived in the valley, had dealt with the water, her whole life long. It wasn't just that she was the kind of person who preferred to solve her problems by herself, not have some people come in from outside in suits and ties and work shoes that weren't work shoes at all, to handle things for her and her neighbors.

It was that she was someone, Miriam Miller. There are just some people like that. Everyone pays attention to what they say, even if they don't even know them well or like them much.

My mother went to every meeting the government people held, but she never spoke, and when people would try to talk to her before or after she was polite but no more, asking after their children or their arthritis but never saying a word about the plans to drown Miller's Valley. I drove up from the city for that one meeting at the church, even though she said there was no need for me to miss school or work, even though my desk was piled high with things that needed to be done. I guess I did it because I'd been there from the very beginning years before, when I was a kid selling corn from a card table outside of our barn, when the talk about turning Miller's Valley into a reservoir first began, when no one really thought it would amount to anything.

It's so easy to be wrong about the things you're close to. I know that now. I learned that then.

When the meeting was over my mother and I drove home together down the dark back roads to the farm, and as I took the curves fast, curves I'd been taking since I'd gripped the wheel of the truck while sitting on my father's lap, she stared out the window so that the sickly green of the dashboard dials just touched the corner of her set jaw.

"You do understand this, right?" I'd said. "If this goes through they'll take the house and the barn and the little house. If this happens you'll have to move. You'll have to pack up all your stuff. You'll have to find a place for Aunt Ruth and pack up all her stuff. You'll have to find a way to get her out of there. Then it's going to be like none of it ever existed. They're going to put the whole place under forty feet of water."

"I'm not stupid, Mary Margaret," my mother said. The night was so quiet you could hear the wood doves comforting themselves with their own soft voices in the fields.

"If this happens they're going to make the valley just disappear," I said, my voice harsh in the silence.

A deer ran through my headlights like a ghost, and I slowed down because, like my father always said, there's almost never just one. Sure enough, two more skittered out. They froze there, staring, then moved on. I was ready to start talking again when my mother spoke.

"Let them," she said. "Let the water cover the whole damn place."

I grew up to the sound of my parents talking in the kitchen on my mother's nights off, and the sound of the sump pump when it rained. Sometimes, all these years later, I wake up in the middle of the night and think I hear one or the other, the faint pounding of the throttle or the murmur of those two low voices. On a wet night the best I could ever make out was a little muttering even if my mother and father were talking loud. If you properly maintain it, and my father did, a sump pump makes a throaty chug-a-chug noise, sort of like a train without the whistle. My brother Tommy always said he liked the sound, but I think it was because it meant he could sneak out at night without anyone hearing. My mother didn't mind it because her shift work meant she was hardly ever at home at night, and so tired when she got home that nothing kept her awake.

My room was in the back corner of the house, right over where the sump pump sat on the cement basement floor two stories below. From the window in my room you could see the path up to the back end of the property and the lights through the trees of my aunt Ruth's house. She kept at least one light on all

night long. I liked looking out and seeing that light in the darkness, something that had always been there, that I could count
on. It was real quiet most of the time around our house at night,
so quiet that sometimes I could tell what Aunt Ruth was watching on television because I could hear the theme song of *The
Dick Van Dyke Show.*

There was a heating vent right behind the head of my bed,
and if you followed it down it stopped at the heating vent behind
the kitchen table before it ended up at the old cast-iron furnace
in the basement. When I was five I thought my room was haunted
because just as I was dropping off to sleep I would hear a moan-
ing sound underneath my bed. Years later my brother Eddie told
me that Tommy had put his mouth to the vent and made the
noise and Eddie made him stop when he caught him, and all of
that made sense, including Eddie saying he hadn't mentioned any
of it to our parents.

The thing was, listening to my parents through that vent was
like a bad radio broadcast, one of those where you've got a song
on you really like but it's from fifty miles away and it drifts in
and out and you have to fill in the gaps by singing along. I was
good at filling in the gaps when my parents talked, and I probably heard a lot I shouldn't have. If it had been LaRhonda listening, the whole town would have known, too. You could close
that heating vent with a little chain at one corner, and I always
did when LaRhonda slept over. But the rest of the time I paid attention to whatever I managed to hear.

She's got cancer in that breast, my mother might say.

That'll be hard on Bernie, my father would say.

Bernie? It'll be hard on her, is who it'll be hard on. From what
I hear Bernie has plenty of female companionship.

Gossip, my father would say. Then silence, and I would fall
asleep.

Or, That baby is going right into the state hospital, no questions asked, my mother might say.

That's a sad thing, my father would say.

Sadder to keep it at home, my mother would say.

Guess so, my father would say. She was always sure of things. He almost never was, except maybe about the government people and their plans for Miller's Valley. Over the years there was a lot of talk about that at night in the kitchen.

Talked to Bob Anderson yesterday, my mother might say.

Got no business with a real estate agent, my father replied.

Asking for you, my mother said.

Fine right where I am, my father said.

Clattering pans in the sink. Tap running.

Why I even bother, my mother said.

"Meems, you up?" Tommy whispered, pushing open the door. When he wanted to he could move through the house like a ghost, even when he was drunk. Maybe especially when he was drunk.

"How come you're home?" I said, sitting up against the headboard.

Not listening to one more word on the subject, said my father.

"Oh, man, not again," said Tommy. He sat down on the edge of my bed and canted his head toward the vent so that a piece of hair fell down on his forehead. It was confusing, having a good-looking brother. I tried not to think of him that way, but LaRhonda wouldn't shut up about it.

"What are they talking about?" I said. "Who's Bob Anderson?"

"Did the water department guy stop by here today?"

"Who?"

"Did some guy in a Chevy sedan come by to see Pop?"

"There's somebody who came by and had some kind of business card from the state. Donald says he talked to his grandfather, too. He says he went to the Langers' house and some other places."

"That's what they're talking about, then. The damn dam."

"Mr. Langer says that all the time," I said.

"Yeah, that's the problem for sure. The old guys say that when they built the dam, when they were all kids, there was a big fight about it. They figure now they put it in the wrong place, or the water's in the wrong place, or something. They want to flood the whole valley out." And both of us looked out toward the light in Ruth's window.

"What about us?" I said.

I knew about the dam. It was named after President Roosevelt, but the one with the mustache and the eyeglasses, not the one with the Scottie dog and the wife with the big teeth. We'd gone to the dam on a field trip. The guide told us it was made out of concrete and was for flood control, which didn't make sense because we had flooding in the valley all the time. A lot of the kids were bored by the description of cubic feet and gallons, but we all perked right up when the guide said four workers had died building the dam. Our teacher said she wasn't sure we needed to know that.

It was probably hard for people to believe, but we didn't pay that much attention to the river, even though it was so big and so close and had a big strong arm that ran through the center of the valley. They called that Miller's Creek because years ago it had been just a narrow little run of water, but once the dam went in it turned into something much bigger than that. I'd spent a lot of time around creeks when I was younger, looking for minnows and crayfish, and that was no creek.

It was mainly out-of-town people who went to the river. The current was too strong for swimming, and it was nicer at Pride's Beach, which was a stretch of trucked-in sand on one side of the lake south of town. The fishing was better in the streams in the valley, although you had to be pretty good at fly casting to get around the overhanging branches.

There was a loud grinding sound through the vent, two wooden chairs pushed against the surface of my mother's chapped linoleum. "Oh, man," Tommy whispered. "You got matches?"

"Why would I have matches?"

Tommy sighed. "I had plenty of matches when I was your age."

"Shut up!" I said, and "shhh," Tommy said. My parents passed by on the way to their room. "I can't ever keep track of where he is or what he's doing," my mother said, and in the moonlight I saw Tom waggle his eyebrows. Both of us knew our parents were talking about him.

Ever since he'd finished high school my brother had been at a loose end. At least that's what my aunt Ruth called it, a loose end. It's not like school had been so great, either: unlike Eddie, who was class valedictorian, Tommy had always been a rotten student. Maybe he had one of those problems they didn't figure out until later, which I see now all the time, a learning disability or dyslexia or something. He had handwriting so bad that there was no one who could read it. Even he couldn't make it out sometimes. The only tests in high school where he had a fighting chance were true and false, although even there he occasionally made an *F* that looked too much like a *T*. He'd squeaked by, but at the time it didn't feel like it mattered much; when he strode across the gym and hoisted his diploma, the cheers were louder than they'd been at the end of the class president's speech.

But then he was out in the world and found it hard to make a living with nothing but his easy ways. He would have been great at politics; instead he'd worked in a car repair place. But he lost his license for six months after he got popped on Main Street late one night speeding, with open beer cans in the car and a girl throwing up out the window; the police officer who stopped him was the father of the girl, and when he looked in the driver's side window it was easy to see that his daughter wasn't wearing any pants. Tommy'd met the girl because her uncle owned the car repair place, so he was twice cursed. A lot of what Tommy got into seemed like a story someone was telling, except that it was true.

He worked around the farm, too, but he made my father crazy. "He's a careless person," my father would say, not even checking whether Tommy was around to hear him. "I ask him to move some hay and two days later I find a pitchfork rusting by the rain barrel."

"Tell the old man I went to get gas for the tractors," Tommy'd say to me, and then he'd disappear for a couple of hours. "You seen your brother?" my father would say, and I'd open my mouth and he'd say, "Don't tell me he's out getting gas again because both those tractors are full." I didn't have a face for lying. "Just stand behind me," LaRhonda always said when we had to lie to her mother.

"You got any money?" Tom whispered after he'd heard my mother go from the bathroom back into her bedroom.

"No," I said, but he kept on staring at me, and finally I said, "Seven bucks."

"I'll pay you back," Tommy said.

"You never pay me back."

He shoved the bills in his pocket, pushed back the shock of hair on his forehead, slid around my door and was gone. I never even heard a car start up. The sump pump was thumping again. That always made it harder to hear Tommy's getaway.

I'd made that seven dollars selling corn. For an eleven-year-old girl it felt like real money. I sat behind a card table by the road on late summer days, sometimes alone, usually with LaRhonda and Donald. It was boring, but it was something to do, although pretty much every day was like the day before. A car stopped, and a woman waved out the window. "How much?" she asked. Her hair was set in pin curls. She had a scarf over them, but the row right around her face wasn't covered and the bobby pins sparked in the harsh August light.

"A nickel an ear," I said. "Thirteen in a dozen."

"I think they're cheaper down the road," the woman said, rubbing at her head. I don't know why pin curls make your head itch, but they do.

"Then go down the road," LaRhonda said under her breath. She had a mouth on her almost from the time she learned to talk.

Donald carried the paper bag to the car. "Thank you, ma'am," he said. The woman handed him a dollar and said, "Keep the change." I gave him a dime from the can, gave LaRhonda another, and put twenty cents in the breast pocket of my plaid cotton shirt.

The shirt had been Tommy's. I got a lot of Tommy and Eddie's clothes, which was made even worse because they were so much older than I was and so the clothes weren't just boys' clothes, they weren't even fashionable boys' clothes. That summer Donald wore a kind of collarless shirt with three buttons in front that I'd never seen before and that I was sure was fashionable, although that was about the last thing Donald cared about. His mother lived in a halfway decent-size city. His father was a shadowy figure. Donald spent a lot of time in Miller's Valley. Visiting, he always called it, but he did it so often and so long that it practically counted as living there. I always felt a little lonesome, the times when he went back home, if that's what it was.

"Dump that poor boy on his grandparents whenever she cares to," I'd heard my mother say through the heating vent. "Her carrying on." I hoped her carrying on wasn't what it sounded like.

LaRhonda was wearing white patent leather shoes with a strap and a very slight heel with her pink shorts and shirt. Her white feet were rubbed red all around, her heels swaddled in Band-Aids over blisters. Most days she was limping by nightfall and her mother would want to soak her feet in Epsom salts and she would say, "Like somebody's grandmother?" and limp off to bed. LaRhonda's mother had been wheedled into buying those shoes for her Easter outfit, and LaRhonda took them off only when she put on her flowered shorty pajamas.

I wore Tommy's old pajamas, too. The worst thing was, all the boys' old clothes fit because I was narrow and sharp-shouldered, more or less built like a boy. I was a straight person, legs, nose, hair, everything long and narrow, up and down. I more or less always would be. When I got older the way I looked came into fashion, but by that time I was past caring. But when I was a kid wearing my brothers' clothes the way I looked was a trial, as my aunt Ruth called things that bothered her. "I won't listen to complaining about what's on your back, Mary Margaret," my mother said. "There's too many fences need mending around here." I remember first finding the expression "mending fences" in a book and being confused because I couldn't think of it as anything but literal. Cows get antsy, or randy, or just stumble sideways, and a section of fence comes tumbling down, and they trudge out onto the road, and you have to fix the fence fast or more cows will follow, and maybe get hit by a truck driven by someone not paying attention. Happens all the time.

My father was a farmer, although I guess that's not what the neighbors would tell you. They would have told you that Bud Miller fixed things for a living. A fix-it man, they used to call it, when things still got fixed instead of just junked. If you had a radio that stopped working, or a fan that didn't turn anymore, you brought it to the little square lean-to stuck like an afterthought to one side of the smaller barn, the one where we kept the feed corn, and you left it with my dad. If he wasn't there you just put it on the workbench with a note. I was always pretty amazed that my father could work out the problem from those notes. They usually said things like "Buzzing noise." If your problem was too big to be portable, a washing machine, say, or even a front-end loader, my dad would come to you, climbing out of the truck slowly because his knees had hurt ever since high school football and only got worse as he got older.

My mother was a nurse. When I was a kid she would leave after dinner and be back in the morning just in time to make sure my brothers and me got on the bus for school, especially Tommy, who usually had a bunch of ideas for the day better than sitting through geometry and civics. She wore a white uniform with a name tag that said MIRIAM MILLER RN. Her name had been Miriam Kostovich, and she was happy to become Miriam Miller, which made her sound a little like she was a movie star. Most of her shift we were asleep, so it was like she hardly left at all.

"You think your mom will take us to town for Popsicles?" LaRhonda asked, rubbing her thumb over Franklin D. Roosevelt's profile on the dime, but she was just winding me up. She knew the answer was no. My mother was thrifty. I wouldn't be getting any white patent shoes until I had a job and could pay for them myself, and even then she would say it was a waste and I should put it all in a passbook account. There was nothing my mother liked more than a passbook account.

My mother was a nurse and my father was a fix-it man. But if they'd ever applied for passports, which they never did, where it asked for profession they probably would have written "farmer," or at least he would have. There were 160 acres of flat, sometimes wet land around our house; it had belonged to my father's father, and his mother's family before that, bouncing back and forth from one side of the family tree to the other. When my father put in a new stove for my mother, when I was eight, he found a limestone lintel in one corner of the wall that had 1822 carved into it as crude as a kid's printing.

My parents had some beef cattle, black and white, and one field planted with hay to feed them, and another planted with feed corn to feed them, too, and another planted with bicolor corn that we sold from the card table in front of the barn, mid-July to September.

"There's no money in it," my father used to say about farming, mainly to get my brothers to stay in school, although he wanted at least one of them to take the place over when he was done. Every once in a while the cows got sold while I sat on a hay bale in the barn, sobbing—"How many times do I have to tell you not to name them?" my father always said—and the sale price barely covered the cost of feed, never mind the hours my father put in in a dark frigid barn before sunrise, filling the troughs while the barn kittens scattered before his boots like dandelion fluff. Our bills got paid with the paycheck from the hospital and the creased dollars a housewife would take out of her expenses tin after my father replaced a part in her old refrigerator. The money in the rusty Maxwell House can where I put the bills after people paid for corn never made much of a contribution, and half the time Tommy would take it, passing by on the way to his rotting convertible and one-handing the can onto his palm, like he was in a big city and stealing a wallet from a tourist.

"I'm telling," I would yell, but he'd wink and rev his engine so the tailpipe made a sound like a wet tuba. He'd always loved the summer. The principal never called the house in summer to say Tom Miller hadn't bothered to show up for school.

"Your brothers are cute," LaRhonda said, and Donald made a retching noise. He didn't like LaRhonda much more than she liked him, but he wasn't as mean about it.

"Both of them?" I said.

"Well, Tommy. Eddie's pretty good-looking, but he always looks at me like I'm in trouble."

"You're in trouble a lot of the time," Donald said.

"You don't even really live around here, so how would you know, Duckface?"

My mother said LaRhonda was jealous of Donald, because she thought of herself as my best friend but could tell I liked Donald, too, and maybe more. My mother said LaRhonda was the kind of girl who wouldn't understand having a boy as a friend. But I thought it was more that LaRhonda didn't know what to make of Donald. Donald's personality was like vanilla ice cream, and LaRhonda was like that weird Neapolitan kind, with the layers of strawberry and vanilla and chocolate, that turned a tan color when it melted in your bowl and you made ice cream soup. Sometimes Donald lived around us and sometimes he didn't. He'd be at school with us for a year or two, living with his grandparents at the far end of the valley, and then he'd go back to living with his mother and disappear for a while and I'd almost forget his face. But I'd always feel like something was missing. Sometimes I thought of him and LaRhonda as sort of like the angel and devil that sat on someone's shoulder in the cartoons. She was always talking and always picking at me, and he was mostly quiet but nice when he did say something. I was working away at the corn table, coloring in the raised flowers on my mother's paper napkins with crayons. LaRhonda said, "That's dumb." Donald said, "That's pretty." That was those two in a nutshell, as my aunt Ruth liked to say.

"I wish I had a brother," LaRhonda added as Tommy pulled away with the squeal of tires that was his trademark. It wasn't true. If Donald had said he wanted a brother I would have believed it, but I'd never known anyone as cut out to be an only child as LaRhonda. "Or a sister," she added. I said nothing. I figured I was never going to get a sister, but I'd never wanted one after seeing my mother and her sister Ruth together or, more often, apart. There didn't seem to be any upside.

Another car pulled over. A man in a seersucker suit got out. We all three knew he was not from around here, since we'd never seen him before and because he got out of the car. People who came for corn asked for it through the window, and people who needed things fixed took the gravel drive back to my dad's shed.

"Hello, ladies," said the man. He was bald and his head glistened with beads of sweat. We were so quiet you could hear the big insects and small birds. The year before there'd been a man in town who drove around asking girls for directions with a map on his lap. When they got close to the car he lifted the map. "Hello, Mr. Pickle," I heard Tommy saying when he talked about it to two of his friends, all three of them laughing, but my mother just told me if a man asked for directions to send him to the nearest filling station and not to get too near the car. I said I was going to have to get close enough for him to hear me. "Everything's an argument with you," my mother said, ironing my father's church shirt. Which wasn't really fair, or true. I was just a person who stated the facts.

"I don't know if my mom's home," I said. LaRhonda stepped on the toe of my Keds. "Mimi," she said, on the lookout for perverts.

"I'm sure your mother is a lovely lady, but I'm here to see Mr. Miller," he said. "Maybe you can give him this." He took a card from his wallet. It said his name was Winston Bally, and he worked for some state office with a long name.

"Not this again," my father said when he looked at it, but he came out and led the man back to his shed.

"He came to see my grandfather, too," Donald said. "About the water."

"What about the water?" said LaRhonda, who didn't live in Miller's Valley, or not really. The town was called Miller's Valley but the real valley was just outside it, a deep pocket with steep stony hills rising around it and a divot at one end that led to the winding road that led to the town itself.

"My grandfather says there's a problem with the aquifer." Donald said the word *aquifer* as though he liked saying it but might not really know what it meant.

LaRhonda spun her dime on the card table. You could tell she didn't think much of the water as an issue. Neither did I. Sometimes mud oozed down the hill during a downpour and wound up on our porch and my mother had to chase it out again with a push broom, and sometimes the basement flooded, which was why we had kept all the important old stuff, like my mother's nursing school diploma and my father's Army uniform, in the attic. Sometimes our water was brown and my mother boiled it and put it in an old Hi-C bottle in the refrigerator, and twice our well had failed and the well diggers had to go farther down. My brother Eddie stood there the first time, saying to our father again and again, "How can there be so much water sometimes, and then not enough?"

Eddie was the glory of Miller's Valley. He was at the state university, on a Rotary scholarship, studying to be an engineer. He wanted to be called Ed now. He belonged to the national science honor society and had a girlfriend named Debbie, whose father was a lawyer in Philadelphia. When she came to stay I got the couch and she got my room. It smelled of Jean Naté bath oil after she was gone, like warm lemonade. Eddie was ten years older than me, and he didn't exactly seem like a brother, not like Tommy did. He was more like a friendly visitor.

"Can I get some corn?" yelled Mr. Brown, who lived down the road, as though he'd been waiting forever even though his car had scarcely stopped moving. Twice that one summer he'd come back the next day with one of those odd ears you get sometimes, the ones where the kernels don't run in a straight line, like somebody with bad teeth. "I want my money back on this one," he'd said. My mother came out of the house the second time. "We'll be happy to give you a refund, Bob, but if we do it'll be the last time you buy corn from us," she said.

Winston Bally didn't stay long. "Nice talking to you," he said to my father as he came back to his car, but you could see the feeling wasn't mutual. My father was standing in the doorway of his shed with his arms crossed on his chest and his chin down.

"I'm going," said LaRhonda, getting on her bike. Her father's diner was only two miles away, and she'd get a ride home from there. When I went in there with LaRhonda we could have anything we wanted free: a cheeseburger, lemon meringue pie, Mason Mints from the candy bin by the register. It felt rich.

"I don't know why she calls me Duckface," Donald said, fingering his upper lip. I would have felt sorry for him except that he was so good-natured that lots of times he didn't even recognize meanness when it was coming right at him. Plus when I looked at how tall and square-shouldered he was turning out to be, I thought he might be one of those guys in high school who played a couple of sports. No matter what those guys were like, things went okay for them.

I stayed at the table for two more hours, coloring some more napkins, reading Nancy Drew, and watching a green caterpillar do tricks on a strand of shiny silk from a big oak branch above my head. Sometimes I went out into the cornfield and walked between the rows with my eyes closed, pretending I was blind, feeling the stalks reaching out to brush me like a pat on the back. But it was too hot for that. LaRhonda swore there was one summer when it got so hot the corn started to pop in its silk, and Donald said that was a lie, and I didn't say anything. You couldn't pay attention when LaRhonda said things like that.

My mother opened the side door a little after five o'clock. "Anybody who's buying corn for dinner bought it already," she said. She was balancing a plate on one hand with a pot lid on top of it. "Take your aunt her dinner," she said.

I was so used to the sump pump that it was more likely to wake me when it went off than when it came on. It was off when my mother woke me that Saturday night. At first I thought it was Sunday morning and she was waking me for church, so I made a noise, a groan and a whine combined. I'd grown four inches in less than a year between my twelfth and thirteenth birthdays, and my legs hurt all the time. The doctor said they were just growing pains. My mother said if I shaved my legs before I turned sixteen I'd be cleaning the bathroom on Saturday for the rest of my life. We only had one bathroom but I wasn't taking any chances. The hair on my legs wasn't that dark anyway, not like LaRhonda's. She had a pink electric shaver she'd gotten for Christmas.

"Up," my mother said, pulling on my arm, hard. "Get your waders on." I couldn't really figure what was going on, so I stood up and started to arrange the flowered coverlet on my twin bed, but she shook her head. "Now," she said.

My mother had two rules: no leaving your room without making your bed, and no leaving your room unless you were dressed. She and Tommy were always fighting about what amounted to making a bed, and what amounted to being dressed. I was leaving my room in my pajamas, my bed all tumbled, so I knew something bad was happening. I couldn't smell smoke and I couldn't hear the sump pump and I knew that if something had happened to Tommy even my mother would be emotional. All I could hear was the sound of rain. It sounded like a truck was dumping a load of gravel on the roof. It had been raining hard for two days, but nothing like this.

The front door was open, and just outside it was one of the volunteer firemen in a black slicker. There were a couple of inches of water in our front hallway, so that the runner looked like it was going to float up and down like the magic carpet in the cartoons.

"Hurry up," my mother said, handing me my waders. And to the fireman, "My sister's back in the house up the drive."

"She won't budge, Mrs. Miller!" he yelled over the sound of water. "She's up in the attic, and when I stuck my head up those stairs she let out a scream. I tried to calm her down but she says she's not leaving."

"Let me go up there," my father said. "She'll listen to me."

"No you don't," my mother said. "No you don't. If she wants to behave this way she can drown." I started to sniffle, but my father heard me and put his hand on my head. "Your mother's just blowing smoke," he said. The water was lapping at the steps.

"Let me try," I said.

"We got to get going," said the firefighter.

"I need my slicker," I said. My mother took it from the hook and put it on me carefully, the way she had sometimes when I was heading to the bus, going to kindergarten. She bent and zipped it up the way she had then, too.

"Go ahead," she said, she and my father standing halfway up the hall steps. I ran back and threw my arms around my father's legs the way I used to when I was a little girl, buried my head in the slippery fabric of his work shirt.

"Don't drown," I muttered.

"Don't be silly," my mother said.

"Not a chance, chicken," my father added.

"It's not safe to stay here," the firefighter shouted over the sound of the rain. He had a good-size aluminum boat, but it still looked flimsy to me.

"We're fine," my mother said as I climbed in, and my father waved. He had his arm around my mother's shoulders. They looked like one of those Norman Rockwell pictures that some-one had hung up on the bulletin board of the home ec classroom at the high school.

"Just give me a chance to talk to my aunt," I said as we rowed off into the darkness. "She'll listen to me."

But she wouldn't. Her house wasn't as bad as ours, anyhow. Except for the runoff from my waders her little living room was dry. It was a one-story house, and the ladder to the attic was down. She was up there sitting on a stack of suitcases, her legs pulled up under her nightgown. My mother was forty-five, which meant Ruth was thirty-eight, but sometimes she looked like a little girl, maybe because she didn't give life a chance to wear her down. I'd always wondered why she had those suitcases. She'd never gone anyplace.

"Just go back down there, Mary Margaret," Ruth said sharply from the half dark, and for just a moment she sounded a lot like my mother.

"Come on with me. The water's getting really high."

"It won't ever get up here. This is the highest spot on the whole farm." I thought she was right about that. My father once said that the little house was built on a kind of ridge so that his grandmother could look down and keep an eye on everyone.

"Then I'll stay here with you," I said.

"I got to get going," called the fireman from below.

"You go with him," my aunt said. "Your mother won't be pleased if you don't." I knew she was right about that, too.

The water was deeper as I climbed back into the boat and we sailed, like a dream, down our underwater driveway and onto what I knew was normally our road. It was hard to see much, no house lights, no streetlights, no moon. What I could make out, it looked as though someone had mistakenly put an ordinary mid-size lake in the middle of an area filled with things that had no business being there. The firefighter maneuvered the boat around power lines that came up suddenly like black snakes spitting and skittering along the surface, and pieces of things, of roofs and fences and strange unidentifiable brown chunks that in the dark might be floating firewood, or a drowned raccoon, or a piece of someone's house. We stopped at the McEvoys', but they were already gone, and we floated past the Derwents' barn, where the cows were standing in the hayloft, mooing loudly. We helped Mr. and Mrs. Bascomb into the boat and they wanted to bring their shepherd dog, but the firefighter said we couldn't take the weight. The dog barked from inside the house. We picked up Mrs. Donovan, who lived alone and was on her front step holding an umbrella that was already in tatters from the wind. You could tell she was afraid, trying to step into the boat, and finally the firefighter took the umbrella out of her hand and laid it down carefully on the edge of her kitchen steps, as though she was going to be back to get it soon. He put out a hand to help her in, but she stumbled, and the boat rocked and a little bit of water slopped in. Mr. and Mrs. Bascomb both opened their mouths but because of the rain I couldn't hear the sound they made. It was probably the same one I did, like a little goat noise.

When we got to the church hall at First Presbyterian, Mrs. Bascomb opened her coat and took out a bag she'd wrapped in plastic and tucked in there. It was full of knitting. "It's the boredom I can't stand," she said as Mr. Bascomb went off to get coffee. Mrs. Donovan found her sister in the robing room. I could hear her crying all the way down the hall, saying she almost fell in and drowned, which I guess was technically true.

Mr. and Mrs. Langer were there because their house was a single-story ranch with a slab foundation; my father used to shake his head sometimes at the foolishness of building that way on low land. Cissy Langer was my mother's best friend from grade school, which I had a hard time imagining even though they had the pictures to prove it, black-and-white photographs with white edges crimped like a piecrust of the two of them in Sunday dresses standing outside of one or the other of their houses, squinting. Cissy and Mr. Langer, whose name was Henry, weren't surprised that my parents weren't there. Cissy said the last time we had a bad flood my parents sat upstairs in their bedroom eating baloney sandwiches and playing Go Fish. I was a toddler at the time and my parents had let Cissy take me and my brothers to the firehouse.

"It wasn't anywhere near as high that time," Cissy said. "Tommy was nine, I think, and he taught the other kids to play poker. I think Eddie did his homework or something."

Donald was in one corner, holding a sandwich in his hand and pulling at his lip with the other. He waved with the sandwich.

"Were you scared?" he said.

"Why?" I said. "You can swim as well as I can." My father had made sure I could swim when I was so little that I couldn't really remember it except the first time I tried diving and got water up my nose. Donald's grandfather taught him, and Donald had such long arms now that he was always ahead of me if we went to Pride's Beach and swam out to the foam bobbles that kept us netted in, away from the deepest part.

"That's just stupid, Mimi. That's not the kind of water you can swim in. The current was strong enough to suck you under.

You should have been scared." He stuffed the last corner of his sandwich into his mouth, so his one cheek puffed out like a chipmunk's.

"What's the matter with you? Don't be so mean."

"Where are your parents?"

"They stayed at the house."

"And you're not even a little bit worried?"

"Where are your grandparents?" I asked, and then I could tell by the strange, pinched look Donald got that that was why he wasn't acting like himself.

"They took a different boat. There wasn't room in the one boat for them and me and Taffy, so I took Taffy and they took the next boat."

"You brought Taffy here?" Donald's grandparents had an old beagle who breathed like she was gargling gravel. Donald's grandfather said he didn't know what his wife would do if anything happened to her, but my mother said that was the kind of dog that lived forever, that lived so long she forgot her housebreaking and made everyone miserable.

"They made me put her in the choir room. There's a goat there, too, and a cat in a cage." Donald looked at the door. "My grandparents should be here soon."

"Maybe they stopped at our house and they're upstairs with my mother and father playing cards," I said.

"Maybe," he said.

"You want to play cards? I bet somebody has a deck. Or checkers. I'm pretty sure there's a set in the supply room." Donald liked to play games and I figured it would take his mind off his worries. He was really attached to his grandparents. The couple of times I tried to get him talking about his life away from Miller's Valley, his other school, his other friends, his mother, he hadn't said much and I just let it go. I didn't even know what his mother looked like. His grandmother had a heart-shaped locket she wore all the time, but the only picture in it was one of Donald.

"Mimi!" LaRhonda yelled.

LaRhonda's father and mother were setting up the big steel dishes they used at the restaurant for wedding receptions and christening parties. LaRhonda's father let me and LaRhonda light the little candles underneath, that kept the chipped beef and the mashed potatoes warm. "Who eats chipped beef?" LaRhonda said.

"I like chipped beef," Donald said, just like I knew he would. He and LaRhonda, oil and water, as my mother liked to say.

The older men were already digging in, ladling chipped beef on slices of toast. "There's more where that came from," Mr. Venti said to each one. Everyone was suspicious of him; he'd blown into town after the Second World War to visit a buddy and just stayed on. "Like he fell from the sky," Donald's grandfather liked to say, shaking his head, as though the sky was a bad place to be from. Besides, there weren't any other Italians in Miller's Valley. There weren't really any new immigrants in Miller's Valley at all. You could tell by their last names that people who lived in the area were originally from Germany or Poland or some of the Slavic countries, but they'd been Americans long enough to have flat vowels and made-up minds. When I got older I realized that the majority of people in Miller's Valley were the most discontented kind of Americans, working people whose situations hadn't risen or fallen over generations, but who still carried a little bit of those streets-paved-with-gold illusions and so were always annoyed that the streets were paved with tar. If they were paved at all.

Maybe that was what annoyed them about LaRhonda's father, too, that it looked like Mr. Venti had showed up out of nowhere and pulled off that American dream. He'd opened a diner, then a steak house two towns over, then a pizza place in the new shopping center. After ten years living in a cinder-block house behind the dumpster behind the diner, he'd married LaRhonda's mother, whose name was LaDonna. He was thirty-nine at the time, and she was sixteen. She finished up at the high school and hustled home from classes every day to do the four-to-midnight at the diner, which actually didn't make her much different from some of her classmates.

Now, though, she was different from almost everyone in town. The Ventis had saved their money, and expanded their businesses, and done well enough to live in the biggest house in the county. It was the only ranch house I've ever seen, to this day, that had columns in front. LaRhonda's mother didn't want a house with stairs, but she did want a house with what she called presence. It had a sunken living room and a kitchen with a wall oven and one wing with Mr. and Mrs. Venti's bedroom and a big bathroom with a round pink tub, and another wing with four bedrooms for the children. But there was only LaRhonda. That was sad to me, because Mrs. Venti seemed like the kind of person who would have liked to have a whole mess of kids. Maybe it would have taken her mind off of Mr. Venti, who liked to make comments about the size of her behind and then, when she started to cry, say that she couldn't take a joke. My mother said she felt sorry for her. "With that big old house?" Tommy always said.

"A house doesn't make a home," my mother said.

One of the cooks from the diner took us from the church back to LaRhonda's house for the night. "What about school?" I said when I heard I wasn't going home.

"Oh, honey, there won't be school for I don't know how long," LaRhonda's mother said as she settled us in the station wagon. "With how bad the flooding is there's no way for half the kids to get there. They're going to have to do something about the valley now, after this."

"You ready to move out, little lady?" Mr. Venti asked me.

"We're never moving," I said.

"I meant you ready to get going? That's military lingo. Move out means get going."

"Hey, Johnny, turn on the radio," LaRhonda said. She leaned into the front seat of the station wagon. In the middle of a natural disaster LaRhonda was flirting with the grill guy. He was kind of disgusting, too, with greaser hair and grubby pants that smelled like bacon and cigarette smoke.

"I'm worried that my parents are going to drown," I said that night as we lay with a white-and-gold bureau between us in the twin canopy beds in her room.

"Your parents are the last people in the whole wide world anything bad will happen to," LaRhonda said, turning off the light. LaRhonda's room was three times the size of mine, and everything matched—the bedspreads, the curtains, the little chair at the dressing table, all covered with the same pattern of big blue and yellow flowers that didn't actually look like any flowers I'd seen growing anywhere. I liked my room better than hers. In my room you could hear my mother humming dance tunes from when she went to the high school and see Ruth's living room light through the arms of the trees. LaRhonda's room was quiet and kind of lonely, with a view of a boring lawn that seemed to go on forever. I lay awake there for hours, listening to the rain thrash angrily against the windows, thinking that a few miles and a few hours could make all the difference between an ordinary day and disaster.

My parents didn't drown. Donald's grandfather didn't drown, either. His grandmother did. I'll remember that date for the rest of my life: August 21, 1966, the day Donald's grandmother died and the day my brother Tommy enlisted in the Marines.

"In a damn canoe," my mother said when my father picked me up and brought me home from LaRhonda's house. That's how I knew it was bad, because my mother swore in front of me. "A goddamned canoe."

Even then I could tell that her anger was a mirror of her love. She loved Tommy so, and so did I, and my father did, too, although it was more complicated with the two of them. Everybody else liked him a lot, mainly in spite of themselves, except maybe the fathers of the girls he dated. He was good-looking, LaRhonda was right about that, but it was more the vitality of him, like a combination of heat and light he gave off. Once I had to find him in the high school hallways, when I'd missed the bus and had no way of getting home, and all I had to do was look for a big clot of kids in front of the lockers. There he was, right at the center.

"Hey, corncob," he'd said, not denying me like most teenage brothers would, and the girls in the group smiled stupidly. He's even sweet to his sister, they were thinking. "She's something, isn't she?" he added, looking around, then making a pistol of his finger and pointing it at one of the guys: "Hey!" A brother warning. No boy had so much as looked at me twice at that point except to ask to copy my math homework, and Tommy in the high school hallway was acting as though I was hot stuff.

When my mother finally spit out the story, in fits and starts, *fits* being the right word because she was ready to have one, I could just see Tommy in a borrowed canoe, pushing the oars through the murky floodwaters as his biceps knotted and smoothed out along with the motion. By the time he got to the house the rain had slowed down and my parents were looking over the flood insurance policy, which my mother always kept in the top drawer of her bedside table. Tommy had steered the canoe right into the hallway and left it there while he went upstairs to sleep. In the morning the canoe was sitting on the hall runner, and the runner was sitting on about three inches of silt. If my mother had been a different sort of person she would have cried.

It probably wasn't the best time for Tommy to say that he'd enlisted, no coffee, no breakfast, two dead cows listed over like spotted dirigibles in the middle of the road. "I joined the Marines," he said as he and my father looped a length of chain around a cow and towed it off to the side of the barn with the truck.

"So he wasn't really in the canoe when he told you?" I said.

"My God, Mary Margaret, what does that have to do with anything?" my mother said as she scrubbed at the dirt on her lower kitchen cabinets and tossed me a sponge.

No one actually handled it particularly well, except for me because I knew to keep quiet. The worst was when Tommy came in from a trip to the barn, tracked mud into the back room that my mother had just finished mopping, and said, "Aunt Ruth says she's thinks it's a patriotic thing to do." My mother dropped the mop so it made a sound like a gunshot when it hit the floor and went right out the back door even though it was still slick mud out there and she was wearing sneakers with a hole in the toe.

"Oh, Tommy," I said.

"Come on, now, Miriam," my father called out the door. You could hear my mother yelling as clear as the sky, which to mock us all had turned sweet baby blue with a big hot yellow ball of sun overhead, like it was saying, Rain? What rain?

"Remind me again how many children you've raised, Ruth," my mother yelled.

What sounded like silence was probably Aunt Ruth replying in a normal tone of voice, but it didn't last very long so she probably didn't get to finish her sentence.

"Let me remind you of how I come by my opinions on this," my mother continued. "I am the mother of these children and if you want to offer your opinions on how they ought to be raised and how they ought to behave then you can do it from somewhere else than the house you live in on my property, on my charity—"

"Oh, man," Tommy said.

"Son, I should beat you with a stick," my father said.

"I'd like to see you try," Tommy yelled, and then there were two yelling fights going on until Tommy stomped out of the house and my mother slammed the door of Ruth's house and they met in the middle of the gravel drive and walked past each other like they were strangers, or invisible.

"I need milk," cried my aunt Ruth out the window, making

me wonder if anyone in my whole family had a sense of when to shut up.

"We got a whole barn full of cows," my mother yelled as she pushed past me. "Milk them yourself."

There was nothing but silence that night through the heating vent. My mother wasn't talking to my father, and neither of them was talking to Tommy, who went to Donald's grandmother's funeral with one of his friends instead of with us. Every once in a while we had to stop the truck so one of us could move something from the middle of the road that had drifted in with the water, and twice we passed cars that were just stopped where they'd been left. But as soon as we got out of the valley it was like nothing had ever happened. There were people cleaning their gutters, little kids running around lawns with balls and bats, one little girl sitting on her front steps blowing bubbles that broke pop pop pop on our car. I waved to her and she waved back.

There'd been trouble over hats: all our dark hats were winter hats, wool or heavy felt, and all our summer hats were hats for a happy day, with ribbons and artificial flowers. "We could not wear hats," I said. My father got a look like, don't, and my mother got a look like, dare you to say that again, so I didn't say anything else.

My mother wore a black straw that she finally found, bent on one side of the brim, and said I could get away with a wide black grosgrain headband, which always gave me a headache. She thought black clothing was unsuitable for young girls, so I had to wear a navy blue dress with red polka dots, which I thought was even more unsuitable. Donald wore a gray suit jacket and tan pants, which didn't look very good, either. He looked at me when he came past with his grandfather behind the coffin but he didn't seem like he saw me. He was changed somehow, just by what had happened. He looked older, walking side by side with his grandfather, like they both were men. Donald's mother walked behind the two of them, holding a handkerchief in her hand.

We were back in First Presbyterian, where we'd been after the flood, and the church smelled like old fried hamburgers and coffee burnt in the urn. Usually after a funeral there was a lunch downstairs in the church hall, but it was still a mess down there, and everyone from the valley was anxious to get back to their homes and clean up. There was another funeral that afternoon, too, but at the Baptist church, a man who had tried to outrun the flooding in his car, and failed. Donald's grandmother hadn't wanted to leave her house, but his grandfather had talked her into it. He hadn't heard or felt anything when she tipped off the back of the boat into the moving water. She'd washed up near her own front steps.

"Did you get to say goodbye?" I asked Donald outside the church. I wasn't really sure what that meant, but people were always saying it after they went to the funeral home, that they got to say goodbye.

"Not really," Donald said. "Have you ever seen a dead person?"

"No," I said.

"They don't look the same. Plus somebody had to lend her a dress to be buried in. It didn't look like the kind of dress she would wear."

"She was a really good grandmother," I said. I didn't have any grandmothers myself, but Donald's grandmother hung his shirts on the clothesline so carefully and was always making pies. When I would go over to the house during the summer she'd bring lemonade out to us at the wooden picnic table in the backyard. "What do you two have planned for the rest of the day?" she'd ask, as though maybe we were going to do something really exciting instead of sitting there smacking horseflies and being bored, talking about our summer book reports. I felt bad because sometimes Donald did his report and then he disappeared again, so it'd turn out that he'd written two pages about *White Fang* and it wasn't even going to count for anything unless that was on the summer reading list at his other school, too. He was teaching me to play chess. "You're getting to be good," he'd said to me after a couple of weeks. "I know your grandfather wishes I could play, but I can never quite get the hang of it," Donald's grandmother said. His grandmother was more the bridge type. When her bridge club met at her house she let us bring out the lunch plates. "Your grandson is quite the gentleman," one of the ladies said once, and Donald got all pink but it was true.

"I didn't expect Donald's mother to be blond," I said when we got home, and my mother snorted.

"She needs her roots done," she said, hanging up my father's suit.

"I feel bad for him," I said. "He really really loves his grandmother. He talks about his grandmother and grandfather all the time but he hardly ever talks about his mother."

My mother sat on the edge of the bed. She looked sad, suddenly, and tired, instead of mad the way she'd been since Tommy's news. There were marks around the edge of her feet where her dress shoes pressed in, like watermarks on a boat.

She took hold of both my hands. "The next time you see Donald, you tell him, I know how much your grandma loved you. That always makes people feel better, hearing that. And in his case it's true, too. That woman loved him to pieces."

"I know how much your grandma loved you," I repeated.

"That's right," my mother said.

But I didn't get to do that because I didn't have a real conversation with Donald again for close to ten years, and then it was in the middle of a busy city intersection and those words had gone right out of my head.

My aunt Ruth asked about the funeral when I brought her her dinner. "Meat loaf," she said, and she didn't sound pleased. She never sounded pleased about beef noodle casserole or chicken à la king, either, but she did seem to perk up at pork chops and ham. I guess she was a pig girl. Her parents had had some pigs, and a goat named Buster that got hit by a truck and died, but not before doing a good amount of damage to the truck. Whenever she talked about her childhood, my aunt talked about Buster and how he would follow her around like a dog, mouthing the skirt of her dress gently.

"That goat smelled to high heaven," my mother always said, but not in front of Aunt Ruth because the two of them were hardly ever in the same room. When they needed to communicate with one another, they did it through me. Get your mother to have new heels put on these shoes. Tell your aunt not to put the heat on so high. Tell your mother those beans were tough as rubber bands. Let your aunt know she can go hungry for all I care.

My mother scarcely ever went to the little house behind ours where my aunt Ruth lived, and my aunt Ruth never left the house. I knew there had to have been a time when she did, because she'd gone to the high school and been sort of engaged, once, to a boy in her class who went to Italy during World War II and came back with a war bride. "Aunt Ruth's heart was broken when her fiancé came home with a wife," I said one night lying on the sofa after dinner, and my mother snorted loudly as though she'd never heard anything so foolish in her life. It was the way she'd snorted when my father had come home drunk one night from the Elks and recited a poem in the front yard. "Under a spreading chestnut tree the village smithy stands," he shouted, and my mother stood in the doorway snorting.

"Pop, you're embarrassing yourself," Eddie had said, standing behind her.

There was a part about the smithy not owing anyone anything, and my father started to cry, and then he sat down in the dirt and Eddie brought him inside. "Leave him on the couch," my mother had said. "I'm not sleeping with him in that condition."

I was the closest thing my aunt Ruth had to the outside world. I dropped off her movie magazines and before I ate my own dinner I brought hers back to the tiny house down the driveway, where it stopped being paved and turned into a gravel path. My father plowed all the way back to Ruth's house on snowy days and shoveled out the narrow overgrown walkway to her front door, which always seemed like a waste of time because Ruth wasn't going anywhere. For a long time, when I was young, I tried to dream up ways to get her to leave the house, but after seeing her up in the attic during the big flood I was pretty sure it would never happen.

Donald used to visit her sometimes, too. He'd listen to her talk without starting to fidget or look at the door the way most people did. LaRhonda wouldn't even go to her house. "She's weird," LaRhonda said. "She likes company," Donald said. "He's got nice manners, that boy," Aunt Ruth said about Donald, "and I knew his mother so I can tell you they didn't come from her." She'd put out a glass of milk and two Oreos on a plate for each of us. Ruth's rules, or one of them: she wouldn't serve us tea, iced or hot, because she said it was a stimulant. She drank it all day long herself.

I spent a lot of time at her house over the years. We must have done a hundred jigsaw puzzles, pictures that the box said were by Monet and Degas or photographs of gardens and houses and barns like ours but nicer. As I got older the puzzles had more and more pieces, so that now we were working on the cathedral of Chartres with pieces so small that we kept losing them and finding them again in the folds of our clothes.

During the day when I was at school Aunt Ruth watched soap operas and read Reader's Digest Condensed Books. She liked the ones by Mary Stewart and Taylor Caldwell. She said they were romantic. When I was in her house during the day, on weekends or if school was canceled because of snow, she turned off the TV and put her little bookmark, the one with violets pressed between plastic and a purple tassel at one end, into her book. I don't know whether turning off the TV was her idea or my mother's. My mother thought watching television during the day was as lazy as staying in bed if you weren't sick. I never ever managed to get up early enough to bring my mother breakfast in bed on Mother's Day. She'd wander in while I was putting a late daffodil in a juice glass and pour her own cup of coffee. "Just stay in bed until seven," I told her once.

"Don't be silly," she'd said.

Aunt Ruth liked game shows, too. One day in second grade I hadn't wanted to go to school because I realized at the bus stop that I hadn't done the spelling homework. I pretended to run back for it and then I hid in the barn until I saw a flash of yellow pass by through the spaces between the warped old boards. Then I went up to Ruth's house. She was watching *The Price Is Right,* yelling "twenty-nine cents" at a bottle of Windex. I don't know why she thought she'd know the price of anything. She hadn't been in the supermarket for years.

She startled when I came through from the kitchen. "No school for you?" She stood and peered out the window. "It can't be a snow day."

"It's April," I said.

"I've seen snow in April, smarty-pants," she'd said as she clicked off the TV and the picture disappeared to a black dot. "I saw snow in May once. We built a snowman on the lawn, your mother and me. We gave him a tulip to hold, that's how late it was."

"Teacher conferences," I said.

"I don't have enough jam for both of us," she'd said. My father usually brought Aunt Ruth her groceries. Sometimes there was a box of chocolate-covered cherries. Chocolate-covered cherries were my favorite things in the world. Later I figured out they weren't so good—the cherries aren't much like cherries, with a consistency more like a pencil eraser and that strange chemical sugary taste of the stuff that surrounds them. LIQUEUR, it said on the foil, but it wasn't. I liked to bite off the top, suck that stuff out, then tap the cherry onto my tongue. They were special then, chocolate-covered cherries. Like shrimp were special. A shrimp cocktail was a big deal. Once LaRhonda's parents had a party for their wedding anniversary. They had enormous platters of shrimp with hollowed cabbages filled with cocktail sauce, and Mrs. Venti had too many White Russians and called her husband a pig and tried to drive off in their Cadillac but couldn't get it out of neutral. But all anyone really remembered was the shrimp.

There was one chocolate-covered cherry left that day, and

Ruth gave it to me, which I knew was a real sacrifice. "If our place caught fire would you run down and rescue me?" I said.

"Your daddy would rescue you," she said.

He didn't rescue me that night, after the school called and asked how come they hadn't gotten a sick note. "I should paddle you," my mother had said, but she sent me upstairs without chocolate pudding instead. "You know where she was all day," I heard her say to my father.

My mother and my aunt Ruth were as different as two sisters could be. My mother was sturdy and strong-minded. She had short hair that got permed in town once a month, first thing in the morning after she got off her shift; she'd sit in the chair trying to kill the smell of the chemicals with a cup of strong coffee Patsy made her in the back room, right next to where she mixed the chemicals.

My aunt Ruth's hair had natural curl, so that it waved around her face, and was the color hair is when you're a grown woman who was blond as a little girl. She was thin and almost unnaturally fair, so that you could see a road map of bright blue veins running up her arms and legs and even beneath the surface of her face, with one vein running crosswise on her forehead and disappearing at the corner of one eye. Once I said that maybe Aunt Ruth didn't like the outdoors because she was afraid she would burn—it was a night when I was sleeping with no pajama top and a back full of Bactine because I'd stayed by the pool at LaRhonda's house too long—and my mother said, "Don't be silly, the woman used to sit out at Pride's Beach all day long in summer in a swimsuit." There was a whole big story in the way she said it, like maybe she was off working or studying or helping her mother while her sister was lounging by the cool water, sunning herself. But it was hard for me to imagine—not the part about my mother, but the part about Ruth out in the wild. When I was younger Aunt Ruth and I had practiced having her leave the house; I would stand at the end of her little walkway with my arms open and a big artificial smile on my face, a school picture smile. One day she managed to take two steps through the door and onto the slate pavers, then said, "Oh, goodness, no," and backed inside.

When my mother said that about Pride's Beach I wanted to ask why Aunt Ruth wouldn't leave the house, but it would have been like sticking my finger into the blades of the fan sending cool air over my hot back. My mother talked about her girlhood as though Aunt Ruth had been her cross to bear from the beginning, making sure she got on the school bus, giving up her milk money when Ruth lost her own. When their mother died she left Ruth the house, but it turned out that with the taxes and the repairs all Ruth could do was sell it and move to the little place at the back of our farm. One of my earliest memories was of being four and going with my father and Ruth in his truck to pick up a few pieces of furniture, of Ruth drifting from room to room—which didn't take long, it was a small house—saying, "Goodbye, stove. Goodbye, cellar," until my father said, "Come on now, Ruth, we got to go."

"Where you going with that rocking chair, Buddy?" she said when we got back to our house.

"Your sister wants that for the living room," my father said.

"She always gets what she wants," Ruth said, which even at four I thought seemed mean and maybe even untrue.

I could remember that day, but I couldn't actually remember Aunt Ruth outside. I must have seen her do it, because it was a year or two after she moved in behind us that she started being balky about leaving the house, which turned into not leaving the house at all. It was one of those things you didn't notice right away, maybe didn't notice at all until one day when she was supposed to go to a party with my parents. "She hasn't left that house for the better part of a month," my mother said, putting a handkerchief in her one good purse, the patent leather one with a handle made to look like bamboo. My mother started to bait her: come with me to the market, let's go to the diner for breakfast. She never wanted to do things with Ruth before, but now she was testing her, taunting her. Finally she said to my father, "You ask her, Bud. She's always liked you better than me."

"Now don't say that," my father said.

"She's always liked you better than anyone, truth be told. Go on up there."

So my father went up the path and he stayed there for a long time. But he didn't have any better luck moving Ruth than the rest of us.

When Tommy came home for a visit after basic training, he'd turned into a grown-up. I didn't like it much. It took some of the old shine off him. His hair had been buzzed down so far that you could see the raw pink of his scalp between the bristles, so that it looked kind of like a baby's head. I'd seen a picture of him in what my mother called his dress blues, although between the hat so low on his forehead and the serious expression it could have been any guy in a fancy uniform. So I was surprised that he came home wearing the old plaid shirt and tan work pants that he'd left in three months before.

We weren't really sure exactly when he would show up but I came in from the school bus and there he was, sitting at the kitchen table and drinking a beer. I threw myself on him and he patted me on the back and said, "I brought you something."

I acted happy when he pulled a doll out of his duffel, a weird little doll made of corn husks and clothespins. But it made me wonder whether, while he was becoming somebody else, he thought I had, too. I guess I figured that that's what it's like when people go away. Donald's mother had stopped at our house three days after the funeral, and she'd told my parents that she was moving to California and with her mother gone Donald wouldn't be visiting anymore.

"We'd be happy to have him here when he visits again," said my mother. "He's absolutely no trouble."

"He's a fine young man," said my father. "He can stay with us anytime."

"California is a long way away," his mother said.

I don't remember Donald saying a word. It was like he was sliding away the longer he sat in one of the living room chairs. I figured if I ever saw him again we would barely recognize one another, that we would both be so different we might as well be strangers. But as they were heading out to the car, he and his mother, he all of a sudden turned to stand in front of me, with his back to her.

"I'm coming back," he said, like he was daring me to disagree.

"Okay," I said.

"I mean it."

"You promise?"

"Promise," he said.

"We need to get on the road," his mother said. "I've got a lot to do."

"I'm coming back," he said again. "Don't forget." Then he got in the car and they drove off.

Even still I was a little surprised that he wrote me so often, although they weren't really letters, just postcards of Knott's Berry Farm or the La Brea Tar Pits or places like that, with maybe two sentences. Donald had always been a person of few words, and writing only made that more so. We have a pool behind our house. I went to Disneyland. There's an orange tree in our yard. I stuck the postcards in the corner of the mirror over my bureau.

I liked Grauman's Chinese Theatre the best. It didn't look like anything I'd ever seen before. A berry farm didn't seem like much even with a Ferris wheel.

My father had been out on a job when Tommy showed up, fixing the clock in the tower of the old train station that hadn't been a train station in years. He came into the kitchen looking beat and then clapped his hands together once when he saw my brother.

"Son," he said.

"Sir," said Tommy.

Then they shook hands, which was what men always did that made me feel like they must be lonely, or at least that made me feel that way. My father scrubbed his hands at the sink with a piece of fine steel wool and some Lava, and then they shook hands again.

"You look good," my father said.

"The food's lousy," Tom said, and my father said, "Your mother's made a nice dinner, believe you me."

It was true. My mother had made a pumpkin pie, and some scalloped potatoes that could be heated up, and she had two roasting chickens all ready to go in the oven. It was a kind of Thanksgiving dinner even though Thanksgiving was two weeks away. My father called her at the hospital, and she got someone to cover the last few hours of her shift.

"Oh, Tom, you're skin and bones," she said when she hugged him.

"You're blind, Miriam, the man's all muscle." That was the first time my father'd ever called Tom a man, I think. Tommy had brought my father a knife with a pine tree engraved on the handle, and my mother a box of saltwater taffy. He brought my aunt Ruth a little crab made out of seashells, and he cracked another beer and carried the crab up to her. "Tell her I'll send her a plate when we're done here," my mother said.

"I wish she would have dinner with us just for tonight," I said.

"If wishes were horses, beggars would ride," my mother said. To this day I'm not sure exactly how that makes a lot of sense, but my mother said it anytime anyone wished for anything. She said her mother used to say it. Ruth said she couldn't recall that at all. She said their mother used to say "Don't trouble trouble," which honestly seemed even dumber to me but no way would I ever say so.

When the chickens were out of the oven and on the stove top under a dishcloth Tom came into the kitchen and put his arms around my mother's waist from behind. "I got an idea," he said. "Why don't we have dinner at Ruth's?"

"Does she have something better in the oven than this? Because somehow I doubt it." So did I. Ruth could make three things: toast, scrambled eggs, and grilled cheese. That was okay because she and I both liked those three things, although sometimes she would put sweet pickle slices in the grilled cheese and I would squeeze them out. Pickles shouldn't be warm. That's just not right.

"We could carry everything up there. It'll be nice."

"Nice for her," said my mother. "Besides, I already had Mimi set the table."

"I didn't do it yet."

Tom picked up the roasting pan. I picked up the stack of dishes. My father came downstairs. "What's going on here?" he said.

"We're all going to eat at Ruth's house," Tommy said.

"That's a nice idea," my father said.

"Nice for you," said my mother. I could tell she wanted to balk in the worst way, but Tommy was smiling his Tommy smile at her, his head on one side, and even without the bangs dropping down on his forehead it worked. "If you drop those chickens you'll be in trouble for sure," my mother said to him.

"This is so nice," said Ruth. I set out to go back for silverware, but Ruth said she had plenty, and she took a big mahogany box out of the bottom drawer of a chest against one wall. The box was filled with tarnished silver.

"I never knew how you wound up with that," my mother said.

"My mother gave me this for my hope chest," Ruth said to me, as though her sister hadn't said a word. "She started piece by piece when I was thirteen. Your mother was in nursing school and she said, Ruthie, your sister is going to be a professional woman, she'll never marry. I'm going to give this to you for when you make dinner for your husband. It just goes to show."

"Did you want it?" I asked my mother.

"I don't see the point, to be honest. Stainless is easier. When we were kids all these women would spend a whole day with a chamois cloth and baking soda polishing the silver. They never used it anyway."

"Mother used hers for holidays."

"I stand corrected. They used it three times a year. Christmas, Thanksgiving, Easter."

"Birthdays, too," said Ruth.

"Your grandmother was a fine cook," my father said to me.

"Buddy, you are so right about that. She appreciated you, too. When you first started coming down, when Miriam wasn't the least bit interested in you—"

"Oh, for pity's sake," said my mother.

"—she would always say, That Buddy Miller, he appreciates a good meal and he's got that big farm, Miriam should be nicer to him—"

"I appreciate a good meal," said Tommy. "I haven't had one

in more than two months. Everything in the mess hall is the same color. Rice, meat, vegetables, it's all the same color as our uniforms."

"—and then when George Lesser left—"

"Mom, this is not only the best meal I've had since I left, it may be the best meal I've ever had," Tommy said, very loudly, and I giggled. My mother got up and put her arms around his neck and hugged his bristly head to her chest, hard. "Thomas Alan Miller, you don't fool me one bit," she said.

The Langers came over next afternoon, and that was nice, too. My father and Mr. Langer were friends in that way that men are who get dragged into a friendship by their wives. But they got along fine. They would sit in the living room and drink Iron City Beer and watch baseball or football on the TV. Cissy and my mom would sit in the kitchen and have cups of tea and vanilla wafers. Mr. and Mrs. Langer didn't have any children, so they always made a fuss over us. You'd hear people talk about them, how Henry was on disability from the foundry and ran a bait shop out of his garage, how Cissy made dolls and sold them at church bazaars and fairs, and then suddenly the voices would drop, and you'd know that they'd gotten to the kid part, those poor people, God's will, and so on. When I was a kid it seemed like God's will was always that bad things happened, mostly to nice people. When Eddie got his scholarship, when LaRhonda's father started to make a lot of money, nobody ever said that was God's will. With Mr. Venti they mainly said it was dumb luck.

"I was there when your brother was born," Cissy said. She was heavier than my mother, and softer, too, with scented talcum powder caught in the creases of her arms like a dusting of snow. When she was happy, which was most of the time, her whole body jiggled. "I was there, out in the waiting room. I can't lie, I wanted a little girl after Eddie, but if I had known how Tommy would turn out I wouldn't have been like that." I saw my mother throw her a look. Sometimes I thought that was how they'd probably been in sixth grade, too, Cissy giggling and jiggling, and Miriam looking at her sideways. Salt and pepper.

"But then we got you, Mimi," Cissy said, raising her voice a little as though I was eavesdropping. Which I was. I figured that most of being a kid consisted of eavesdropping, trying to figure older people out and understand what they were going to do next, because whatever they were going to do next was surely going to have some effect on you.

I went down to the other end of the hallway to listen to what the men were saying in the living room, but all I could hear was the guy on television saying somebody needed to punt because it was a fourth down. "That's for sure," Mr. Langer said, and they all went silent.

Men silences could last forever, so I went back down the hallway to hang around outside the kitchen again. My mother and Mrs. Langer had a big bag between them and were emptying it onto the table next to their teacups. There were swatches of fabric, bright flowered stuff, polka dots, plaids. My mother was sorting them into piles.

"You don't like that navy print?" Cissy said.

My mother rubbed the fabric between two fingers and frowned. "It won't hold up," she said.

That was probably what they'd been like in sixth grade, too. My mother was the practical one. Even choosing material for doll dresses, she was on the lookout for something that wouldn't wear thin in a year or two. My mother had never bought me a dress that didn't have a hem three inches deep so it could be let down, with a tidewater mark that showed where the old hem used to be.

"I've got a new line," said Cissy, reaching into another bag. She always said that, like she was running a big doll factory instead of sitting in a tiny back bedroom of her house, hand-sewing button eyes and a thick zigzag of red embroidery thread for a mouth.

My mother turned the doll over in her very clean, very large hands. My mother had a nurse's hands. You could eat off her palms. They were almost big enough to hold a full meal, too.

"Cis, I could be stating the obvious, but this is a pig."

It actually was pretty clever, how she'd done that. Cissy usually made a doll face with a soft white sock, and somehow she'd puckered and pulled with thread so the doll had a little snout with pink floss nostrils and lips. The pig had pigtail hair and shoes that looked like little hooves with black felt triangles. Cissy sure knew how to make a cute doll. My mother said that if you figured how long she worked on each one, she was making about a dollar an hour. I was still young enough that a dollar an hour sounded like real money to me. I made that selling corn.

"I think people will like them. The three little pigs, but girl pigs."

"Hmmm," my mother said, like she did when I gave her a composition to read and she was going to tell me to take another shot at it.

I went back to the living room. I could tell by the television sound it was halftime. "It's not going to amount to a hill of beans," my father said.

"I wouldn't be so sure, Bud," Mr. Langer said. "We been down this road before. They can come right in and take your place. Imminent domain."

"They still working on that water deal?" I heard Tommy say.

"It's the damn dam," said Mr. Langer.

Tommy laughed.

"What's so funny, son?" said my father.

"Nothing, sir."

"He calls me sir now that he's in the service," my father said to Mr. Langer. "I'm his superior officer." I didn't need to see my father's face to know he was smiling.

I'm not sure I'd ever seen my mother happier, either, but it didn't last. After a few days Tommy didn't seem to know what to do with himself. My father would say things like "I guess they work you men pretty hard," and Tom would say, "They sure do," and then they would read the newspaper until my father said, "There must be men there who don't have the kind of fire-arms experience you have," and Tom said, "Some, that's for sure." Tommy had never been a hunting fanatic the way my father and Mr. Langer were, mainly because it required being up at dawn, which Tommy only managed when he'd been out all night the night before. Then he never got a deer anyway. I think half the time he fell asleep waiting in the blind.

It was funny: before my parents had been upset that Tommy went out so much, but when he was home for those ten days they were worried that he didn't go out enough. I could hear them through the heating vent. My father wouldn't stand for the heat going on until after Thanksgiving, as though no one got cold until they'd had turkey and stuffing.

"I wish he'd have some fun, maybe take out that Jansson girl he used to like," my mother said. I lay in bed and shook my head. Tom hadn't had anything to do with Meggie Jansson since tenth grade, when she gained all that weight. He liked small girls.

"Leave him be," my father said.

My father liked the notion that Tommy spent afternoons walking the property, although it seemed pretty sad to me. One day I followed him up to the ridge. He was sitting on a big rock, smoking a cigarette. Even though the rock was cold and hurt my butt I sat and leaned into him a little bit. It felt like his whole body was hard. My father said that's what basic training did to a man.

Tommy held his cigarette toward me, but I shook my head. "Mom'd kill me," I said.

"I'd say she wouldn't need to know, but she'd know. She'd kill me, not you."

"Not now she wouldn't. She's so happy you're home."

He inhaled smoke, blew it out, then said, "You like it here?"

I looked around. "Where?"

"The valley. I was just wondering if you like it here."

"I guess."

The truth was, I never thought much about it. My name was Mimi Miller. I lived in Miller's Valley. Everyone I knew lived in Miller's Valley. I wasn't ignorant; I knew there was a world outside. I just had a hard time imagining it. We went on a field trip to Washington, D.C., but between the museums, the monuments, and the White House it didn't really seem like a place where people went bowling and had dinner and lived a real life. On *The Beverly Hillbillies* they were supposed to live in Beverly Hills, but their house didn't look that different from the Ventis' house. Donald's postcards made his life in California sound not much different from his life here, except that it was warm all the time. Finally I said, "I guess every place is pretty much the same."

"Nah, that's the weird thing. Every place is really different. Like where I am in South Carolina, the food's different, the houses are different, even the flowers. But the people now— they're pretty much the same. You got guys from all over and it seems like they should be real different, but once you get to know them they're a lot like the guys I knew in school, you know?"

I didn't know what to say to that. This was the most adult conversation I'd ever had with Tommy, and I didn't want to say the wrong thing and have him all of a sudden look at me and remember that I was barely a teenager.

"You got to be smart," he finally said, not looking at me. "You walk around thinking everything's going to stay the same, you know? But everything changes all the time. Ten, twenty years, this whole place will be different than it is now. It's like, how come we're so stupid, to think that things are going to stay the way they are forever? We should know better, right?"

"Nothing changes around here," I said.

Tommy laughed. "Yeah, I hear you. I know it seems that way. I went into the diner the other day and it looked like the same guys were sitting in the same booths they were in the last time I was there eating the same food."

"They probably were."

"Yeah, probably. But you can't be like that, you know? You don't want to get stuck. You don't want to wake up someday and just be sitting in the same place doing the same stupid stuff. Especially not somebody like you. You need a plan."

"Like what?"

"You know what I mean. Like Ed. He was gonna be an engineer, he went to school, now he's doing it." I didn't want to say that Ed's life seemed about as boring to me as a life could be, even more boring than mine, so I said, "What's your plan?"

"Uncle Sam has a plan for me," Tommy said, with a little barking laugh. "I don't know exactly what it is yet, but it's all up to him. You come up with your own plan, Meems. No matter what happens." That last sentence froze me, like it might be the beginning of a hole opening in the ground around me. I was too young and stupid to realize that the hole had already opened. But sometimes now when I think about that day, the two of us sitting close so our rib cages were almost touching, I think that Tom saw it right there at our feet.

He took a deep drag on his cigarette and then rubbed it out on the rock. "You're smart," he said, and he stood up. "You'll figure it out. I don't know much about much, but I know you're going to be okay."

"Yeah?" I said, wishing I did, too.

"No question. No question. How's that crazy LaRhonda?" he added, and I knew our real conversation was over.

"Still crazy," I said to make him happy.

"The military makes you grow up," I heard my father say that night. "He'll get himself some discipline, come back here and run this place."

"Oh, for pity's sake, Buddy. If the government has its way there won't be a here to come back to anyhow."

"Don't you be saying that. The government talks and talks. They don't do. This farm will be here long after I am, and Tom will be taking care of it the way I did."

"It's a different time," my mother said, and I heard my father push his chair back and go out the back door.

When Tommy left it was one of the only times I'd ever seen my mother tear up, although she got it under control before my brother got in the car. But I hung back in the kitchen doorway, in the shadows. There was a story in our family about me, about how when I was real little we all went to a birthday party. The big kids had been playing Farmer in the Dell, which I liked at first because I thought the song was about us. The farmer, his wife, the cow. There was even a nurse in it. But when we were driving home I started crying in the backseat of the car, and when my mother asked why, I'd said, "The cheese stands all alone. Poor cheese." The boys thought that was hilarious. Poor cheese, they said for a while, whenever I would cry. That was me, standing in that dark doorway. Donald gone, Tommy going again. Poor cheese.

"Don't start smoking, corncob," Tommy called to me. "It'll stunt your growth."

My mother glared at me over her shoulder, probably glad for a reason to be mad instead of sad. "If I ever smell cigarettes on you, Mary Margaret, you're going to wish you'd never been born," she said.

"I'm just teasing, Mom," Tommy said, putting his arms around her.

"You be careful, son," she said.

"Always, Mother," he said seriously, and then he winked at me over her shoulder and I finally ran out of the house and put my arms around his waist.

"You have to come back," I said. I kissed Tommy on the cheek and it felt like a man's cheek, rough and bristly.

"Of course he's coming back," my father said, putting Tommy's duffel in the back of the truck. "Where else would he go?" But I noticed Tommy didn't say a thing, just looked straight ahead through the windshield, that same look Donald had had when he drove away, that I thought of as the leaving look. And when I turned, my mother was sitting down on the back step, and I went to sit beside her, both of us quiet and still, neither of us wanting to break the silence.

The summer I was fifteen LaRhonda's father gave me a job at the diner. I was off the books because I wasn't old enough to get working papers, which meant that he could pay me even less than he paid the regular waitresses whose vacations I covered. Mr. Venti made it sound like my reward would come later. "You do a good job at the diner, someday you can work at the steak house, where the real money is," he said. Like being a steak house waitress was my goal. Which it wasn't. Ever since that talk with Tommy I'd been thinking about a plan, although I had no idea yet what it was, just what it wasn't. No diner. No steak house. Everyone said I should be a nurse because my mother was. I was leaving that open for the time being.

"You'll make your money on tips," Mr. Venti said, and there was some truth to that, but not so much. When a kid you've known since she was playing in a mud puddle serves you pie and coffee, you're disinclined to do more than put a dime under your saucer. Some of my father's old friends didn't even do that. "She don't need the money," I heard one of them say to another as he hoisted his big belly away from the counter and off the stool, like my parents were rich people and I was just playing at working. On the other hand, none of them ever tried to put his hand up my skirt. I was shocked the first time I saw that happen, as one of the younger women walked past a booth carrying a tray of breakfast specials. Dee saw the look on my face and said, "Grab-ass, baby. The waitress's cross to bear." Not just from the customers, but the grill cooks, who would mess your orders up but good if you didn't play up to them. Except for me, again, because I knew the boss.

Mrs. Venti worked at the steak house as a hostess. My aunt Ruth said she didn't understand that, that the Ventis surely had enough money that she could afford to stay home. "I'd just sit around and play cards," said Aunt Ruth, who had played more hands of solitaire than maybe any person on earth. But Mrs. Venti was at the steak house most nights, in black high heels and a satiny dress with some sort of sparkle on the neck or the skirt, saying "Right this way" and cradling a pile of menus as though it was a newborn. I think she just did it to have something to do and somewhere to go. Unlike my mother, who couldn't go to the market without running into someone who wanted to pass the time, Mrs. Venti didn't have a whole lot of friends. Maybe not any. I told my aunt Ruth that I figured she wanted to get out of the house at night.

"Getting out of the house is overrated," said Ruth, putting down a line of cards slowly and then squinting at the result. By my calculation my aunt Ruth hadn't gotten out of the house for ten years by then.

Of course, Mrs. Venti getting out of the house had turned out to be part of the problem, and was one reason why I was waiting tables at the Villa Venti Diner ("Good food, good folks, good prices"). LaRhonda was the one supposed to be covering the vacation shifts, but she was two thousand miles away on some special ranch for incorrigible girls. Word in town was that she was in trouble, taking one of those trips to an aunt that ended with a secret adoption and a permanent reputation. But she wasn't. LaRhonda was one of the few girls in town whose reputation was much worse than the reality, so bad that my mother had stopped me spending the night at her house six months after the big flood, although LaRhonda was still allowed to stay at our house.

"I couldn't let her if Tommy was still around," my mother had muttered at the sink.

The problem was that LaRhonda always had to be ahead of everybody else. She was sure ahead of me: heels, makeup, hose, padded bra, home permanent. She was the first one to have a little stereo in her bedroom, that she could fold up into a kind of suitcase and tote to pajama parties. She got the first Beatles albums and the first transistor radio. "What's that?" someone would ask, usually a boy because the other girls didn't want to give her the satisfaction, and she'd flick the radio dial with her thumbnail, which was painted pink.

So she acted as though she was first to do a lot of other things, too, and she did a pretty good job of convincing people. You'd cut under the bleachers at a football game and there LaRhonda would be talking to one of the seniors with barely a playing card's worth of space between them. Or you'd see her in some boy's car sitting way in the center of the front seat. "It looked like there were Siamese twins driving," my mother said one day when she'd stopped at a light on Main Street behind a yellow Mustang.

I guess I was the only one who knew that it wasn't what it looked like, that when the Mustang's driver would try to feel LaRhonda up she would slap his hand, that when the guy under the bleachers tried to stick his tongue in her mouth she would turn her head away. "They are disgusting," LaRhonda would say, and if you'd heard her you would have known that she was telling the truth. But those guys were angry that she promised something and then didn't deliver, and so they made sure everyone thought that she'd delivered plenty. I don't know how her parents heard, but the day after freshman year ended LaRhonda was on a plane to a place where she was going to learn to ride a horse and cut hay to build character, two things I'd learned how to do almost as soon as I could walk. Although come to think of it my character might have been exactly the sort the Ventis were trying to build in LaRhonda. I'd learned to think of myself as not that kind of girl because boys never acted as though I were, and it wasn't until I was older that it occurred to me that that was because they were afraid of what Tommy might do to them. Which he would have.

"You're a good influence on her, Mimi," Mrs. Venti sighed, handing me two of the pink uniforms the diner waitresses were assigned.

"There's not one of us looks good in those things," said Dee. "Plus it's hard to get stains out. Did she tell you you have to take them home and wash and iron them yourself?"

"I like to iron," I said.

"Save me," Dee said, picking up a coffeepot.

The women I worked with were hard women, widows with kids who lived with their parents, middle-aged never-marrieds who'd given up on something better, women who wanted factory jobs but couldn't get them because they paid more and men wanted them, too. But they were nice to me. I got to be an okay waitress faster than most, at least according to them, but there were still times when the place would get real busy, breakfast after church or early bird dinner on bowling league nights, and I'd get overwhelmed by a four-top with four different dinner orders, Salisbury steak (no gravy), fried chicken (no vegetable), open-faced roast beef sandwich (extra gravy), fish cakes (extra tartar sauce), and one of the others would pick my plates off the grill shelf and help me out. I think they were glad I wasn't LaRhonda, who they'd have to be careful around all the time and who they knew from experience was not a bit friendly.

They were always teasing me about the love letters in my apron pocket that I would pull out when I was putting my tips in my bag in the back. But they weren't love letters and they were always from the same people: Tommy, LaRhonda, Donald.

Hey sis, it's hot in Bancock. I got you something. See you at xmas.

Your brother, Tom

(How come I was in Miller's Valley and knew how to spell Bangkok and Tommy didn't? Why did he say he would come home at Christmas when he hadn't been home in more than a year?)

What's up, MM? It's not as bad here as I thought. There is a girl named Sandy who is from Chicago and has even more albums than I do. She tweezed my eyebrows and they look a MILLION times better! What's up with you-know-who?

(Which who was you-know? The basketball player, the guy from the construction crew, Pete Walker, who sat behind LaRhonda in English? And why did her parents think it would do her good to spend the summer with a whole lot of girls who had been in the same trouble that she was, most of them probably the real thing?)

Dear Mimi,

I am learning to play golf. My mother got married. My step-father is a salesman and he plays golf, too. How is everything there? My grandfather says he sees you some times. Do you still play chess?

                              Sincerely, Donald


Sincerely?

"Cheap bastards," said Frances, the waitress who'd been around longest, looking at my piles of quarters and nickels as I put the letters back in my apron pocket. There were two bills from two tables I'd had first thing, one of them from the Reverend from the Baptist church who always left a nice big tip because he never had to pay for his food. "Roman collar, no check," Frances told me my first day. I hadn't known what it was called until then.

"I have to go," I said, scooping the money up. I had two jobs that summer, and I couldn't be late for the second.

Tom hadn't been overseas for long when an old friend of my father's named Pete Fenstermach showed up at our house in his truck. He'd pulled into the driveway with a sound from his tires that didn't look good for the visit, had gone around to the passenger side and pulled his seventeen-year-old daughter from the cab by her arm. It was January, but she wasn't wearing a coat, just a big old man's shirt and a pair of jeans underneath. She tried to pull away but her father was stronger than she was. I knew her to say hi to—she was a couple of years ahead of me at school, the kind of girl, pale and big-eyed and thin, who looked pretty sometimes and other times just looked plain. It took me a minute to remember that her name was Callie.

"Daddy," I said.

Mr. Fenstermach and Callie came in through the back door, into the kitchen. My mother put her hands on her hips and looked the girl up and down as though she knew just what she was looking for, and then she sat down hard in one of our kitchen chairs. She put up her hand as Mr. Fenstermach, red in the face, started to open his mouth.

"Pete," my mother said in a way that shut him right up, and then to Callie, "How far along are you?"

I remember I leaned so hard against the refrigerator that I could feel it humming through the backs of my legs.

"Go see your aunt," my father said.

"No," my mother and I said at the same time.

"Six months," said Callie.

"You know who did this to her?" her father shouted.

"Don't be ridiculous," my mother said. "You wouldn't be here if it was anybody but my Tom."

My Tom. My mother never called me her Mimi, or called my brother her Eddie. It was always her Tom. I couldn't even argue with it. He was my Tom, too. Since he'd left, the house had seemed like a baby's rattle with all the jingly things inside gone.

"He's gotta marry her."

"I hear what you're saying, but he's over in Asia someplace and we don't even know when he's coming back or whether the mail's getting through to him."

"You get him back here," yelled Mr. Fenstermach. "I'll go over there and drag him back here myself."

Callie whispered something. "What's that?" my mother said.

"I'm not marrying anyone," she said.

"You're not planning on giving this baby away to strangers, are you?" my mother said.

Callie shook her head. "I can handle it," she said, and, quiet as it was, she said it in this kind of voice that made me believe her. The men argued some, but my mother kept quiet, and Callie wouldn't budge. And then it was all over, or just beginning.

I got the impression that my mother had known long before that afternoon. She was discreet, my mother. She had to be. You can't be a nurse in a small-town hospital, know who has a crooked spine and who has a killing cancer and whose hysterectomy is because she used a Lysol douche to try to keep from having an eighth child in ten years, and not be the kind of person who can keep a secret. My mother had two texts on the wall of her bedroom in gilded frames, the Lord's Prayer and the Florence Nightingale oath. "Hold in confidence," it says about a nurse's obligation. It was never my mother who gave things away; it was the looks on other people's faces when they saw her.

I had a fifth-grade teacher who I could tell my mother didn't like, and who didn't like her, and it wasn't until the week my mother died, when I was telling her stories to take her mind off the pain in her gut, that she said to me, "That Mrs. Prentiss? She beat her boy. I was sure of it. She or her husband. But I couldn't prove a thing." I don't think she would have told me even then if both Prentisses hadn't been dead, and their son living somewhere out west. I remembered the wary look Mrs. Prentiss had had those few times my mother had come to school.

Callie gave my mother a look that day, but it was more an exchange of understanding, and that's what they came to. Callie was going to need help, and my mother wanted a hand in the raising of her grandchild. I think my mother kind of admired Callie, admired her nerve, admired her determination to keep her kid at a time when a pregnant teenage girl either got married or gave her baby away. But it made her start watching me even more than she normally did. She needn't have worried. Every time I thought of what Tommy and Callie had done, it gave me a funny feeling, and not a good one. I liked kissing and even then some, although I'd done very little of it, mostly in the hallway at mixers with a boy from my homeroom named John Gellhorn, who said "wow" each time we came up for air. But what came after just seemed strange to me. And Callie and Tommy were such a mismatch, him all fireworks and her so not.

But I got to admire her, too. She'd had to leave school before Clifton was born, and when he was three months old she'd gotten the job at the diner. My aunt Ruth said the baby was named after some movie actor I'd never heard of, but Callie said she'd just seen the name in a book and liked it. Her grandmother took care of him sometimes, and so did her mother. Her father told my father that he was washing his hands of the whole business, and it seemed like he was standing by that. "I've lost respect for Pete," my father said, and that made me proud, that my father felt that way.

I asked Ruth if she'd help with Clifton, but she looked shaky and said, "Oh, good gracious, Mimi, I'm not up to all that." So I worked eight to four at the diner that summer, and then Callie came in and handed Clifton over to me before she started her shift. She always insisted she pay me a dollar an hour. At first I said I wouldn't take it, but my mother said, "People need their pride," so I caved. LaRhonda said that was cheaper than the going rate, but I don't know how LaRhonda would have had any idea what the going rate was. She never did any babysitting. All the other girls said it was because she didn't need the money, but I'm not sure anyone would have asked her. She didn't seem like the kind of person who liked kids much, and she seemed like exactly the kind of person who would go through your under-wear drawer and jewelry box and eat all your ice cream while you were out.

"Me! Me!" Clifton always said when Callie handed him over, reaching out his arms and putting them around my neck. "You be good," Callie said as she tied on her apron. "I'll pick you up in the morning." I fed Clifton at our house, gave him a bath, and put him to bed in a secondhand playpen in Tommy's old room. "Da," he said, pointing at a picture of Tom in his dress uniform on one corner of the bureau, but only because I'd told him that.

The diner was a couple of miles outside of town. Mr. Venti said that that was where the future was, that downtown was dying. He said that at a Chamber of Commerce lunch and some of the business owners wanted to throw him out but he owned too many businesses for them to do that. Besides, I thought maybe he had a point. My parents talked all the time about how they used to go shopping on Main Street, for my mother's wedding suit, for my father's tools. Now there was nothing but a Christian Science reading room with books open in the window and no one inside, an insurance office with travel posters and a sign that said PLAY IT SAFE WITH MUTUAL OF OMAHA, and the sporting goods store that stayed in business because of the high school teams and the Little League and because it sold guns. There was one place that opened as one thing or another, a used book store, a bakery, a gift shop, and then closed so quickly that sometimes it seemed like you'd imagined it.

There was nothing close to the diner except for a big parking lot where I waited with Clifton on my hip for my father to pick me up after work, a big sweaty spot on one side of my uniform where the baby sat. He was starting to walk now and didn't like being held, but if I put a couple of barrettes in my hair they could keep him quiet, playing with them, trying to yank them out, at least until my father pulled in. My mother usually had Clifton's dinner waiting. Callie didn't let him get away with much, so for a baby he was pretty well behaved. We sent Tommy pictures. He was in Vietnam, a place I'd had to find on a map, fighting the Communists. I asked Callie if she wanted to send him a letter, but she didn't.

"It wasn't any big thing," she'd said to me once, but at least she'd let us share the baby.

I sent Donald a picture of Clifton, too, although LaRhonda had said it was a well-known fact that boys didn't care about babies. "Only how you make them," she'd said, like she knew. But I was pretty sure Donald was going to like Clifton when he met him. He'd finally sent a real letter, although it was typed, as though it was more business than personal. "I am coming to visit for a week on August 2," it said. "My grandfather is picking me up at the airport. Maybe you could come with him so he could stay outside with the car and you could come in and find me." He did make it sound a little bit like business, but I was still happy. "Your Friend," he signed that one.

"I sure will be glad to see that young man," his grandfather said when I saw him at the diner. "I can't call him a boy any-more. He's a young man now."

"I hope he still has that nice way about him," Ruth had said when I told her.

I shifted Clifton from one hip to another. My work uniform usually smelled like hamburgers and donuts, and I think Clifton liked the smell, because sometimes he'd put his nose to my chest and inhale loudly. I always had to check afterward to make sure he hadn't left a snail trail of snot behind.

"You're good with that child," my aunt Ruth said. After din-ner but before he was due to be put down for the night I usually walked him up to her little house and let him toddle around a bit. My aunt Ruth had a lot of dolls on shelves in the dining room, and Clifton always pointed up at them like he wanted to look at them. She had a doll dressed like a nun, which was the only way I knew what a nun looked like because there weren't any in Mill-er's Valley, and a doll that was supposed to be a figure skater named Sonja Henie that had belonged to her mother. She had one dressed like Scarlett O'Hara and one dressed like Florence Nightingale, and she had some Cissy dolls, too. Clifton seemed to point at those the most, but Ruth just ignored him. She ig-nored him when he put his arms in the air to be picked up, too. One day he even took her hand and tried to get her to walk him outside, but that led nowhere.

Ruth's well was acting up that summer, and my father spent a fair amount of time behind her place, tinkering. He'd put in a new sump pump, too, because the last time there'd been a heavy rain, water had wound up really flooding the basement of her house for the first time.

"Your father can fix anything," Ruth said. "Gaga," Clifton shouted, his hands on the sill, his face to the screen so that there was a grimy grid pattern on his nose after. That's what he called my father, Gaga. "Right out here, little man," my father shouted back.

"I don't care so much for children when they're small," Ruth said.

"What about me?"

"That was different," she said, finishing up the crust of a tuna sandwich. It had been maybe a year since my mother had stopped sending meals up to Ruth's house. "She can look after herself," my mother said flatly, and a couple of nights later when she caught me with a ham steak and some macaroni and cheese on a plate she took it wordlessly out of my hands and dumped it in the trash.

"That's a waste of good food," my father had said.

"I made it, I paid for it, I can do what I want with it," my mother said. I thought I saw my father wince.

The two of them were at war because the older Clifton got, the more my mother wanted to move him and Callie into the little house where Ruth lived. I didn't even have to eavesdrop on the heating vent to know about her plans, or my father's upset with them. They'd fight about it right there in the living room.

"Callie's doing fine living over there with her mother," my father would mutter.

"She and the baby are in one room," my mother countered. "What's she going to do when he's out of the crib?"

"We can't turn Ruth out onto the street."

"No one is talking about turning anyone out onto the street. There's always vacancies at those garden apartments down by the hospital. One of the girls in the ER lives there, and her place has a nice big living room, and a little balcony. Not that Ruth would need a balcony. God forbid she should go out on the balcony, the world would end."

"This is her home."

"This is our grandson."

"Ruth's not a town girl."

"She's not a girl, she's a grown woman and it doesn't matter where she lives as long as it has walls. It's not like she's going to miss the scenery."

Then my father would play his trump card: "How the heck would we get her out of there?"

And my mother would fold: "I don't give a rip." Or a hoot. Or, if her feet really hurt and Callie's mother had been bragging at the beauty parlor about how much time she spent with the baby, a damn. Even she couldn't find an answer to the idea of Ruth screaming her lungs out, holding on to the doorjamb as someone tried to drag her into the open.

"I'm her only flesh and blood she's got in the world and your mother treats me like a boarder," Ruth said to me, tears running down her cheeks onto her floral blouse.

"I'm pretty sure I'm her flesh and blood, too," I said.

"You know what I mean. I don't know why you all make such a fuss about that child."

"He's flesh and blood, too."

"Oh my God, Mary Margaret, you are the most literal girl I've ever met. You're worse than my sister. You think it's right for her to talk about throwing me out?"

"What if Clifton and Callie moved in here with you? You've got two bedrooms you're not even using. It would be company for you."

"I like my privacy," Ruth snapped. "Besides, your father

won't let her do anything. It's his place. She forgets all about that. Your father's the boss, pure and simple."

I didn't want to take sides, but the older I got the more Ruth seemed childish to me. Sometimes someone who had known her when she was a girl would say that that was because she was a youngest child, but I was a youngest child, too, and I didn't sit around waiting for someone to make me cinnamon toast and put it on the end table with a cup of tea.

But I still brought her food, only from the diner instead of my mother's kitchen. We were allowed to take things that wouldn't look pretty on a plate, lopsided cakes, the end piece of a pork roast. Sometimes I made her something, a cheese omelet ("Not runny inside, Mary Margaret," she would call from the living room) or a BLT.

"Ruth has always been a soft sort of girl," said my father one day when we were riding in his truck. "I remember when I first met your mother, Ruth was maybe ten years old and was always saving baby birds. She'd put them in a little shoe box with some cotton, feed them bits of things."

"Did she save them?" I asked.

"She sure tried hard enough."

"But did it work? Did the birds live?"

My father thought for a moment. When my father was thinking it was like an aerobic exercise, like he was putting his whole body to the test. "I'm thinking not," he finally said.

It was a hard time, the fall just before I turned sixteen. August 2 had come and gone, and Donald had never arrived. He sent me a postcard saying he couldn't get off work, but his grandfather had already told me he wouldn't be coming. "It's that mother of his," he'd said. "Don't get me started." He looked so sad. I knew how he felt. Our house was built for five, and now it was down to three. My brothers' old shirts hung in their closets like the ghosts of people who'd once slept in their beds. I missed Tommy. I missed Donald. I even missed Eddie sometimes, and Donald's grandmother. Sometimes I thought about her lavender smell and her warm pies. I think maybe more than anything I missed the Mimi I used to be. Getting older wasn't working out so well for me. My brother's words had made me think a lot about what I wanted, where I wanted to end up, and the truth was I had no idea in the world. I figured it should be clear, like that big strip of yellow tape they held across the end of the course for the sack race at the volunteer fire department picnic: this, here, this is how you win.

I did well in school. I'd always done well but now I moved to the head of the class because I didn't have much to do except homework and helping Callie out. There were things we studied that I couldn't see the point of, like poetry and ancient history, and there were things that made perfect sense to me, like algebra and biology. First term of sophomore year I got highest honors. The list was in the paper: three of us, the other two boys. "Don't let it go to your head, Mary Margaret," said Ruth, who got the paper a day late, my father taking it out to her when my mother was done with it. But my mother made me sit down at the kitchen table after it had been cleared and wiped, and she put her finger on my name like she was marking a point on a map.

"This is your road to something better than this," she said. It was the only time I'd heard her say one single thing that made it seem as though her life wasn't just what she wanted it to be, except that one night after a Jansson wedding at the firehouse and a couple of whiskey sours when she had talked about how all through high school she had gone out with an older boy named George who had gone away to the state university. "That one had a high opinion of himself," my father had said. The next day I asked Ruth if she remembered a boy named George that my mother had dated. "Of course," Ruth said. "That was a time." And she wouldn't say more, which for Ruth was saying a lot.

My mother's finger tapped my name in the paper. She had made my father buy extra copies. "You're a smart girl," she added. "Don't waste it."

That's who I was by then: the smart girl. But it was hard. When you look back on your life there are always times that you remember as the hard times, even if they're the hard times a girl has, not the hard times of a woman, with grief and loss and real hardship. "I might come to visit this summer," Donald had written on his last postcard (a picture of the Hollywood Bowl) but I wasn't going to count on it again. I figured it was what Ruth called wishful thinking.

LaRhonda and I had never been a perfect fit as friends, which my mother and Aunt Ruth and even Cissy Langer had told me more than once, but sometimes, I've found there are people you get to be friends with accidentally and then stay friends with because you've always been friends. But I only saw LaRhonda now when she didn't have anything better to do. After she'd come back from the ranch she seemed a lot older than I did, and for the hour or two that we'd been at her kitchen table, eating fried chicken from the diner that her mother warmed up in the oven, I figured that it was because she'd learned a lot from the other girls there. Once Mrs. Venti went to work, leaving us with a banana cream pie and a pitcher of iced tea, I'd found out what was really going on.

"I've accepted Jesus as my Lord and Savior," LaRhonda had said solemnly, clutching at the neck of her blouse and finally pulling a gold cross on a chain from underneath.

I'd seen a lot of that growing up, from Mrs. Bascomb, who spoke in tongues at a church that held its services under a tent in a used car lot, to Donald's grandfather, who had once told him that he'd been traveling a dark dark road before the Lord lifted him up. For LaRhonda finding Jesus took a different form. She became friends with a group of girls in our high school class who had all found Jesus, too, and who all spent a lot of time on the phone each night planning the outfits they would be wearing next day. They also managed to incorporate gossip and meanness into their religious tradition, like this: "I'm praying on Cheryl because I hear she drank six beers after the football game and puked in the bushes outside Cathy Barry's house."

There's a particular kind of way I've noticed people, women mostly, act with one another when they're pretending to be nice but they really don't like each other. That's how those girls were with me. They were town girls, and it was like they could smell the farm on me, or maybe they made me smell it on myself. For a while I hung around the edges of all this, but there was a girl who kept saying she was praying on Callie because of Clifton, and I thought Callie needed a second pair of hands and a job that paid more than minimum wage a lot more than prayers, and at one point I said so, and although LaRhonda said she had told the group I was expecting a visit from Aunt Flo—which I wasn't— they were concerned about the state of my soul.

Even Tommy wasn't Tommy anymore. When he finally came home on a visit it was like he was someone else again, jacked-up and hard. He'd let his hair grow down the back of his neck and refused to shave, and he and my father had a fight about it. "I'm waiting for a gook bullet through my skull and you're worried about hair?" he'd said. He had a tough little barking laugh he laughed now, a mean second cousin to a real laugh, a poor substitute for the way he used to throw his head back and let loose. His first dinner home he said, "There was one night when the guys and I were crawling through some mud—" And my father cut him off and said, "Son, I don't think your mother and sister want to hear that." Then we all sat silent until my mother put butterscotch pudding, Tommy's favorite, on the table, but he pushed back his chair and said, "I'm going over to see Jackie." In the middle of the night he came in and started crashing around his room, banging his knee on the playpen. "Goddamn," I heard, and then a thump, and silence.

When it was time for him to leave again my mother hugged him hard in the kitchen while Tommy sobbed on her shoulder like some tormented version of his old self. For weeks afterward I could hear that sound, the hoarseness like his guts were coming up, the gasps like his heart was going to explode. I'd been waiting for Tommy to tell me what to do with myself, but as his tears turned the shoulder of my mother's plaid shirt black I knew that he was more lost than I was. He pulled himself together and tried to pretend like nothing had happened, but it was one of those moments you can't ever take back, that you remember forever.

I was crying, too, and Tommy said, "Hey now," like there was no reason for it. He kissed Clifton on the forehead and said, "Stay cool, little man," but he hadn't really seemed to know what to do with his son when he was home, and Clifton didn't recognize him and kept pointing to the picture in the bedroom and saying "Da."

After Tommy left, my father must have realized that I was having a tough time, or maybe he was having one, too, because he started to take me along on some of his fix-it trips when I wasn't working or at school. He said he liked the company, but I think it was more for my sake than his. He wasn't much of a conversationalist, my father; when people would stop by to have something fixed he would mostly listen. But he liked telling me stories. He would talk about being in the service, not about fighting but about being on KP and meeting men from Brooklyn and Tulsa and other places he'd scarcely known existed. "There were two Jewish boys," he once said, as though you couldn't get more exotic and unexpected than that. He talked about how his father decided dairy was too much work and switched to beef cows, and how his mother's father had trained as a taxidermist and how my mother's grandmother had been a teacher in a one-room schoolhouse up the slope of the mountain.

My father told me a story about a great-uncle of his who was a dowser, who could stand in a yard and sniff long and hard, the way Clifton sniffed my uniform dress, and then tell you where to sink a well. Sometimes I thought Winston Bally could do that, too, sniff out, not the water, but where the water was causing trouble. As far as I knew he hadn't ever come back to our place, hadn't talked to my father since I was an eleven-year-old kid selling corn out front. But sometimes I'd see him driving on the back roads of the valley, in his navy blue government sedan, and sometimes I'd hear that he had been around, telling people that plans for the reservoir were moving ahead slowly but surely. There were two farmers at the other end of the valley who had already agreed to sell their places if the government plan went through, and a husband and wife who had taken over his mother's place and had plans to finish the basement until they found out that no builder could keep the water out. They put a For Sale sign at the end of their driveway, but it was hard to sell a house in Miller's Valley, and they were talking about discussing some kind of deal with the state.

Mr. Bally showed up at my aunt Ruth's door one day when it was in the nineties for the second straight week and she was sitting in front of a fan watching *Days of Our Lives*. Nothing irritated her more than having someone interrupt a soap opera, and nothing unsettled her more than hearing a knock at the door, which had to mean a stranger because all the rest of us just walked in.

"Can I speak to you for a moment, ma'am?" Winston Bally apparently said, and Ruth replied, "Not on your life," although when she told me that, it sounded like the kind of thing you wish you had said at the time but dreamt up afterward.

The screening on Ruth's front door was thick and a little dusty. Looking through it was sort of like looking at something through a sheet of heavy rain, so Ruth said all she knew was that Mr. Bally suddenly backed up off her steps. That was because my father had grabbed him by one shoulder and pulled him down to the scrubby patch of dirt and struggling lawn in front of the little house behind our bigger one.

"I've been as polite as I know how to be," he said—"hollered," said Ruth later—"but I'm not going to tell you again to stay away from this property. And if you ever bother this lady again I will be doing more than telling you."

"You'd better be careful, assaulting a government agent," Mr. Bally had said, straightening the front of his white shirt.

"You are trespassing, mister, and you're upsetting this lady and I won't have this lady upset."

"The law says I am allowed to visit citizens at their homes for this purpose."

"I don't care what the law says, I want you off," my father told him.

The story made the rounds in town in the next week. I heard people tell it at the diner, but it got bigger and better in the telling, the way things do. One man said my father had punched Winston Bally, and another said Winston Bally had threatened to have my father arrested. When Winston Bally came in and ordered the lunch special on Saturday, a bowl of Scotch broth and an egg salad sandwich, the place got real quiet for a minute. It so happened that he was at my station at the counter. He left me a two-dollar tip but I didn't know whether he was a good tipper because he wasn't from around here, or whether it had something to do with the fight with my father.

"You can't stop progress," one of the other men at the counter said after he was gone. It was the first time I'd heard that sentence in the conversation about the water, but it sure wouldn't be the last, or the last time I heard the sound of my mother's voice through the vent at night as I fell into a deep and exhausted sleep: Face facts, Buddy. Just face facts.

Four months into junior year Mrs. Farrell, the chemistry teacher, asked to see me after school. "Ooooh," one of the boys said, but I knew it was nothing bad.

"You're Eddie Miller's sister?" Mrs. Farrell said, and I nodded. "And Tommy Miller's, too, then, I imagine."

They must have had some time figuring that out, all the teachers at the high school. The boy who gets straight A's and the boy who can barely read. The boy with the slide rule in his shirt pocket and the one who has the circle of a rubber permanently imprinted on the leather of his wallet. They all probably thought little sister was going to wind up somewhere in the middle, but by junior year they knew different.

"There's a summer science program at the university that I'd love to see you enroll in. You've got a real natural facility for the subject."

"I can't, Mrs. Farrell. I work at the diner full-time during the summers. I'm saving money for college."

"Well, I guess I have to respect that. Where are you thinking?"

"State, I guess. It's cheaper than anyplace else except the community college."

She nodded. "I don't think you need to think about the community college, although I've had some fine students spend a year or two there. I've got some thoughts about other places and about scholarship opportunities, but it's early yet. You want to take physics next year?"

"Yes, ma'am."

"The advanced section? It'll be pretty small, and it won't be easy, even for you."

"Yes, ma'am."

"Can I talk to your mother?"

"I'm pretty sure she doesn't know anything about physics," I said, and Mrs. Farrell smiled.

"I wouldn't put anything past your mother," she said. "When your brother was struggling with bio she came in here one day, sat down, and said, 'Tell me how we fix this.' And we did. He wound up with an A minus at the end of the term. It would have been a solid A if not for that first bad month."

"Tommy aced bio?"

"Not Tom. Edward."

I would have thought she was confusing my two brothers, except that that was impossible.

"I think maybe I just spoke out of turn. Obviously Edward was an excellent all-around student." She paused. "But not as good as you are, I don't think."

"I've never heard that before," I said.

"I was so glad to hear that your brother Tom came back safe from the service," she said. "Your mom and dad must be relieved."

"They are," I said, which was sort of true and sort of not.

"I always thought Tom was an untapped resource."

"I've definitely never heard that before."

She stood up, and so did I. I knew that soon she would give me harder textbooks, extra-credit work, college catalogues, contest entry forms. I was beginning to know the smart-girl routine.

"Eddie almost failed bio?" I said that night after dinner while my mother and I were washing the dishes.

"Never you mind," said my mother.

"What else don't I know?" I said.

"You should assume you still have a lot to learn, Mary Margaret," said my mother, and then she dried her hands on a dishtowel and said, "Although not as much as some." It was the closest my mother had ever come to paying me a real compliment.

"Mrs. Farrell wants me to go to some summer program at State," I said to my father next morning in the barn while our breath froze in front of us.

"Oh, Mimi, that's a tall order," he said.

"I said I couldn't."

You can tell time by a farm, a day's worth of time, a year's worth. There's a particular kind of quiet on a farm in the morning, which isn't really morning the way other people think of it. It's still dark, with just the smallest idea of black sky getting lighter around the edges, and unless there's a moon the only light comes from the bare bulb hanging like its own moon from the center of the barn ceiling. It's a place where it's just as easy to feel lost as it is to feel contented. I felt lost most of the time now, but I never said so, even to myself: in that same way I knew it was odd for a grown woman not to leave her own home, I knew it was odd for a teenage girl to feel like there was a big rattly empty space between her stomach and her heart. But it made me wonder whether other people felt the same way without showing it, whether Tommy felt the same now that he was back in town, whether my father felt the same way when my mother gave him a hard time about not taking the reservoir plan seriously, or about kicking Ruth out and moving Callie and Clifton in. I helped my father out in the barn some mornings at least as much to make sure he wasn't feeling sad as to cut down on his work time.

It was always warmer in the barn than it was outside because of all the cows crowding together, breathing and snorting and farting, making a fug that hung in the place like cigarette smoke over the poker game my father used to have once a month in the dining room, before my mother told him he needed to stop smoking and move the game to the VFW. Cows at dawn are different than cows at dusk. A farm in winter feels different than a farm in summer. The whole year passed in front of me on the farm. The cornstalks with yellow edges that meant summer was over and the classroom getting ready to close around you. The pumpkins of October that squatted where the yellow flowers sprouted on the vines in August. The mornings when you could hear the cattle complaining like a bunch of old men with tobacco throats and you knew, you just knew, that it was February and their water trough was frozen solid and you were going to have to go out there with an old shovel and beat a hole into the ice until it fell apart like a broken window.

The one constant all year round was the sound of my father, in the foggy mist of summer or the dry-ice mist of winter, taking care of business in the barn. My father liked to whistle while he worked in there. He had a strange whistle, more like a breathy thing that came out between his teeth than that full pursed-lip sound my brother made, or used to make. My father usually whistled from the time he slid the barn door open until he slid it closed. On Saturdays, when I'd sleep in a little bit, I'd roll over in bed sometimes and hear it, faintly, unless it was raining hard and the rain was bigger than my father's whistle. Then it would wind up drowned out completely by the thunk of the sump pump.

My father took a lot of pride in keeping a neat farm. He never said much but you could tell he had contempt for people who had messy knock-around farms, with broken hay wagons falling apart in the corner of the field and moldy straw to one side of the barn door. My father even dug a big trench down one edge of the barn and into the far fields so that when the groundwater was deep, which happened more and more the older I got, the cows wouldn't get foot rot. There was an order to running a farm right, and my father appreciated it, and so did I. It was a little like math, one thing in front of another until it was solved. Sometimes I would pull on a pair of dungarees and a sweater and give my father a hand before I got the bus to school. Sometimes he'd drive me to school so I wouldn't have to take the bus at all.

I was already halfway across the road one morning in March, stepping carefully because of the black ice slicks on the tar, my wool gloves frozen into hand shapes because I'd left them to dry outside by the door, when I heard my father stop whistling and say, "Lord give me strength." I came up behind him and saw that where our big tractor always sat there was an empty place, and an empty forty-ounce bottle of Pabst Blue Ribbon beer. My father favored Iron City or, when he was feeling flush, Rolling Rock.

We were less than a mile along the road when we found the tractor overturned down the side of the shoulder. The engine was still running but it made a grinding noise, like it was butting up against something it had no business touching, and Tommy was lying half under it with blood on his face and all over the front of his shirt. I could hear the tractor but no sound of breathing but my own, and I made a fluttery motion with my hands in their old gloves, then put them under my armpits to make them stop. Tommy wasn't even wearing a coat, and there were two other beer bottles near the tractor, although they could have been from anyone since there was a lot of racing down our road at night and throwing beer bottles from the window, which was probably why my father hadn't noticed the sound of the tractor starting up in the first place.

"Don't try to move him or you might make it worse," I said.

"I couldn't if I tried," my father said.

We were a family that didn't use the rescue squad, figuring we could handle most things ourselves with a first aid kit and iodine, but my father sent me back to the house and I called for an ambulance. I called the hospital, too, and told my mother we were coming in. "I'm going down to emergency," she said in her nurse's voice, calm and cool, which was noticeable because I was crying and my nose was running and I was having a hard time catching my breath.

"He can't have lived through all that in Vietnam and then die drunk on a damn tractor," I sobbed.

"Take a deep breath, honey," said my mother, and I cried even harder because my mother only called me honey when things were really bad. Then I heard the sirens and got off the phone.

"Mary Margaret, what's going on?" my aunt Ruth called from her living room window, and I realized it was getting light and that I was going to miss school.

"Tommy," I called back, and ran onto the road.

When my brother had finally come home for good, people said he was a changed man. That wasn't true. He looked a little like Tommy Miller, and sometimes he even talked a little like Tommy Miller. But the real Tommy Miller was gone. I don't know where he left him, but that guy didn't live in Miller's Valley anymore. One day a car had dropped him opposite the barn just as I was getting home from school. I wrapped my arms around his neck, but it was like hugging a mannequin. He peeled me off as soon as was decent, or maybe sooner.

"Who was that?" I said as the sound of the car's spitting muffler receded. "Damned if I know," said Tom, picking up the military-issue duffel at his feet.

We weren't even sure where he'd been. He'd been gone more than three years, but Eddie was certain he hadn't been in the service all that time. It was funny, Tom had changed so much but Eddie hadn't changed much at all, still serious and a little anxious. He was working as an engineer at a big real estate development company, had bought a nice little house just outside Philadelphia. He'd gotten married a couple of years after college;

Tom was supposed to get leave to be his best man but just never showed up. I was a bridesmaid; my dress was purple and a little big on me, and they did my hair teased and lacquered into some kind of updo. As soon as we got home I tore it all down and my mother changed into slacks and a summer shirt. It was like we had been visitors in Eddie's life, and we were glad to be back sleeping in our own beds.

"They seem like nice people," my father kept saying about Debbie's parents.

I guess you could say that it was the other way around with Tom after he got back, that he turned into a visitor in our lives. He got himself a place near town and we didn't see him a whole lot, and when he came to dinner or stopped by to use the washing machine we had nothing to talk about. "What have you been doing?" I'd say, and he'd say "Not much," and where do you go after that? He even scared me a little. He'd grown a big mustache and his hair was even longer now, and everything about him had coarsened, his skin, his body, his language, his eyes. The light in his eyes was gone, and so was the grin. That broke my mother's heart, I think. The fact that he was living in a falling-down trailer on the other side of the valley and yet always had enough money hardened my father's. I was glad we lived so far from anyone else so no one could hear him and my father yelling at one another after they'd had a couple of beers, or more than a couple. My father might drink six beers during the course of an evening and just get quieter and quieter, until finally he'd say, "It's the sandman for me." But Tommy was one of those drunks who went through all the stages: sociable, silent, sulky, mean, nasty, violent. He tuned my father up, although he'd probably say it was the other way around.

One evening after Tommy had been back a few months Callie asked me to pick her up at work because her car was in the shop. She'd been a good friend to me, Callie, when I'd found myself without anyone, Donald always promising to come back but never showing up, LaRhonda off with God and the Goddettes, Tommy smelling of smoke and whiskey and unwashed clothes. Callie had her evening shift at the diner and she was taking classes in the mornings at the community college and there was Clifton and her grandmother had emphysema and was always wanting her to do this or that, but she somehow made time every week to stop over and spend an hour with me, or ask me to walk her through any of the schoolwork she needed to know for a test.

Callie brought a slice of German chocolate cake out to the car from the diner and we put it on the seat between us and picked at it with our fingers as we drove. We both had coconut under our fingernails.

"How's chemistry?" I asked.

"I'm never going to be a whiz like you, but since you went over that last chapter with me I've got a better idea of it. I'm going to pass, at least."

"Of course you're going to pass."

"They grade on a curve. They have to. There are some real dummies, although some of the girls are smarter than you'd think."

I licked some frosting off my finger. "Your grandmother's okay?"

"If you listen to her she's at death's door. One of the things I like about your mother is she never complains about her health."

"She's never sick," I said. "I don't know why. Willpower, I guess." And we both laughed, and then Callie sucked in her breath the way people do when they're getting ready to say something they think you won't like.

"I just needed to talk to you without your mom and dad around," she said.

"You're moving away," I said.

"I wish," Callie said. "What would I do with Clifton without you and your parents and my mom and grandmother and every-body? I need to stay put at least until full-day kindergarten. It's about Tommy. I need you not to leave Clifton alone with him."

It was quiet inside the car. Someone was honking a couple blocks over, but then they stopped. Finally I said, "Don't worry. I never would. Never ever." Saying it like that made me know it was true, and why it was true, and it must have showed on my face because Callie put her hand on my arm and rubbed it the way she did with Clifton sometimes when he was crying.

"I know this has to be hard for you, Mimi. I know you love the guy. But I just don't think he's reliable with a little kid, you know?"

"I know. It must be hard for you, too."

"Not really. I got to be honest, I didn't really know him that well. You know the way he was, like he could sell ice to the Es-kimos. He picked me up at the Dairy Queen one night, and the next thing I know I'm in the backseat with my feet out the win-dow. In a way I don't regret it because how could I regret Clif-ton? I knew from the beginning that I was going to be on my own. Well, not really, because your mom was a lot nicer about the whole thing than I thought she'd be. But you know, Tommy and me, it didn't amount to much. I'd like it if he liked Clifton and Clifton liked him, but I'm not so sure what's going to hap-pen at this point."

"Is he giving you any money? He has money."

"It's fine. Your mother has been great about stopping by with groceries and buying Clifton clothes. She buys him the cutest things." I knew that. I knew, too, that my father had told her to stop doing it. "A father should support his own son," he'd said to my mother. "You shouldn't let him off the hook."

"Don't let Tommy off the hook," I said to Callie.

"Really, it's okay. Sometimes he drops over some milk, or toys. He doesn't really know what to do, you know? He brought

Clifton a bike. Like, a big bike. I don't think he knows that he's three. Or what three-year-olds like. Or something. So that's another reason. I'm fine with him seeing Clifton at your house, or when he's with you. But not taking him out, you know? I'm not sure what he'd do with him."

What could I say? She was right. Even when I was around, Tommy looked at Clifton like he couldn't quite figure out what to make of him. Half the time when he was supposed to come to the house and see him he never showed up. Once or twice I ran into him by accident. The day after I talked to Callie I saw him when I was coming out of the library. Mrs. Farrell kept saying that she wanted me to enter the state science fair and I was searching for something I cared enough to spend six months studying. I kept thumbing through books about diseases and space exploration, but I hadn't found anything I really wanted to do yet.

"What are you doing here?" I said when I saw Tommy in the parking lot between the library and the high school.

"Meeting up with a guy," he said. He acted like he barely knew me, kept looking around the lot as he smoked a cigarette. He didn't offer me a ride, and I wondered if he was nervous because he figured our father was coming to pick me up and they might get into it again. I wouldn't have driven with him anyhow. His eyes looked funny.

"What are you doing here?" he said. "Isn't it late for school? What, you have cheerleading or something?"

"You're kidding, right? I'm working on a topic for the state science fair."

"So, no cheerleading I guess." He sucked on his cigarette like it was oxygen. He had a skull tattooed on the back of his hand. Every time I looked at him something inside me felt jagged, like I'd swallowed a razor blade and just had to hold really still so it wouldn't move around and slice my insides up.

"You should come see Clifton," I said.

"I saw him."

"When?"

"I don't know, a couple days ago," he said. "You were there. I brought him that thing, what was it?"

"That was two weeks ago. He's your son. You should see him every day."

He flipped his cigarette to the ground and mashed it with his heel. "Who died and made you God?" he said.

"What happened to you?" I said. I must have been crazy to ask that question, or really tired. Between work and studying and helping my father with the farm and looking after Clifton and looking after Ruth, I didn't get that much sleep a lot of the time.

Tommy smiled then, but it was that kind of hard humorless smile that's worse than no smile at all. "Little sister, you have no idea," he said.

"Try me."

It was like for a moment a mask was lifted and from his eyes shone the old Tommy, the piggyback-ride Tommy, the bring-me-a-tadpole-in-a-jar Tommy, and the razor sliced at my gut and he must have seen it. For the first time since he'd gotten out of that rattly car in front of the house he really looked at me like he saw me. I could feel a sweet-sour smell coming off him but I could see Tom in his eyes.

"I wouldn't do that to you, Meems," he said. He hadn't called me that for a long time. He called me that again a week later after I got back to the slope where the tractor lay, its engine quiet now, the ambulance guys working with my father to get it off him. I saw the old Tommy again just for a minute, even through all that blood. "I really blew it this time, Meems," he'd said, and he coughed, gagged, spit a big maroon clot onto the ice, and then passed out.

One day I came home from school and there was a strange car in the driveway, an Oldsmobile 88 with a faded blue paint job. It looked like an old-lady car, which was what it was. Mrs. Jansson's mother had driven it for a few years and then had died suddenly of some heart thing. So it was a dead-old-lady car. And now it was mine.

"You deserve it for sure," my father said, as though it was a brand-new convertible. But I didn't care. I could get myself where I was going now. I couldn't ever remember feeling so free.

"It will come in handy," my mother said, by which she meant Tommy. She had an idea that I would be driving him around to doctor's appointments so his leg could improve. They said in town that the doctors wanted to amputate, but my mother had crossed her arms across her shelf of a chest and said, "Not my Tom, you won't." They'd airlifted him to the big hospital and spent hours reattaching his leg where the skin had been split open and the bone splintered, and while they weren't optimistic, over time the join had taken. My mother hardly slept at all for almost two months, first using her vacation time and staying with an old nursing school classmate who worked at the big hospital, later putting in her shifts at our hospital and then driving an hour north and sitting by Tommy's bedside. Maybe she saw some of that old Tommy, too, as she sponge-bathed him. Or maybe she saw the Tommy I'd never even known, the baby she'd cradled, the small boy she'd chased around the yard.

"He's going to need a lot of rehab," she said at dinner, big blue thumbprints of tired under each eye, dishing out the packaged mac and cheese. There hadn't been a whole lot of cooking since the accident. We'd eaten what I brought home from the diner on weekends, and sandwiches and canned soup during the week. Good thing my father wasn't picky.

"Dear Mimi," Donald wrote. "I hear your brother is doing a lot better. Tell him I said hi. I'm on the swim team so I don't get home until late most nights so sorry this is so short. I'm going to one of the University of California colleges but I don't know which one yet. You will be the first person I tell when I know."

When I took some brownies I'd made back to her place, my aunt Ruth said with her mouth full, "And to think, your brother made it through the service just fine and almost gets himself killed on your father's tractor."

"I don't know how you can say he made it through the service just fine," I said.

"Well, he's still alive, isn't he? Lots of those boys aren't. He's still alive and he's got all his limbs and his faculties."

"Never mind," I said. I was losing patience with Aunt Ruth's certainty about the things she thought. It was easy to figure out how people ought to behave out in the world if you never went out in the world yourself.

People said Tommy made a miraculous recovery, which is to say that even with a cast and crutches he was soon showing up at the Rusty Hammer with a woman on either side of him, soon promising my mother he would come to Sunday dinner and then not showing up while the roast curled hard and dark around the edges in a warm oven. To tell the truth, I think that's another reason why my mother kept pushing for Callie and Clifton to move to the farm, to reel Tommy back in, although he was just as likely to blow off a visit with Clifton as a Sunday dinner.

Once he got pulled in for a drunk and disorderly and my father went and got him and let him sleep it off on the couch. The second time the cops called, my father said, "He's all yours." The police let him out anyway, because he was a veteran, because they'd known him in high school, because he was Tommy and sat in the little holding cell and got them laughing, even changed as he was.

I never drove him in my new car to the doctor after all; he never even saw the inside of my new car. When he went to the rehab facility, I guess he had some girl drive him, and my mother complained that he'd stopped going long before he ought to. LaRhonda rode in my car a few times when hers was in the shop; she was always driving over the curb on Front Street or backing into a tree. At the body shop where Tom had worked, briefly, I heard the guys called her car the cash cow. I could tell she wasn't enthusiastic about my old sedan. "I'm praying on your brother," she said one day, touching up her blush in the rearview, and it reminded me of why we weren't really friends anymore.

She'd given me a small box of books that day because, she said, she was putting away the things of the flesh, although it seemed kind of insulting that it was all right for the things of the flesh to wind up with me and I noticed she'd left out *Forever Amber,* that we'd read together in her bathroom when we were both twelve. Instead there was a book about cowgirls called *Giddyap!* that was pretty much all sex scenes except that the sex seemed ridiculous if you knew anything about what it would feel like to lie on the floor of a barn with no clothes on. There was a book called *Human Sexual Response* that was creepy because it took some of the stuff from the cowgirls book and turned it into science, with black-and-white drawings. And there was a really sad book about a bunch of college girls who thought they were going to be someone and then just turned out to be married and unhappy. There was one good sex scene in that one, though. The book was called *The Group* and it was the only one I wanted to keep, but I couldn't figure out how to get rid of the others. They felt like boomerangs, that would somehow find their way back to me and, more important, to my mother's attention.

I stashed them behind the dolls Cissy had made for me over the years, even though I'd never been much of a doll girl, but then I thought better of it. My mother was always taking the dolls down from the shelf and batting them against the wall to shake the dust loose because my mother felt about dust the way the evangelicals at the Church of the Living Lord felt about the devil: everywhere, and the cause of all evil. So finally I hid all three books behind the little door at the back of my closet that led to the pipes and wiring, although I kept taking the one about the college girls out and rereading it, trying to figure out why they'd all had plans but the plans had amounted to nothing, and whether the one at the end was really having sex with another woman. I bet LaRhonda hadn't even read that one. I didn't have much time to read myself, what with Clifton and the diner and my school assignments, and I wasn't much for made-up stories, but it was a good one, so good that somehow it didn't feel made up at all.

The only person who was really happy about my car, other than me, was a boy named Richard Bachman, who was first in our class to my number two. "Dear Mimi," Donald had written. "My grandfather says you're going to be the valedictorian. Wow! I'm not surprised." But that was just Donald's grandfather talking out of loyalty. There was no question that Richard was going to beat me out, which was fine. He was the youngest son of the Presbyterian minister, and while his five brothers and sisters were

fair-haired, fair-skinned, almost transparent people of Scandina-
vian appearance, Richard was Korean. His parents had adopted
him, and it showed how idealistic the God crowd was that they
thought he would fit right in in Miller's Valley. I don't know how
he survived high school; I had two classes with him each year, science and English, and I heard more slant-eyes comments than I
knew what to do with. "Don't feel sorry for that boy," my mother
said. "He'll leave the rest of them in the dust." Last thing I heard
Richard was the chair of the neuroscience department at one of
the big state universities, so as usual my mother sussed out the
future correctly. Although not about Tommy, who she said would
surely have learned his lesson once and for all from his accident.

One afternoon a week Richard and I had special permission
to drive to the state capital to work on our science projects. It
was a little over an hour's drive, and we kept the radio on so we
wouldn't have to make much conversation, although from time
to time Richard would say, "Great song," to show that he wasn't
a total loser. We had even been given a parking permit card for
the Office of Mines, Soil, and Water. Richard was doing a project
on plant life and the development of coal deposits in the region.
I said I thought that sounded interesting, but I didn't really think
so. I had decided to do my project on the water table in Miller's
Valley and the effect the dam had had on it since its construction.

"So, what about it?" Richard said.

"I'm not sure yet."

"You're going to need a hypothesis soon," he said.

"Well, hello there, young lady," said Winston Bally.

I don't know how Winston Bally knew I was working in the
water offices. Maybe they let him know any time someone asked
for information about the Roosevelt Dam. On our third visit to
the state capital he walked into the conference room with a big
smile as though we were old friends. He started picking up the
dusty microfilm boxes stacked on the table next to the microfilm

machine, which came on a little cart with wheels like the one we kept desserts on at the diner, so we could roll the cakes and pies around and show them to people. Finally he said, "I knew you were the smart one. I could tell from the beginning."

"I'm doing a science project," I said.

"So am I," said Richard, reaching across the table for a handshake, like he was a grown-up, which is how he'd always acted. "Coal deposits. Are they a product of compressed plant material?"

"That's not exactly a new idea, son," Mr. Bally said.

"I'm going to show it's false with data."

"Good for you. And what about you, Miss Miller?"

"I don't know yet."

"You looking at the data, too? At this data? The dam and the valley? That should be interesting for you."

"I haven't decided what I'm doing yet."

"I'd be happy to help," Mr. Bally said. "I'm an expert on the subject you're studying." He picked up one of the microfilm boxes. "Judges in these contests like primary sources."

I knew that. Judges in these contests always liked primary sources. I was already using one. "Tell me about Andover," I'd said to Cissy Langer, sitting in her back room with a wall full of piggy dolls staring at me.

"Oh, my goodness, Mimi, what a question," she'd said.

I took the glass of iced tea, and I took the plate of chocolate chip cookies, and I set my tape recorder between them. I'd borrowed it from the school librarian.

"I've already got some primary sources," I said to Winston Bally in the conference room.

We all pick and choose the things we talk about, I guess. I'd listened to my mother and Cissy talk about growing up together for maybe hundreds of hours, about sharing a seat and red licorice ropes on the bus, about getting licked for wearing their Sunday dresses into the woods one day, about the years when they both moved back in with their parents while their husbands went to war. And somehow I'd never really noticed that all the stories started when they were ten, that there were no stories about the four-year-old Miriam, the six-year-old Cissy, about the day when they were both seven when Ruth came home from the hospital, a bundle of yellow crochet yarn and dirty diaper. It made sense, I guess, since it turned out Cissy had grown up in a place whose name I'd never even heard because it had been wiped off the map before I'd ever even been born.

"My whole family lived in Andover," Cissy said. "My mother and father were both born there. There wasn't a real church, or a school, either. My grandfather used to say Andover was nothing but a wide place in the road. The next biggest place to Andover was the valley, if you can believe it. But we had a little store that sold all kinds of things, pots and pans and cheese and newspapers, you know, and there was a little chapel that some Shakers built in the woods and that's where my parents were married. I've got pictures somewhere."

She'd gone off and came back with a shoe box. "White patent," it said, "size eight." There were photographs of a family group standing in the woods, the men in white shirts and dark pants, the women in dark dresses and big hats. Cissy pointed at a woman who looked just like her. "Mama," she said.

"I don't have a whole lot to tell you, Mimi," she said. "I don't even really understand why you're dredging this all up in the first place. Andover wasn't like Miller's Valley. There was hardly anyone who lived there, maybe a hundred people or so, and there weren't any farms. The ground was terrible for planting things. My mother would force petunias from seed on the dining room windowsill and when she went to plant them outside she'd get herself a spadeful of rocks every time. She always got those flowers to grow but it was hard work. I love the soil in Miller's Valley.

When my mama lived here she did a beautiful job with the garden. I remember one day, you were real little, and you were out at their place looking at the hollyhocks. You kept putting out your little finger and saying 'flower.' It was the cutest."

She put the lid back on the shoe box. "We moved here when I was ten, after they built the dam and backed the river up so it flooded Andover. It was sad to leave, and then the very first day here I met your mother on the road, and that was that. I was content."

"What about Andover?"

"What about it, sweetie? It's gone. Even when there's drought the water's too deep to see any of what's left. Or maybe there's nothing left at all. I'm fifty now, so it's been down there under all that water for forty years. You know what water does. It gets to where it makes things just disappear." She picked up the last cookie, held it out to me, then popped it in her mouth when I shook my head. My mother said Cissy had always had a sweet tooth.

"You know what they call a place like that?" she said. "A drowned town. It's a drowned town, Andover."

"But when you go past there what do you think?"

"I don't go over there no more, Mimi. I don't go anywhere near that place."

"Who is your primary source?" Mr. Bally said in the water offices.

"I'm still doing my preliminary work," I said.

"I'd be happy to sit down and talk to you. That would look good to the judges."

"Do you know much about coal, sir?" said Richard.

"No, son. But I know everything about water and Miller's Valley." He picked up one of the microfilm boxes. "You talked to your father about your project?" he asked.

"Preliminary project," I said. "It's just preliminary."

I believe in love at first sight. I remember the day it happened. Any time I want I can make myself feel that feeling again, although I don't anymore, haven't for years. But I could if I wanted to. There were times when all someone had to do was light a match for a birthday candle, start the fireplace in the living room, burn some trash at the dump down the end of the road. All I had to do was smell smoke, and I was there, I was there. The smell of smoke could get me going good.

Clifton was kissing the cows. I don't know why, but that summer his favorite thing was to slip his head between the rails of the fence and kiss each one on its damp square nose. Cows can be skittish, but they hardly ever were with him.

"I like this one the best," he said.

He was almost four, a good-looking little boy who was smart and watchful. Minding him now didn't consist of much. He knew the rules, and he was good at keeping them. He was more like me, more like his aunt Mimi than his father. Of course his aunt Mimi had been around from the beginning, and his father—well, he just wasn't.

I could see a thin ceiling of whisper-gray smoke over the entire valley. There'd been hardly any snow that winter, and little spring rain, which everyone had said was a good deal until the brush on the mountain got dry as typing paper and some passerby dropped a lit match or maybe a cigarette and set it alight. My father was back at my aunt Ruth's, spraying her roof with the garden hose so that stray embers wouldn't nestle between the asphalt shingles. The volunteer companies from six or seven towns were on top of the mountain, coming in on one of the old logging trails, sending a state helicopter over to the deep cold waters behind the dam to lower buckets and bring them back and upend them over the blazing brush.

"Don't let anything happen to my house, Buddy," Ruth had yelled out her window.

"It's not your house," my mother had yelled back, but Aunt Ruth couldn't really hear her at that distance. I tried to remember the last time my mother and her sister had had a real conversation, a knees-touching-under-the-kitchen-table, eye-to-eye, pass-the-sugar conversation, but I couldn't.

"This one is his wife," Clifton said as he stood at the fence looking at a cow with a black eye and swollen udders. When he tried to kiss her she backed up and rumbled a low warning.

"No, no, I like you, cow," he said. He had a big orange sucker Ruth had given him, but she still wouldn't let him take any of her dolls down to see up close. "Those are just dolls to look at," she said. "We don't play with those dolls."

I was sitting on a stump reading a book, *The Construction of Water Containment Units in the Continental United States.* I'd done so much research on my science project that I could have written a book myself, but maybe not the one I'd originally intended. "You don't like that guy much," Richard had said after Winston Bally had stopped by the conference room for the third time, and I didn't like him any more for being right about most of the things he said about the valley. If you didn't take the people who lived there into account, he had the right idea.

The helicopter came overhead, its bucket dripping water that I figured had a little bit of Andover in it. Clifton looked up. "Daddy was in a chopper," he said.

"Really?" I said. Every once in a while Tommy would get drunk and say something like "The bugs, man, you can't even believe the size of the bugs. They'll eat you for breakfast." But you couldn't ask him a direct question about Vietnam. On the news they showed some boys who had burnt their draft cards, and Tom said, "I wasn't even drafted, I signed up of my own free will." Then he laughed and laughed, and then he started to cry and he fell asleep on the couch before dinner and had disappeared by morning. Sometimes at the diner one of the old guys would say, "They make it look pretty bad out there, son." And Tom would say one of two things, either "You have no idea" or "You don't want to know." Then someone would say that we had to beat the Communists or they would take over everything, and Tommy would stand up and leave. He always got comped because Mr. Venti had told the waitresses we had to honor his service to our country, even though I wasn't sure Tom felt that way himself.

Most of the time when he came to visit he would fall asleep in the living room, and my mother would cover him with an old quilt and leave him there. Tommy took a lot of pills, some to help him sleep, some to help him get up in the morning, some to help with the pain in his leg. He took something that was supposed to make him puke if he drank, and he took it and drank anyway and got so sick it seemed he would turn his insides inside out. "I always start the day with good intentions," he said to me once. Sometimes he even fulfilled them. He would help my father deliver a heavy engine in the truck to someone, or he would pick up groceries for Ruth. He would sit with her and watch television and he would make the two of them baloney sandwiches with mustard and potato chips. And then he would disappear and we wouldn't see him for days, maybe longer, and Callie would say she hadn't seen him, either. Usually when he turned up again he looked exhausted, and sometimes he was bruised, or cut up.

You don't want to know. As far as I was concerned he was right about that part. Sometimes I thought what I imagined was worse than the reality, most of the time not. I would sit in the living room chair and watch him sleep on the couch, not looking at his face but at the rise and fall of his chest under a grimy T-shirt. I wondered what his plan was now. Getting through the day, I figured.

"Daddy!" Clifton would holler when he would finally turn up, and there Tommy would be.

"Daddy," Clifton hollered, turning away from the cows at the fence, and there he was moving through the smoke, my big brother, swinging his bad leg out the way he did so he wouldn't have to bend it much. He slung it along with him like a long narrow sack of cement. The funny thing was, a lot of people had come to believe it was a war wound. I guess it was. I guess Tommy's whole life now was a war wound.

"Who are you?" Tommy said as he bent down slowly, like an old man.

"I'm Clifton."

"Clifton who?"

"Clifton Miller. Clifton Miller!"

"Clifton Miller? That's funny—my name's Tom Miller. Maybe you and me are related."

"We *are* related," Clifton always said, and he always garbled the last word a little bit, like he couldn't quite get his mouth, with its tiny pearl teeth and pursed pink lips, around all of it. "I'm your boy!"

"You are?" Tom would say. "Hell, yeah, you are! You are my

boy!" And then he would pick Clifton up, trying to keep the pain that cost him out of his face, and look him square in the eye, foreheads almost touching. It never got old for Clifton. I wondered when it would. Or if it would. My mother's lips clenched when Tommy got to the "hell yeah" part. Her crazy love for him was always at war with her disapproval of what he'd become. Whenever anyone would say how hard it was to watch him limp, she would say, "He's lucky to have that leg at all."

"Hey," I said to him.

Tommy put Clifton down slowly, picked up my book and looked at the title. "It's summer, it's your day off, what the hell is wrong with you?" he said, rolling his eyes, which were bloodshot, but maybe just from all the smoke. "You want to come up the mountain with us? The fire guys want to cut down a line of brush and shrub to make it harder for the fire to jump any further. I told a couple of them I'd give them a hand with the chain saw and the brush hog." I looked down. His hands weren't shaking so much today.

"I've got Clifton," I said, but just then my dad came down to the road and said, "Clifton can help me with the hose."

"I can help Gramps with the hose!" Clifton said. He made everything sound like an adventure. I guess we were all like that, once.

"I'm coming back to take you to the diner for dinner," Tommy told him. "You want to drive the tractor?"

"Yes sir!" said Clifton.

"Not you, bud. Your aunt Mimi. You help Gramps with the hose."

Quick as you could say Tom Miller just showed up, we had things happening all around us. My father came out with a box of sandwiches wrapped in wax paper that my mother had made before she left for the hospital, and he hitched the brush hog to the back of the tractor. "Take your finger out of your mouth," he said to Clifton, who put his hand behind his back, embarrassed. My father noticed Tom had a case of beer on the passenger seat of the truck, and he shook his head and said, "Don't you be driving my tractor all lickered up," and Tom said, "I'm never driving that tractor again," and there was a noise from the back of the truck and it was only then that I saw there was a guy asleep back there, wearing jeans and a white T-shirt with a baseball cap covering his face.

"Who's that?" I said, climbing up on the tractor and handing Clifton my book, which he held carefully in his small square fingers. Callie was doing a good job with him. Even my mother said so, and my aunt Ruth. It was the one thing they agreed on.

"Oh, hell, I almost forgot. We'll wake him up when we get there. That's Stevie. You'll like him. Everybody likes Stevie."

Tom was right; everybody did like Stevie, although Tommy was the only one who called him that. I wound up calling him Steven. "The woman makes me sound respectable," he would say, his arm hooked around my neck. "The woman makes me sound dignified."

The smoke woke him up that afternoon, smoke lying so low that it swamped the flat bed of the truck and killed my view of the valley, which from the tractor usually looked miniature, like the village Donald's grandfather had for his HO train set. The truth was, the fires were never really that big a deal, but everyone acted as though they were, maybe because the fires they could fight and the flooding they couldn't. You could put out flames but you couldn't stop the water from running into Miller's Valley when it wanted to. Twice the copter dragging its water bucket went over again, and both times, as soon as the sound started, Tom stood still and let his head drop down low, like he was waiting for it to be done. I didn't say anything about that. I didn't want to ruin this time we were having, which felt more or less like normal.

I dragged out a long line of brush with the tractor and Tom cut up some dead branches with the chain saw. Then we finished off the sandwiches, except for plain cheese, which no one really liked much, and balled up the wax paper into the empty slots in the beer carton. We were sitting on an old stone wall when there was a groan from the truck, and then the slow grinding metal sounds of someone standing in the truck bed and using it as a springboard to the ground.

"This's my kid sister," said Tom, mustard in his mustache.

"Good to meet you, kid sister," Steven said, putting out his hand and looking straight into my eyes like he was trying to see what was inside my head. It was a good thing I was sitting down because if I'd been standing I would have staggered, maybe even fallen.

"That's not love," my aunt Ruth had said one day when we'd been watching *The Guiding Light,* nodding at the screen, where the blond nurse was kissing the blond doctor next to a sign that said SURGERY. You could see how red their lips were, like they were painted on.

Maybe she was right, although there was a part of me that wondered why she would think she knew anything about it. But whatever it was, I was in it, surrounded by smoke, just like that.

For the rest of my life he would always be the guy:
Who first French-kissed me.

Who first felt me up.

Who first put his hand down my jeans.

Who first took my virginity.

Nah, that's not true. He didn't take it. I gave it to him. I shoved it at him with both hands. There was a routine the girls went through in high school, and I'd heard about it enough to know how it went. I'd heard it once spelled out like a science experiment to a whole bench full of girls in their underwear after gym by a senior named Nancy Fuller. "You don't let him put his tongue in your mouth for at least four dates," she said, adjusting her breasts inside her bra to make sure they were even. "You wait at least three months before you let him get under the shirt. If he's really your boyfriend you can let him go below the waist. But that's it. And don't ever take your clothes off because he won't be able to stop."

When the time came I felt like Nancy had missed an important part of the whole deal. I couldn't wait to get my clothes off.

I would have died if he'd stopped. I don't know why I wasn't embarrassed or ashamed or sorry, but I wasn't. Sometimes I thought there was something wrong with me, that I was just bad and I'd better stay with one guy because if they let me loose there's no telling what I'd do. Mostly I thought it was because Steven was so damn charming. He wore charm like a three-piece suit. He knew his way around a girl.

The first time he came to the house to take me out he brought a box of peanut brittle. My aunt Ruth was still a sucker for a chocolate-covered cherry, but my mother loved peanut brittle more than anything on earth. I guess Steven had gotten that out of Tom, because he sure hadn't heard it from me. A whole pound of peanut brittle, hand-packed in a white box with a gold elastic around it and fancy gold-and-white patterned wax paper inside that looked like the wallpaper in the Ventis' dining room. He would have been three steps ahead of any guy in Miller's Valley if he'd just handed my mother that box, but not Steven. He had to put whipped cream on the sundae. "Maybe you haven't had dinner yet but I sure would like it if you would try a piece and give me your opinion," he said to my mother. "Someone told me it's the best peanut brittle in the state, but I'd like to know what you think."

"That boy went out of his way," my father said next morning at breakfast.

"He is in no way a boy," my mother said.

He was twenty-four, almost seven years older than I was. He worked construction all over the county and the map of his arms was as sharp as the contours of Miller's Valley: bicep, tricep, shoulder muscles, all as hard as the tire on a semi. He told me he was taking me to a steak house, and I thought we were going to LaRhonda's father's place, but he drove for almost an hour to a place off the highway with a big aquarium in the center of the room. He told me they aged their own beef. He ordered surf and turf for the both of us. It was the first time I had lobster, and he cracked the claws for me. "So fill me in on this project you're working on," he said. I hadn't told him about that, either. It was like he made a study of people. We were sitting side by side on a red-leather bench against the wall, and he put his arm along the top of the bench but he never let it touch me, which made me even more conscious of the fact that it was there.

"It's pretty boring," I said.

"Try me."

He was the first person I told about what I had learned, that all the history and all the science and all the simple common sense made it pretty clear that someday the government was going to buy up all the houses in the valley, or take them if they weren't freely sold, to extend the water storage area behind the dam and increase the size of the reservoir. He listened like he was really interested, which may or may not have been true at the time. That was the thing about Steven: you couldn't always tell what was him and what was his idea of how he ought to be. He was a high school graduate framing in walls and laying shingles, but he had plans, big plans, not school plans or job plans but money plans, success plans.

I don't know how I managed to keep up with my schoolwork. Maybe it was because Steven acted as though it was a part of me he thought was important. We would be at the dumpy apartment where one of his friends lived, up a rickety set of wooden stairs to the second floor of what you could tell was meant to be a one-family house instead of a collection of weird apartments with half kitchens and sketchy bathrooms, drinking beer, or gin and orange juice for the girls, someone in the bedroom passing around a joint, and Steven would announce, "This woman? Top of her class. You wouldn't know it to look at her, but she's more than a pretty face. She's a brain. Calculus, man."

"Precalculus," I might say under my breath, but no one lis-

tened to me much, in those apartments or in the bars. Steve Sawicki's girlfriend. Tommy Miller's sister. That was all I was, no
matter how often Steven told people otherwise. "Ladies and
gentlemen," he'd say, putting out his hand, "Mimi Miller." It
was embarrassing, but there was a part of me that liked it, too.
He made it feel like life was a party, and he was hosting it. Sometimes when I wasn't with him and I thought about him he seemed
unreal to me. But then he'd be sitting next to me and I'd look
down at those little dark hairs on his arms and they were the
realest things in the world. I know some people wondered why I
was with him, and part of it was because he made it seem like he
was training for the Olympics and I was the gold medal. No one
had ever acted like I was the gold medal before, or not so I'd
noticed.

But I know now that some of it was simpler than that. It was
the sex, although I spent a lot of time pretending we weren't having it. I wouldn't go into one of the bedrooms at those crappy
apartments the way those other girls did, so you could hear them
through the thin hollow-core doors. Some of them sounded like
they were pretending to me. I wasn't pretending, not one bit.

None of the people Steven hung out with were the kind of
people who cared if you took calculus, or precalculus. Some of
the girls seemed just shy of low-dull normal, although maybe
that was what they thought their boyfriends liked. One or two
were nice to me. Brenda, who was a beautician, was always telling me how good my hair would look if I let her put streaks in it.
She said she could do it right in the kitchen, but I thought my
mother would go nuts. She was already suspicious of Steven.
Maybe she could smell the sex on me. Maybe that's why I was
keeping up with my schoolwork, too, because my mother kept
watch, was always going in my bag and looking at the grades on
my quizzes. They didn't give her any ammunition: A A A A. Even
the English essays.

Once Steven insisted on driving me to the state capital when I was planning to do research. I tried to get out of that by saying that I had to take Richard, too, but he insisted on giving Richard a lift. The three of us were sandwiched in the cab of his truck, Richard and me with our notebooks on our laps, Steven with his hand on my knee.

"He seems like an okay guy," Richard said when we got inside. "He has a lot of plans," I'd replied, but that sounded lame even to me. Although it was true. Steven could talk about his plans for hours at a time, until Tommy, who liked him less now that I was with him, would tell him to shut up. His plan—his business plan, he always called it—was to buy a run-down house cheap, fix it up, then resell it at a profit and buy another one. He would take long drives to look for the right areas, "up-and-comers," he'd call them. I'd go with him, if I wasn't working at the diner or doing extra credit after school, and study in the truck while Steven walked around the main street, checked out the parks and playgrounds, picked up the local paper to read the real estate ads. Sometimes he'd see a house in an ad that looked promising and he'd drive over and sit at the curb, saying things like "I just want you to picture that painted white, with green shutters. That real dark green, kind of a classy color. Like, country club, you know what I'm talking about?"

"Hunter green?" And he'd look at me like I'd invented fire, and kiss me, first a smacking kind of kiss, then a long kiss that made me go all soft. "That's why I need you to help me with this," he'd say. "You understand this. You're on the same wavelength." At the end of the day, if it wasn't cold or raining, or even sometimes when it was, we would drive to some gravel road off the main drag, where the trees closed in, and he would put a sleeping bag on the bed of the truck. We would take off our clothes as fast as we could and jump on each other like crazy people. It's been a long time, and I know more now than I did then, a lot more, but I'm not sugarcoating anything when I say that the charm didn't fail him there, or in the twin bed in the room he rented from an elderly man the other side of town from the valley. Maybe that's why I kept up with my schoolwork. A long line of correct equations, a physics test with the number 100 at the top in red ink: they made me feel more like my old self. My old self believed all the stories about how boys had to talk you into it, about how you had to just smack them down or put up with it. I'd never heard anyone talk about putting up with dinner and a movie just so you could get to the part where the warped wooden door was closed and locked and your boyfriend had to put his hand over your mouth so you would stop making so much noise.

"Dear Mimi," said the postcard I'd just gotten from Donald. "I'm here. Hope I will do okay. Donald." On the front was a picture of what looked like an apartment building with palm trees and the ocean behind it. It was in Santa Barbara, but it looked like the Garden of Eden only with tennis courts. "California," Steven said when he took it out of my purse. "That's an idea." The next time he saw LaRhonda he said, "Who's Donald?" LaRhonda rolled her eyes. "Loser," she said. "That's mean," I said. "But true," LaRhonda said, and I'm ashamed to say I didn't say anything after that. I told myself that he was just a boy I'd known when we were kids, who I hadn't seen in years.

It was funny—LaRhonda's interest in me had revived. It didn't hurt that her boyfriend knew Steven from construction. His name was Fred, and he had red hair and freckles and bright green eyes, so depending on your taste he was either good-looking or just plain weird. He and Steven liked each other, maybe because, unlike the other guys on the jobs they worked together, Steven didn't mock the little inspirational palm cards Fred liked to hand out. Sometimes I would find a card in Steven's pocket with a picture of a bird or a flower or something, and then some verse:

"Out of the ground the Lord God formed every beast of the field" or "All we like sheep have gone astray," something like that.

LaRhonda was still part of the God Squad, and so was Fred, but the numbers had gotten smaller and smaller since LaRhonda had first taken Jesus as her personal savior, or what her father sometimes called "lost her tiny mind." One of the girls had gone the other way and become part of the new hippie group, kids who had moved from skirts and sweaters to bell-bottom jeans and Indian print blouses. "All of them smoking that pot in Lizanne's basement!" LaRhonda said, and Fred frowned and tapped her on the knee, as though I was the only one in Miller's Valley who hadn't heard that my brother was the man to see for marijuana.

LaRhonda's mother loved Fred, and I could tell why. He was so agreeable that it sometimes seemed like he didn't have an opinion about anything. He'd order whatever LaRhonda did at the Dairy Queen, go along with anything Steven said. "Definitely!" was his favorite word, and about as close to a sentence as he usually got, unless you counted "Praise God." But even praising God he was the guy who would buy beer for the fifteen-year-olds who hung around the package store after every other guy had passed them by and said "Get lost." Sometimes we would go to LaRhonda's house and swim in her pool, lie on the chaises, and ask Fred to bring out iced tea or sandwiches, see if there were more towels in the laundry room. "Definitely," he always said.

We usually left if the Ventis showed up. Even with the four of us there, a situation where most parents went out of their way to pretend to like one another, they were uncomfortable to be around. Their conversation went like this:

"You need more ice cream like you need a hole in the head."

"What difference does it make what I look like? Unless I was twenty and wearing a waitress uniform, you wouldn't even notice."

"You're crazy."

"You're disgusting."

LaRhonda was working as a hostess at the steak house during the shifts when her mother was off, and she said she didn't know what her mother was talking about, but at the diner we all did. After Callie shut Mr. Venti down and told him that if he fired her she would tell Tommy why, he'd turned to a girl whose mother was also a waitress at the diner. It caused all kinds of problems because both daughter and mother let Dee know that while she made the station and schedule assignments they would change them if they didn't like them. Plus when Mr. Venti would stop by there were always angry customers wondering where their club sandwiches were when they were sitting right up on the to-go shelf waiting for a waitress who was in the back office doing who-knew-what, usually on her knees.

"The man is almost sixty!" Dee would mutter to herself sometimes, but the rest of us kept our mouths shut. I had to admit, Mr. Venti was right about one thing: Mrs. Venti was getting really fat, and to make it worse she was wearing the clothes she'd worn when she was thinner. "She's a total mess," LaRhonda said. "She imagines all kinds of disgusting stuff about my father." Once Mrs. Venti came in and spilled hot coffee down the front of the uniform of the girl at the diner, but that only made things worse because then everyone was talking about what had happened. Mrs. Venti laughed so hard, in a kind of odd and uncomfortable way, that everyone knew the coffee was no accident. That was the last time we saw her at the diner. When I came over she would try to ask me questions about what was going on there, but I stayed vague. The glass of orange juice she always had in her hand smelled like it had gone bad, and Steven said that was because it was half gin. "I thought things would be different," she said to me one day looking out the kitchen window to the big back lawn, and after that I tried not to be alone with her.

M r. Bally came into the diner at least once a week. He was spending a lot of time in the valley. One Saturday he waited until I'd changed out of my uniform and then asked me if I wanted to join him at his table. A busman's holiday, he called it, which I'd never heard before but looked up after. "Can I offer you a soda pop?" he said, when I slid into the booth, looking wary.

"A soda pop?"

"Why is that funny?"

"I'm sorry, but the only person I know who calls Coke soda pop is my aunt Ruth, and that's because she hasn't left the house in thirteen years."

"She hasn't left the house?"

"It's a long story. I don't really need anything, thank you. I've got to get home."

"To work on your science project, correct? I'm still not entirely clear on the thrust of your science project."

"Me neither."

"But I can tell you're a smart girl or you wouldn't be doing all this research. So you're smart enough to have a handle on what's going on here. Let me just ask you one question: what was the biggest mistake they made in the original Roosevelt Dam project?"

I knew the answer, but I wasn't going to give him the satisfaction. It got so quiet at our table that you could hear the clink of knives and forks all around us. "Adam and Eve on a raft," Dee called to the grill cook, one of her customers having eggs for early supper.

Finally Mr. Bally said, "You must know there are two ways this can go. There's the easy way, and there's the hard way."

"The easy way."

"The homeowners are offered a fair market price for their properties as well as compensated for the cost of relocation."

"The hard way."

Mr. Bally leaned back and didn't say anything. He made his fingers into a little steeple. He had a tie clip with the state seal on it, and an old Timex watch, and a wedding band. He looked like he felt sorry for me, which made me angry. Plus I felt like he was using me somehow to get what he wanted. That made me angrier.

"You know what I've noticed about you, Mr. Bally? You have two different voices. You have the voice you're using with me here, and then you have the voice you use when you come out to the valley." It was true: when he was talking to the men at the diner, or arguing with Donald's grandfather, or talking to Mr. Langer, Mr. Bally used a kind of folksy voice and vocabulary. It seemed practiced, and natural, and I wondered whether it was because that was the voice he'd grown up with and this, here, all business, was the voice he'd grown into.

"So do you, young lady. You just haven't noticed it yet." He stirred sugar into his coffee. "Someone from the valley who understood the process and the science behind it could be extremely helpful to me and to the state water board in terms of bringing others around to a reasonable point of view. Do you have any thoughts about your plans after graduation?"

"They're holding a spot here for me at the diner," I said.

"Very funny."

"Are you offering me a job, Mr. Bally?"

"Would you like one? I know you're planning on college, but we could give you a job for the summer. It would be a lot more interesting than waiting tables. And state employees get a break on tuition at the university."

"A job flooding my family's farm?"

"That's going to happen one way or another, Miss Miller," Mr. Bally said. "The easy way or the hard way. Why don't you discuss my offer with your mother?" He put a ten-dollar bill on the table, then put his coffee cup on top of it. "You still didn't answer my question," he said. "What was the biggest mistake they made in the original dam project? I know you know the answer."

I sat there saying nothing, watched him pick a mint out of the bowl at the register and walk out the double glass doors. "Too smart for your own good," Ruth said about me sometimes when she was irritated, and I felt that way then.

There was something I wanted to say to Winston Bally, and the simple fact was I hadn't had the guts. One afternoon near the end of summer I had spent three hours on the banks of the river, waving off the gnats with a hand in front of my face, thinking about what I'd do if I were the engineer, the manager, the person calling the shots on Miller's Valley. The dam was big, bigger than it needed to be. The reservoir was big, too, but not as big as it could be or maybe ought to be. The air was as thick and still as tapioca, and I felt like I might as well be the only person in the world, it was so deserted and silent except for the sound of rushing water and the occasional bullfrog thump. Until I followed

Miller's Creek pretty far in and broke through a thick line of trees, there was no sign of anything human or even alive, and then not much of one until I'd hiked so far that I could almost see our place down below. Which was the point, I guess, as far as the government people were concerned, so few people who needed to be moved to do what needed to be done.

I'd gotten to a spot on the creek where I used to build dams myself, as a kid, and I'd stood and stared at it for a long time. As wide as that spot was now, as deep as the water lay, as fast as it ran, there was no way that any kid could build a dam there on their own the way I had when I was younger. Slowly I'd walked back the length of Miller's Creek from that point to the river. It had always been bigger than a creek, but now it was much much bigger. Not from groundwater coming up, but from river water coming in. It was like a knock on the head, realizing that instead of reading books in some state office building I should have been here, that what Winston Bally knew that I didn't wasn't in maps or charts but in the way my feet were sinking deep into ground that used to be dry and now was wet.

Sometimes I wonder whether it would have made any difference if I'd said anything, if I'd leaned across the diner table to Winston Bally and said, "You all rigged it. Years and years ago, maybe before I was even born, you decided you wanted more water and less land. You blocked off the flow of the river out of the dam locks. You block off a little more each year. What we thought was nature letting more and more water take over the valley wasn't nature at all. You all made it happen. It was slick and it was smart, deciding that one way to convince people to leave was to drown them little by little, by inches instead of all at once."

Maybe I would have added, "You killed Donald's grandmother, too."

I wonder what he would have said. He would have known

that there was nothing in all that microfilm, in any of the documents, that said, If we make the valley wet and then wetter, sooner or later all those dumb farmers will give up and move out. Besides, it was a different time then, when lots of people still believed the government always did the right thing, had our best interests at heart, and so he might have pretended to be shocked and amazed at my suggestion.

But maybe not. We'd developed a strange relationship, me and Mr. Bally. I think he liked the idea of talking things over with someone who'd been born and grown up in Miller's Valley, who loved the place and would mourn it forever but who also knew that its time was past. He got a strange look in his eyes sometimes when he was talking to me, like he got a kick out of what I knew, and how I knew I couldn't do anything about what was coming.

So maybe I would have spit out all those things that I had figured out while slapping the gnats away, and when I was done, my voice choked, my face all balled up in a battle against the tears, he would have leaned toward me and said, again, "I always knew you were the smart one."

Out in the diner parking lot Mr. Bally pulled down the car visor to shade his eyes. I sat in the booth watching him and said, so low no one could hear me, "The biggest mistake they made in the original dam project is that they didn't flood a large enough area."

I stood up and handed Dee the ten. "Your table," I said.

"Hot dog," she said, shoving the bill into her pocket.

Eddie came for a visit. My mother took the day off to make dinner: lamb stew, green beans, a cake. He was in the area on business, he said, which is why Debbie wasn't with him. He was wearing a tweed sport jacket and a plaid shirt and looked like someone from a Van Heusen commercial. Eddie was good-looking in a kind of average way, and his personality was not so different. He never got really angry, and he rarely got really excited. Or maybe he did. I didn't really know him very well. By the time I was eight years old he was already gone at college. The difference between fifty and sixty is nothing; the difference between eight and eighteen is more or less a lifetime.

"Mom says you're doing great at the high school," he said as he dug into his stew. "What are you thinking about after?"

"She's going to college," my mother said from the stove. "I told you that." My mother talked to Eddie on the phone every Sunday evening after the rates went down. Every time she got off the phone she said two things: I'm certainly proud of my son, and I don't understand why they haven't started a family.

"I know that. I just meant in terms of a course of study. You can't go wrong with a teaching degree, Mimi. Debbie had more job offers than she knew what to do with. She's working in her father's office because he couldn't get anyone reliable to answer the phones, but she'll go back to teaching school someday."

"I'm not sure," I said. I was sure I wasn't going to get an education degree or teach school, but I didn't want to start a fight. Good morning, Miss Miller. I'm sorry I'm late, Miss Miller. I didn't do the homework, Miss Miller. There was just no way. I'd told Steven about Mr. Bally's offer of work, but he just waved it away like a fly at a picnic. "A government job? You're better than that." Of course I hadn't said anything to my parents. My mother might have thought it was a good idea. My father might have beaten the man until his fists bled, and then where would we be? Four landowners had made deals with the state and four others had put their places on the market to see if someone who'd never heard of the water and the dam would be foolish enough to buy them. They kept lowering their prices but no one bit. In history class our teacher had talked about the domino theory because of Vietnam, which he stopped talking about after just one class, maybe because someone told him about Tommy or because he was afraid of getting in trouble with the principal, who had the tallest flagpole in town on his front lawn. But you could see the domino theory at work in the valley as the sales and the sale signs spread. And I was pretty sure I had seen the domino theory in the woods between our place and the river. A little more water in the reservoir made a little more in Miller's Creek made a little more in the valley. Until soon it was a lot more.

"You could run this place, the way you work around here," said my father, tapping his fork on the edge of my plate. "I should have known neither of your brothers were going to come around to farming."

"Can I get a glass of milk, Mom?" Eddie said.

"There's nothing wrong with nursing," said my mother.

"No question," said Eddie. "There'll always be jobs for nurses."

"Everybody wants to eat, but nobody wants to farm," said my father. "Where the heck do they think beef comes from?"

"Did you see Aunt Ruth?" I asked Eddie.

"If she wants to see him she knows where he is," my mother said. "She can come down here and sit at the table like the rest of us."

Eddie looked sideways at me. No wonder he never showed up. He'd arrived in a Toyota and had to spend fifteen minutes standing outside discussing whether it had decent pickup and whether my father had fought the Japs so that they could take over the automobile business from the Americans. Eddie said it was a company car, but my father had been in a touchy mood ever since. I think deep down inside he didn't know exactly how to feel about Eddie. He was proud of how well he'd done, but the way in which he'd done well made my father feel like Eddie was above the life he'd been raised in. I wondered if he'd feel the same about me if I went to college, especially if I didn't become a teacher or a nurse. Sometimes LaRhonda said she was going to get a business degree, but I didn't think she really knew what that meant. Maybe LaRhonda should go to work for Mr. Bally; she'd foreclose on a farm without thinking twice. Her father thought a girl going to college was a waste of time. "Look at this," Mr. Venti would say, sweeping his arm out over the restaurant the way Ed Sullivan did when he introduced an act. "You'll never want for anything. You'll never even have to cook for your family."

My mother had cleared the dinner plates—"don't get up"— and was dishing out cake when the back door slammed and Tommy came in. The look on his face, and my mother's face, made me realize right away that he hadn't known anything about dinner and Eddie.

"Well, hell," he said, slow and low and with an undertone.

"Look what the cat dragged in," said Eddie, and he stood up and the two of them shook hands, as though they were strangers meeting in an insurance office or something. My mother used to say sometimes that when they were little they were close, but it was hard to believe. Looking at them you couldn't even imagine they were related. One looked like a cop and the other like a criminal.

"What brings you to this neck of the woods?" Tommy said, pulling up a chair while my mother made him a plate.

"Work, believe it or not. We're doing the engineering on a new development off 502."

"Off 502? None of the construction guys have said anything about that."

"It's early yet," said Eddie, and the way he said it made me understand he didn't want Tom to mention it to anyone.

"How many houses?"

"A good many," said Eddie, shutting the discussion down and chasing cake crumbs with his fork. "What's happening with you, brother?"

Tommy mumbled with his mouth full, "Ah, a little of this, a little of that." It was small-talk city, but that was the way my brothers liked it, I guess.

"How's your wife doing?"

"She's good. You should come down and visit. She's teaching herself to cook. She's getting pretty good. Mom and Dad drove down and she made them a roast beef dinner."

I remembered. My mother said Debbie had gotten the wrong cut of meat, made mashed potatoes from a box and gravy from a jar. "The carrots were good," my father said. "Frozen," my mother said.

"Maybe I will," said Tom, in that way you say you're going to do something you're never going to do. He handed his plate back to my mother, who refilled it. Eddie asked for a second piece of cake.

"I want to take you two for a ride," Eddie said to my parents when he was done with his cake, standing up and taking his jacket off one of the hooks by the back door.

"We safe in that tin can?" my father said.

"Ah, man, don't get him started on Japanese cars," Tommy said.

"I bet you'd feel the same if people started driving Vietnamese cars," our father said.

"I don't care who drives what as long as no one is trying to kill me."

When we were alone I said to Tommy, "You don't look dressed for a wake."

"Yeah, right?" he said. "You want to make a pot of coffee?" He went upstairs and when he came down he was wearing one of my father's sport shirts, a dark plaid with short sleeves. The fabric pulled across his wide shoulders. I didn't know exactly what Tommy did with himself all day, but he was still in basic-training condition. All the other guys at the VFW had big bellies sloping over their belts. "Baby likes beer," they would say, rubbing their midsections like a genie would show up and they would get three wishes. The wishes being three more boilermakers lined up on the bar.

Tommy still didn't look like he was going to a wake. No tie, hair curling down around his collar and over his ears, mustache drooping around his mouth. He poured himself some coffee and his hands shook just a bit.

"So you and Stevie," he said.

"So?"

"I didn't see that coming," he said.

"Are you okay with it?"

"I mean, yeah. I'm just not sure he's right for you. Don't get sidetracked."

"From what?"

"Anything. Everything. Be like Ed. Get out of here. Don't get stuck."

"What about you?"

"Never mind about me, Meems." He took two sips of coffee and put his cup in the sink. "I'm rolling out," he said.

A boy three years ahead of me at the high school had joined the Army earlier in the year. He'd been in Vietnam for three weeks when he got killed. Nobody knew exactly how, except that it was a closed-casket wake, and Miller's Valley wasn't a place that was big on closed-casket wakes. He was the second soldier from Miller's Valley to die there. Tom was so far the only one to come back alive.

I did the dishes and thought about whether Tommy was going to make it to McTeague's Funeral Home and figured that he wouldn't. There were two bars between here and there, and a little cinder-block box of a house that one of Tommy's semiregular girlfriends lived in. He'd get sidetracked. He usually did.

I walked back to Ruth's with a slab of cake on a paper plate. I figured my mother would think Tommy had eaten it. Aunt Ruth was watching *The Beverly Hillbillies*.

"You know, Buddy Ebsen was a big song and dance man when he was young," Ruth said, reaching for the cake without taking her eyes from the TV. "He was supposed to play the Tin Man in *The Wizard of Oz,* but he got hives when they put that silver makeup on him." Aunt Ruth said that every time she was watching *The Beverly Hillbillies,* just like every time she watched *The Andy Griffith Show* she said the little boy was cute and Andy Griffith should have won an Oscar for *A Face in the Crowd,* and every time she watched *The Carol Burnett Show* she said,

"Honey, I love her but that woman has no chin at all." Aunt Ruth subscribed to movie magazines, and nothing ticked her off more than when my father would forget to bring them back to her when they showed up in our mailbox. She had her own mailbox, right on the road next to ours, but the mailman knew better than to put her mail in it.

"This cake is a little dry," Ruth said.

"Beggars can't be choosers." As I'd gotten older I'd refused to side with Ruth in her spite war against my mother.

"Just get me some milk before you go home, okay, honey?" she said, which was my cue to stop distracting her from some argument Jethro and Elly May were having on the television.

I was at our kitchen table taking notes for a history paper on the medical techniques developed during the Civil War when I heard a car door slam and my father yelling. When my mother yelled her sentences were sharp and tight, but my father did it seldom and his words got loose-limbed and ran together so he was hard to understand. From inside the barn you could hear the cows mooing loud but low, and that made the whole thing even more confusing, like when the school band tuned up in the practice room.

"Oh, for goodness' sake, you know Eddie never intended any disrespect. The opposite. The exact opposite. You know that boy. You're being ridiculous."

"I feel goddamned ridiculous, I can tell you that. He's twenty-eight years old and he thinks he knows every damn thing." I kept my head low over my paper and pretended to be writing something. "To take us out there and start talking about ranch houses and bathrooms with two sinks and attached garages and all that—what the hell was he thinking, that I was going to say, Well, gosh, Edward, sign me right up?"

"He's worried about you. If you've said it once, you've said it a hundred times: running a farm is hard work. And what's wrong with living in a nice new house with wall-to-wall carpeting? You may not want to hear this, but I'd like some wall-to-wall carpeting."

"Miriam, you want carpeting, I'll have it installed tomorrow. In this house. Which, in case you've also forgot along with that snot-nosed son of yours, was built by my great-great-grandfather. Built good, too, with four-by-fours and plaster over lath, not this sheetrock crap they'll be using for those houses out there. You imagine my customers bringing lawn mowers out there to one of those nasty little nowhere roads to get fixed? Or no, I guess they won't be doing that because, as Edward James Miller says driving around in his Jap car, maybe I might want to retire."

There was a picture in the book in front of me of a doctor dressed in a kind of cutaway jacket with a white apron over it. He was holding a saw. I just kept staring at the saw. It was bloody and looked dull. My father said a dull saw was worse than no saw at all. My brother must have lost his mind with this idea, or he'd forgotten where and who he came from.

"You made it clear where you stand on that, and on all the rest of it. Just put it to bed."

"You put it to bed. You were the one standing there in an empty field, looking around and smiling and nodding like some goddamned beauty queen."

"You've let loose with enough profanity to blow the roof off this place for the next ten years," my mother said. "Put that to bed, too. Speaking of which, I'm going to bed."

The door slammed twice, her, him. She didn't even look at me as she stomped up the stairs.

My father sat down hard at the table and glared at me, then down at my book, like he was mad at us both. "What the hell is that?" he said, still kind of yelling.

"Amputation," I said.

"You want to live in a new house with all the modern conveniences?"

I tried to imagine anyone in my position at that moment who would say anything different, even LaRhonda or Tommy. "No," I said.

My father walked out the back door and let it slam behind him. "Get back here," my mother called from their bedroom window, but my father just kept walking down the back path and into the dark.

I was happy that only the valedictorian gave a speech at the high school graduation. My mother was annoyed, though. "Every other school, they both speak, number one, number two," she said. "How will anyone know you were the salutatorian if you don't get to speak?"

"It's in the program," I said. It also said I'd won the 1971 Chamber of Commerce Mathematics Prize. Richard got the science prize, although neither of us had placed out of our region with our projects. He'd been very disappointed, but I knew I wasn't going to win with "Andover, Pennsylvania, 1921–1930: A History of Water Management in a Drowned Town."

"You pulled your punches, Miss Miller," Mr. Bally had said after he'd polished off a western omelet at one of my tables the week after the regionals. "I thought you were going to be taking a good hard look at the water situation in Miller's Valley, not go over ancient history."

"I did take a good hard look," I said as I refilled his coffee cup. "I don't know that you would have liked much what I saw."

That was as close as I ever got to saying that I suspected what the government people had been up to. I stood at the table with the coffeepot in my hand and looked at him with my eyes narrowed.

"Aha," he said. That was it.

"Oh, Mimi, you took me right back to when I was a girl!" Cissy had said, clapping her soft little hands.

"It turned out a little more like a history project than I expected," Mrs. Farrell said. I could tell she was disappointed in me, and since she'd seen Steven pick me up a couple of times in his truck I was betting she thought he was the reason I hadn't done better. I couldn't really tell her what had happened. I wanted to say, Mrs. Farrell, if you did research and found out that someone you really loved was going to die, would you publish it or keep it to yourself? But I just came up with my own answer, and did what I did, and didn't do what I couldn't bring myself to do.

I got a check from the Chamber of Commerce for a hundred dollars for the math prize, and a check from the PTA for a hundred dollars for being salutatorian, and Mr. Venti surprised me by giving me a hundred dollars in new twenty-dollar bills in a card shaped like a mortarboard. With the money I'd saved from my job and a scholarship I'd gotten from the Pennsylvania League of Women Voters, I'd be able to make it through at least two years at the state university, and Mrs. Farrell said she was sure there was more scholarship money out there for a woman in math and science. I liked it, when she said that, like I was actually a woman, and in math and science.

My parents had a party in our yard, the tables set up between the back of our house and the front of Ruth's. If you talked to my mother she said that was the best place because there was plenty of room and some trees for shade. If you talked to my father he said it was the best place because then Ruth could sit in a chair by her window and hear most of what was going on. Steven insisted on walking with one arm around me, telling people to take a good look at the gold heart with the diamond at its center he'd given me as a gift. "It's a quarter carat," he said over and over again. "When she graduates from college there'll be a bigger stone, and it won't be in a necklace." He'd already bought one house and then resold it. He'd made almost two thousand dollars and said next time it would be more when he was finished with the two new places he was working on.

"Ed, I'd like to talk to you about an investment that I'm pretty sure will interest you," he said to my brother, backing him up against the dessert table.

"Now, son, this is a social occasion," my father said to him after a few minutes. Eddie took his business card out of his wallet and gave it to Steven. Steven did the same. "I'm going to make your brother rich," he said.

He'd talked about calling his company Steamy or Misty, both names that combined his and mine, neither of which made any sense at all and sounded more like a dirty movie than a real estate business. "I guess I'm just a sentimental guy," he said when I shot them down. Finally I'd come up with Home Sweet Home when I was having lunch with Aunt Ruth and staring at a fake sampler she had on her wall in the kitchen. Steven had gone right out and had cards printed up. He was still working construction, then knocking off to go over to work on the places he was fixing up. I helped him some, pulling up stained carpeting, chiseling Pepto pink tile off the bathroom wall. I'd panicked him a little bit in one of the houses when the toilet ran slow and I said the septic might be failing, but I had an old plumbing snake of my father's, and once I snaked it it was fine.

"Sometimes I wonder why you're paying for college," he said, lying beside me in a sleeping bag on the breezeway floor, both of us stripped to our underwear and smelling of sweat and spackle. "With two of us we could make twice as much money on this. We could clean up."

I didn't say anything. My mother had ordered a sheet cake for my graduation party that said GO GET 'EM MIMI! which for my mother was pretty whimsical. I knew it didn't mean GO GET THAT OLD TOILET OUT OF THE BATHROOM AND PUT IN A NEW ONE!

"That young man of yours is a keeper," said Cissy Langer, fingering the heart around my neck and listening to Steven tell Mr. Langer about an apartment building that he was really itching to get his hands on if only he had the cash. She leaned in and whispered, "He is good-looking, too." There was no question. The black curls, the dark eyes, the broad mouth. I still wasn't sure why he'd chosen me. That was another thing that made me hang on to him.

"Mary Margaret, bring me a piece of cake," Ruth called. "A corner piece, with one of those big frosting flowers."

"I'll take it to her," my father said.

"You stay where you are, Bud. I asked your daughter and that's who I want." Good thing my mother was across the grass talking to the Ventis, whose big party for LaRhonda at the steak house wasn't until Saturday night. "I'm closing the whole place for you kids," Mr. Venti had said. "Do you know what kind of a loss I'm taking doing that?"

"Oh, Daddy, don't start," LaRhonda had said. Her father talked all the time about how much college was going to cost him and how LaRhonda was just going to waste it by getting married anyhow. "Give the girl a ring and save me a whole lot of money," he was always saying to Fred. LaRhonda kept saying she was mainly going to State to spite him, but she also kept talking about the sororities, spent most of my party sitting over in a lawn chair talking to Ed's wife, Debbie, who had been a Kappa, which was what LaRhonda wanted to be, too. Fred was next to her, empty beer cans lined up in a nice neat row at his feet. He'd given her a wallet for graduation. "I already have a wallet," she'd said. "Not one I gave you," he said. "Take a look inside." There was a picture of Fred and LaRhonda in the photo compartment, and a hundred-dollar bill in the bills compartment.

"He's a decent guy, but he does not know the way to a woman's heart," Steven said, running his hand up my arm and nodding at my neck, then putting one finger in the frosting on the piece of cake I was holding. "That's mine, young man," Ruth called.

"Just testing it to make sure it's good enough for you, ma'am," he called back as I went inside.

"I haven't decided yet if he's trustworthy," Ruth said, taking the cake from me.

"When will you know?"

Her mouth was full; she looked like a squirrel storing nuts, like the sheet cake on the table wasn't big enough to feed half the county, and another sheet cake in Ruth's refrigerator because my mother had run out of room in hers, what with the Jell-O molds and the potato salad.

"Don't get smart with me," she finally said, a blob of frosting on her upper lip. I reached over and took it off with my finger.

"What am I going to do without you around?" she said, and she started to cry, really cry, like she had finally said out loud something that had been eating at her for a long time.

"I'll only be two hours away," I said. "I'll be home all the time."

"It won't be the same," she said, shoveling in some tearstained cake and licking the plastic fork.

From Ruth's window the party looked fuzzy, like maybe it was a mirage, but with plenty of balloons. I could see my mother talking to Mrs. Farrell. "You invited a teacher to a party?" LaRhonda had said when she saw her. My mother and Mrs. Farrell had become friendly, united in their determination that I better myself. My mother was holding the gifts that my father had given her, a sweatshirt and a hat from the university. The state university took itself so seriously that all its stuff had a big *S* on it for State, as though there weren't forty-nine others out there.

"Dad did the same thing when I graduated," said Ed, who was standing by the cake when I went to get Ruth another piece. I think he was happy that I'd left him the only family valedictorian. "You're too young to remember."

"I remember."

"Mom invited Mrs. Farrell?" he said, squinting.

"Wasn't she your teacher?" I said.

"She was just starting out," Ed said. "Maybe she's a better teacher now." I laughed, just a little. "What?" he said.

"Nothing."

"Where's our brother?"

I shrugged. Steven was talking to Mrs. Farrell's husband, who worked at a bank. I could see his face freezing while Steven talked. My mother put the State hat on Clifton, who started to strut a little bit, that way little kids do when they think they're really something. I looked around and it was like I was seeing everything frozen into a still photograph, like I was seeing my whole life but in one of those shots you look at later and think, Yeah, that's what it was like, once upon a time. Once upon a long time ago.

Time passed, and I had a chicken leg and some of my mother's quick pickles, which were really just cucumber salad. I didn't really care for bakery cake, but I had one of the homemade cookies Cissy brought with her, chocolate chunk and coconut. There were all those conversations you have at a party like that, about when I had to leave for school and what I thought the chances were for the football team, which any idiot knew you were supposed to say were good. Every once in a while one of the adults would stuff a bill in the patch pocket of my dress. My white patent heels got dusty, and finally I put them on the back steps and walked around barefoot, hoping my mother wouldn't notice.

Some people started to leave, LaRhonda's parents, Donald's grandfather. He'd brought me a package from Donald. "He was trying his darndest to come, Mimi, but it's real expensive, flying from out there, and it's too far to drive," he said. Inside the package was a lacquered jewelry box. When you opened it the blue fairy from *Pinocchio* popped up and "When You Wish Upon a Star" played, tinkly little notes you could barely hear over the sound of people talking in the yard. I knew that Donald had sent it because his grandmother had taken us to see *Pinocchio* when I was ten and Donald was eleven. LaRhonda hadn't come with us that day, and afterward she made her mother take her, and spent two weeks saying it was the stupidest movie she'd ever seen. But Donald and I loved it. We both started to cry a little bit when Pinocchio died, and Donald's grandmother had put her arm around me.

"What's he think, you're twelve?" said Steven, poking the blue fairy with his finger. I knew what he meant, but he was wrong. It was the perfect gift, and just the kind of thing the Donald I'd once known would think of, not something that would impress other people but something that would send a message just to me, that he hadn't forgotten.

"It's great," I said to Donald's grandfather. "I'll write and tell him so. Now I have a place to keep my necklace."

"Hey, hey," Steven said. "Don't take that necklace off."

"That's some gift," Donald's grandfather said, about the necklace, not the music box.

I think a fair amount of time passed between that moment and when the state police pulled up. But when I thought about it that night, after I went out and had a couple of rum and Cokes with Steven and found myself staring at the cracked ceiling of a stuffy room in somebody's apartment, feeling like I was going to throw up the quick pickles and the cookie, it all ran together. My shoes, the cake, the bills in my pocket, the blue fairy, the glass bowls with the last spoonfuls of potato salad, the chicken bones that had fallen underneath one of the tables, the pink paper tablecloths flapping a little, and then police car cherry lights. No sirens. Thank God no sirens. My mother's face got white enough when she turned and saw the car.

"You stay right where you are and take care of the guests," my father said in his low voice, and he and Mr. Langer walked over to the troopers together. We didn't have local cops out where we lived. The Miller's Valley police only took calls in town proper. Otherwise it was the staties, who came from miles away, so that everybody who lived in the valley said that before you called the police about someone breaking into your house you'd best call your closest neighbor with a gun. My father had taken more than a few of those calls over the years, although usually the burglar turned out to be a bear trying to turn over a trash can.

The men standing by the police car were talking low, but everyone else had stopped talking, so we could catch a word here or there. Clifton ran to my father, and my mother tried to catch him as he went by. But he got past her and threw his arms around my father's leg, and my father absently picked him up, although he was getting so big that his legs dangled halfway down the length of my father's body.

"Dear God, no," said my aunt behind me, but I knew she couldn't hear a thing and was just offering up some general badnews prayer. Then there was some shaking of hands and nodding of heads, and the two state police guys got back in their car and drove down the road.

"Everything's okay," my father called, but the party broke up pretty fast after that and there we were, sitting in the yard on lawn chairs, waiting for my father to spill it.

"They're looking for your brother," he said to me and Eddie, and Debbie put her hand to her mouth. "He beat somebody up pretty bad last night."

"So they say," said my mother.

"Oh, come on, Mom," said Eddie.

"Don't you 'come on' me, Edward. The police have been known to accuse all kinds of people of all kinds of things they didn't do."

"That's right," said Steven.

"Dad, you want me to go look for him?" Eddie said.

"Let them look, son," my father said. "They'll find him, or they won't. Then they'll put a warrant out, or whatever they do. We can't do anything until they find him, and talk to him, and charge him."

"Maybe charge him," said my mother. "Maybe not. We don't know."

"Miriam, if it wasn't this it would be something else. Everyone in the county says he's dealing drugs, and he's torn up the tavern twice, and I wouldn't be surprised if some other girl turns up here in trouble, and who knows what else." He looked around suddenly, but Clifton was across the road, talking to the cows. "Be realistic."

"You give up on your own son, you do it alone, Bud." She went inside, the screen door slamming. My father called over his shoulder, "Ruth, if that boy is in your back bedroom again, you better come clean about it right now. Don't make me search your place."

"He's not here, Buddy, I swear." She sniffled, loud enough to be heard outdoors.

"Maybe I better go looking for him," said my father wearily, using both arms to push himself out of the chair. "Mimi, you stay here in case he shows up, but don't go soft and let him leave. Ed, you've got a ride ahead of you. Get on the road so you're home before dark."

"I'll go with you."

"Best not." And Debbie stood up, too, looking as though she

couldn't wait to get out of there. She gave me a big hug. "I can put in a good word with the Kappa rush chair for you, Mimi," she said.

"Thanks," I said. What else was there to say? I just wanted to sit by myself somewhere and let my mind go blank. "Why don't you go to your place and see whether anyone has seen him?" I said to Steven. "It would mean a lot to me." The fact was, I just wanted to be alone for a while.

That was when people still believed that one thing caused another to happen, when someone would have a heart attack and the guys at the Elks would say it was because his daughter had just come home with a hippie boyfriend with girl hair, or someone would have cancer, which no one called cancer because apparently if you said the word it would make things worse, and the women at bridge club would nod and say she'd been worried about her husband losing his job for six months and now look what happened.

Because my mother was a nurse she was always having to argue with people about stuff like that. I remember, when I was eight, listening to her rant all through dinner about a woman whose baby had been born with a port-wine stain on one cheek and who swore it was because she ate strawberries during the summer.

"What's a port-wine stain?" I said, but my mother just kept on ranting. The woman could rant when the occasion demanded.

I'm probably the last person who should say this, given my work, but I think maybe there was some truth to what people thought, although no baby gets a birthmark because of anything its mother ate or saw or dreamt, that's for sure. And maybe it was just coincidence that a week after they arrested Tommy I heard Ruth screaming my name and I came out the back door in my pink waitress uniform to see my father lying at the foot of her front steps. He was crumpled up like a pile of old clothes and so damp that it felt as though he'd been there all night and was covered with morning dew. My mother had pulled an early shift because of taking off for my graduation, and either he hadn't been lying there then or she'd missed him in the dark.

"You couldn't even come out of that goddamned house to help him?" I screamed, and Ruth just wailed back without words, useless, useless as always. I was mad because I was scared, too, scared as I'd ever been.

The good thing about a small town is the same thing that's a bad thing about a small town, and that's that everybody knows your business. So it wasn't long after I came through the emergency room with the rescue squad guys, my hand clamped on the gurney, that someone said something to someone in the diner and Dee knew I was going to miss my shift, and somebody said something to somebody on the site of the addition to the middle school so Steven knew to come after work to the hospital. Although knowing Steven, I was pretty sure he was wondering whether he had time to put in a couple of hours on the house he was working on, which already had an interested buyer.

Maybe the latest news would even make it to Tommy in the holding cell, and Ruth in her little homemade prison. My mother called Eddie and told him to stay put until we knew more. But she took one look at my father on the gurney in the elevator and said, "Stroke."

People were so nice to us that first week. Henry Langer came over every morning to let the cows out, clean the barn, make sure there was water in the trough, check on all the fences. Our refrigerator was full of food, ground beef casseroles and chicken pies, the counters crowded with zucchini bread and blueberry muffins and angel food cakes. Cissy said she'd taken some out to Ruth, although she said she didn't think Ruth was eating and she mainly just cried. My mother and I were of one mind about poor Ruth and her crying, and turned hard-faced and turned away. Ruth had the leisure for tears. The two of us had work to do.

Dee switched me to a four-to-midnight shift at the diner, and I went to sit by my father in the ICU before and after. My mother worked six to six. She spent her lunch and dinner hour in my father's room. I took over the farm. At dawn I'd be opening the barn doors and checking that the culverts weren't jammed with branches and leaves. The barn cats were wild, nobody's idea of a kitty on a pillow on a couch, but they always came running when I showed up with the food. Sometimes I sat on the barn floor, my back against the wall with splinters picking at my spine, the bowl between my knees so that I could run my fingers over their fur. I was good with being alone, always liked it, but there's something about doing a job alone that you've always done with someone else that just doesn't feel right. Maybe it's like making Christmas cookies by yourself. There's nothing wrong with it in theory, but you're really supposed to be doing it with other people, and not just any other people.

"Your brother should be here helping out," Ruth said, and I just spit out, "Well, you could give me a hand, too." But I knew that there was no one else, that I was on my own.

I think that was when I really began to like hospitals. There's an orderliness to them. Your life is a mess and there they are, clean, organized, white as white, each bed in each room in the same place, everyone with a clipboard and a job to do. I hear what people are saying, when they complain about the nurse who comes to take your blood pressure at six in the morning even though you're having a terrible time getting any sleep, complain about the lousy food and the tinny intercoms and the smell of disinfectant. They're right about all that. But what I liked was that there were a series of problems, and the hospital figured out what they were, and how to solve them.

That's up to a point, and up to a point is what they did for my father. They got him a bit better, and then they sent him to a rehab place, and then they sent him home after Steven and some friends of his built a ramp up the steps and moved a rented hospital bed into the middle of the living room. They taught my father to walk, but he walked like Tommy only worse, like the right side of him was the sidecar on a motorcycle. I brought him home while my mother was at work, and when he saw the ramp and the bed he started to cry. I don't know that I'd ever seen him really cry before, even when Tom was under that tractor. But he cried all the time now, and that was terrible. So was the fact that when he talked he made no sense, but you could tell he thought he did. Usually he repeated the same word over and over. One day it was *bat*. Another day it was *rattle*. He said *shit* a lot, too, which upset my mother so much she would leave the room, although his mouth was such a tangle that unless you knew what the word was you might not figure it out.

Usually once a day I'd get him into the truck and ride him around the valley. It was a production, walking him out to the drive, heaving his one side into the passenger seat. I couldn't even tell if he liked it. I would see him staring out the window, his head turned from me, looking at the old house where my mother and Ruth had grown up, the turnoff for the river and for Andover, the high school where he'd played football, the Dairy Queen and the Presbyterian church and the cemetery where everyone we knew who was dead was buried, and I'd figure he was watching his whole life passing in front of him, bit by bit, building by building.

To fill the quiet in the car I'd talk about the price of beef cattle, the straw someone had dropped over to our barn, who'd been into the diner. I took him to the diner for lunch one day, and all the guys at the counter crowded around our booth, the big booth we weren't supposed to give to anything less than a party of four but Dee had put us right there as soon as we came in, me holding the door, my father holding up the people coming in behind us. "Bottle," my father said, leaning across the table surface toward me. "Bottle bottle."

"We'll both have iced tea," I said. "With some straws."

"What's he saying, Mimi?" said Mr. Jansson, which was the kind of question that made me tired and angry at the same time. He's saying "bottle," which makes no sense, which is the way he is now. Instead I said, "He's still working on his speech, Mr. Jansson. It takes a while."

"Bottle," my father whispered.

I ordered chocolate pudding for both of us because my father couldn't chew and swallow real food anymore. No hot dogs, no pork chops, no ham and egg on a bun with a piece of American cheese melted on top. There's not a lot of food for grown-ups that doesn't have some heft to it except for pudding and soup, and because the one corner of his mouth still hung low the soup was a disaster. The pudding wasn't a whole lot better, and after he knocked over his tea and leaned his elbow in the wet spot I took him home. There were chocolate blotches on one shoulder of his shirt, and a wet area on the front of his pants that made me shiver, looking at it, until I realized it was tea. My mother helped him get dressed in the morning, thank goodness, and I figured it wasn't going to kill him to have some iced tea on his fly until it dried there. After I helped him out of the truck in our driveway, I took his hand in mine, and he whispered something.

"What, Pop?" I said.

"Bottle," he said, and as I turned toward the house he moved away from it, down the path to Ruth's place. The truth was that since he had gotten home that was where he seemed most settled, sitting in Ruth's front room in front of the television. No ramp, no hospital bed. She'd moved the furniture around so that there were two chairs side by side, with a little end table in between. Ruth would talk nonstop the way she always did, going on about nothing, Bob Barker's female assistants, the evening gowns on a masked-ball episode of *The Guiding Light,* who should get picked on *The Dating Game.* My father seemed to recognize some of the people—Mary Tyler Moore, Merv Griffin. Sometimes my mother came to get him for dinner and he would pull away and she'd leave him until it got dark and she wanted to go to sleep. A couple of times I noticed she let my father stay there, sleeping in the chair in Ruth's living room. I would look in the screen door after I was done with the cows and the culverts in the morning, and he'd be asleep, his head thrown back, his mouth open, an old afghan tucked around him even in the heat. Ruth would be sitting at the dining room table with a cup of tea and a copy of *Life* magazine. She'd put her finger to her lips, and I'd go into our kitchen and make myself a second cup of coffee, and put my head down on my arms and cry.

"We need to talk," I said to my mother one day at the end of July. We were never in the same place at the same time. When she was at work, I was at home, and when she was at home I was at work or in an empty house somewhere with Steven. I noticed that there were two times when my father and my brother Tommy weren't going round and round in my head. One was when I was asleep, and the other was when I was having sex. I had a lot of sex that summer. "Babe babe babe," Steven would repeat over and over, and I would close my eyes so that he wouldn't sound like a sex version of my father, repeating the same stupid word over and over.

"I have to go grocery shopping, Mary Margaret," my mother

said. "I had to throw half those casseroles out and now there's barely anything to eat in this house."

"I'll go with you once we talk."

"I don't want you leaving the two of them over there all on their own."

"Mom," I said, loud, and she put both her hands down on the kitchen counter and dropped her head. Then she hammered on the counter with her palms, one two three, hard hard hard.

"I talked to Mrs. Farrell the other day," I said. "It's all taken care of." She beat on the counter again.

"I wanted better for you," she said, and her voice sounded like she was trying not to cry. She never cried, either. I don't even think she cried in my father's hospital room, or maybe she did when she was alone, when there was no one to see, like that thing about a tree falling in the forest. If Miriam Miller cried and there was no one to see it, were there really any tears?

"It's not the end of the world. I'll go to the community college for a year or two until he gets better. Mrs. Farrell says she already talked to one of the deans at State and they can just hold my admission for a year. She talked to him about what courses I can take at the community college so I won't get behind."

My mother shook her head back and forth, but she still wouldn't turn to look at me. "Mom, I can't go away right now. It's just a fact. I have to be here. You can't leave the two of them alone all day. When Dad was here to look after Ruth it was one thing—"

"Oh, to hell with Ruth. To hell with Ruth. I'm not having her ruin your life, too."

"Nobody's life is getting ruined," I said, strong and even, like I really believed it. "I'll take classes and in between I'll look in on the both of them. I'll take him to his appointments and he'll get stronger and then we can make other arrangements."

I'll remember the quiet in that kitchen for the rest of my life. It felt like it went on and on, filling the room from floor to ceiling, almost like it was a gas or a fog or something. It had weight and mass.

"I have to get to the supermarket," my mother said wearily.

"Get a lot of tomato soup," I said. "It goes down easy and he seems to like it."

"Callie's bringing Clifton over to see him later."

"Get Clifton some Fudgsicles."

"Maybe he can spend the night. Your father seems to like that." We used the word *seem* all the time because we couldn't really tell what was going on inside his addled brain. Bat. Bottle. Shit. Who knew what he thought when his grandson showed up and yelled "Gramps!" Maybe he didn't even know what that meant, or who that was.

My mother took her purse from next to the phone and fished out her car keys. As she left she put her hand on my shoulder and I felt a shaking go through her and into me. Then she was gone to town.

Callie said Clifton had gotten sad and quiet, but I couldn't see it. I was worried that this new Gramps, the one with the draggy leg and sandbag arm and funny mouth, the one who couldn't talk and sometimes cried, would freak him out, but Clifton seemed to like him just fine. I guess that made sense. My father had turned into a giant toddler. Maybe Clifton, who I thought ought to be in nursery school with other kids, believed he was finally with someone his own age. Sometimes he would climb into my father's lap and try to lift the low loose corner of his lip, and it always made my father laugh a little, a deep heh-heh laugh that almost sounded like his old one. Sometimes the two of them would sit out on the steps of Ruth's house and eat Fudgsicles. Clifton would count cars on the road, which was easy because there weren't many, and my father would turn the Fudgsicle stick around and around in his hands as though he was trying to figure out what he was supposed to do with it. His workbench in the barn was the saddest thing you ever saw. It was so clean and tidy, but with a faint smell of motor oil and mildew, so that it seemed like whoever once used the tools on the pegboard hadn't used them for years. The ghost of the old Bud Miller was nowhere to be found there.

When Clifton stayed at our house he would take that picture of Tommy in his dress uniform from the bureau and kiss it before he got under the covers. He thought Tommy was still away in the service, and none of us told him different. "God bless Daddy," he said when he said his prayers, "and make him come home to Clifton soon." That's when he looked sad to me, not when he was with my father.

If a prisoner at the state penitentiary doesn't want to have visitors, even if the visitors have driven two hours and emptied their pockets and filled out a form and gone through all the riga-marole you have to go through to sit on the other side of what looks like glass in the movies but is really plastic, then he doesn't have to come out. The guard comes back and says, "I told him you were here but he wants to stay in his cell."

My mother tried. My brother Ed tried. Steven tried, or at least he came with me, and he said to the guard, "Go back and tell him his sister will wait in the car and it will just be me." Nothing.

Steven and I went to the trailer Tom had been renting, and that was when I finally cried over him, my big brother in jail and his sad, nasty little life for anyone to see in a shoe box of white vinyl siding with one cracked concrete step to the front door. Inside there were some jeans and T-shirts in old plastic milk crates, a drawer full of rolling papers and condoms, and nothing in the refrigerator, which was one of those half-size dorm room numbers, except beer, a lemon that had dried out to a yellow marble, and a half of a ham sandwich that wasn't even wrapped in paper and that smelled like rot. "There aren't any drugs here," I said, and Steven looked at me like I was crazy. "He flushed his stash as soon as he saw the red lights outside," he said. "The staties are so damn dumb that they let you know they're com-ing."

The guy who owned the trailer, who owned the one next door, too, wanted us to take Tom's stuff, but except for the picture of Clifton stuck in the edge of the mirror in the medicine cabinet, we pitched it all. I almost left the picture, too. It was maybe two years old, Clifton as a toddler. There were a dozen prescription bottles, but they were all empty. I looked at the labels. "All the others are happy pills or chill pills, except that one," Steven said, pointing. "That one revs you up."

"You seem to know a whole lot about all this stuff."

"Guys in construction don't live such clean lives," he said.

Even Callie got in her little junker, which was ten thousand miles away from rattling to a stop forever, and drove up and tried to get Tommy to see her, although she just did it for my mother. But she wouldn't bring Clifton along. "It's okay that he thinks Tom is back in Vietnam," she said.

"I almost wish he was," I said.

Callie was dropping Clifton at the house a lot more, and I'm sure part of it was to make my mother happy because it was pretty much the only thing that did. But I knew there was another reason, too. I'd been helping Mrs. Venti out at the steak house when she had to go to the hospital in Philadelphia to have some female surgery that turned out to be, far as I could tell, something that made her face look really tight and not at all younger. One night I was seating people and there was Callie with a man in a jacket and tie who looked familiar to me, although I couldn't tell from where. "Mimi!" she said, as though I was the last person in the world she'd ever find with a wine list and a menu under her arm, but I just said quietly, "Good evening," and led the two of them to a table as far away from the podium as I could. Callie had on a blue dress and heels, and she was carrying one of those little purses that doesn't hold anything except a lipstick and some tissues. She was wearing makeup, too, and she looked so pretty, like a twenty-one-year-old girl whose only care was what to wear to a restaurant dinner, which she'd never gotten to be. Or maybe was getting to be now, every once in a while.

"Please don't say anything to your mom," she said the next time she dropped Clifton by, making him blow his nose into a tissue before she let him loose. "It's not a big deal."

"I think your date thought it was a pretty big deal," I said, remembering how the man had pulled out her chair and then settled himself, leaning across the table so that when I glanced over I was worried the votive candle was going to set his shirt on fire. Halfway through their dinner I'd realized I knew his face from the community college, that he had some kind of suit-and-tie job there, although I wasn't sure which one. I didn't spend enough time there to find out. I had four courses and they were harder than I'd expected, especially the history seminar on America between the world wars. Trig was fine, but there was an intro statistics course Mrs. Farrell had insisted I take that was kicking my butt, and the bio had a lab that required me to stick around the building, which was one of those pale cinder-block boxes from the 1960s that looked like a middle school only more so. It was strange that I'd gone from the Miller's Valley high school, a serious red-brick building that looked like it belonged on some Ivy League campus—it actually had ivy, although they were always tearing it off so it wouldn't mess up the pointing—to a place that looked like a municipal building and had actually been built by the same people who built the municipal building, probably from the same set of plans.

A girl from my high school class named Laura was my lab partner. "I thought you were going to State," she said the first day. We hadn't really known one another in high school because she was prealgebra when I was algebra, geometry when I was precalculus, so our class schedules were out of sync all the way along. It was funny, how that kind of thing could make all the difference in who you knew, and who you just knew by sight.

"Next year, I guess," I'd said. "My dad is sick."

"Me, too," she said. "My mom."

She was a good lab partner, careful and hardworking. I was afraid in the beginning that she might try to let me carry her, which had happened sometimes in high school, but she put in half the work for sure. We would have been friends if I'd had time for friends, but I didn't. School and the farm, the farm and school, and Steven when I could, which he said wasn't half enough. My mother wanted to sell the beef cattle, but I thought that might level my father, and he was leveled plenty. So I kept on doing what I needed to do every morning and evening in the half-light of the barn. Cows are companionable animals to cry around. Dogs notice and they run over and try to lick your face and cheer you up. But when there's no hope of cheering up, give me a couple of cows any day.

I have clear memories from that time, but they're not the ones you'd think. They're never the ones you think. When I walked across the stage at graduation, that's a blur. Even that morning when I found Tommy under the tractor isn't real sharp in my mind. My mother said she could barely remember her wedding day, she was so jittery.

No, it's strange little moments that live inside you and keep peeking out the windows that open suddenly in your mind. One morning outside the barn my boot got stuck in a suck hole made of water, mud, straw, gravel, and hay, with maybe some cowpat thrown in. It was like quicksand, and I pulled and pulled and pulled back until I came loose with a wet sucking sound and fell on my butt with my bare foot in the air, the boot and even my sock still in that hole. I can still see my toes, white and a little wrinkled from the humidity in my boots, and I can still feel the water soaking into the seat of my jeans and the empty feeling I had inside that was just plain hopelessness.

I guess there are times in your life that tell you what you're made of, the weeks after you bring a colicky baby home from the hospital, the year when you lose your job and the number in your checking account just gets smaller and smaller until it looks like it's going to wink out like daylight on a January afternoon. This was my time. There were record rains, and the two sump pumps we had now because one just wasn't enough went day and night, a chunk-a-chunk noise from the basement, and one morning I woke up because the sound had changed and I thought, Thank God, because it meant sunshine. But what it really meant was that one of the pumps had failed. You'd think that the saddest day would be the one when I found my father all folded up outside Ruth's house, but instead it was the one when I had to hire a guy to come and fix that pump. "My father's sick," I said, "otherwise he would do it."

"It's an antique," said the guy. "I'm not sure I can even get parts for something this old." My father used to make the replacement parts for sump pumps himself, which was something I just took for granted until I figured out how remarkable it was in the basement that morning, tapping my foot because I was afraid I was going to be late for class.

"We need to buy a new sump pump," I'd said to my mother, and she passed over the coffee can from the summer's corn. It had a couple hundred dollars in it, in singles, mainly. The price had gone up since I'd been a kid selling corn with Donald and LaRhonda, but the same card table was there, with the coffee can on top of a sheet of loose-leaf that said 10¢ AN EAR. People pulled up, filled a bag, and left the money in the can. I imagined someday Clifton would sit there and sort out thirteen-ear dozens for people he'd known his whole life. I'd figured out a long time ago that it had been busywork for me as a kid, but busywork seemed like most of my life now.

The weeks went by, each day the same as the one before it, and my father didn't get any better at all, although he seemed a little happier when Clifton came by. Ruth tolerated Clifton better now that my mother had stopped talking about moving Ruth out and moving her grandson in, now that my father was spending so much time at Ruth's house. He sat in front of the television, and he ate soup and pudding and ice cream, and his nice flat stomach went all slack and soft. "Bell," he said some days. "Wall," he said on others. "Me!" he shouted when we were out in the truck. "Me!" It was like when Clifton was small: I couldn't tell whether he was using what he could of my name, or trying to tell us that he was still there, that Buddy Miller was still inside there somewhere, lousy balance, no words, but still there.

The swearing was really bad some days. "Oh, put a sock in it, Mimi," Ruth said one day when I made a face. "You're just like your mother. Let the poor man say whatever he wants."

"Shit shit shit!" my father yelled.

"That's right, Buddy, you go right ahead," Ruth said, taking his hand, but he pulled it away.

I liked to sit with him and pretend everything was just the same. "Pop, we're reading about the Depression in this course, and I have to say, I had no idea how bad it was. You were, what, fourteen or fifteen or something? Maybe it wasn't as bad for farmers. At least you could grow your own food. I guess that's always been the advantage of having a farm, right? You might not have money but you've always got food."

"Not in January you don't," Ruth said.

"I wasn't talking to you," I said.

"I know, honey," Ruth said. "There's a car pulled up on the drive."

It was still pouring, but as soon as I saw the dark sedan through the window I went outside. My shirt soaked up the rain like a sponge, like it wanted to pull me down into the mud, like my foot and the boot had been just the beginning and the farm was going to eat me whole. I went over to the driver's side window of the car, and Winston Bally rolled it down.

"Get off my property," I said.

"I just wanted to check in on your father. I was sorry to hear about his illness."

"Get off his property," I said.

"I need to talk to your mother," he said.

"Get off her property."

"I'll go to see her at the hospital," he said. "I guess your father's not really in a position to make decisions anyhow, is he?"

"Just stay away from my family," I said, turning my back on him. It was the rudest I'd ever been to anyone, and I didn't care one bit, not after what he'd said about my father. It made me feel good, to talk like that, better than I'd felt in weeks.

My least favorite part of the fall was listening to people tell me how much their kids liked it at the state university. Mrs. Venti said that LaRhonda had the prettiest roommate, a girl from outside Pittsburgh whose father worked at Alcoa, and that the two of them were both figuring on being Kappas. The only thing worse than hearing that was listening to the woman who worked in the steak house kitchen and went on and on about how homesick her daughter was. I wanted to tell her that if her daughter really wanted to know homesick, she should stay home in my house. I felt like my head was always full of things like that, that I felt like shouting but could never get away with even saying out loud.

LaRhonda came home at Thanksgiving, and the next thing I knew she was asking me to be her maid of honor, telling me that she was getting married over Christmas break, showing me a good-size diamond ring. "I'm telling you right now, there's no way Fred bought that unless it's a cubic zirconium," Steven said. It always amazed me, the things he knew. A cubic zirconium. He was right about one thing. Fred hadn't paid for the ring himself but with a loan from his future father-in-law, who took one look at the chip Fred had gotten at the new mall and said, "You'd need a microscope to see that thing."

"I guess there are some girls at school who are married, right?" I said, but LaRhonda frowned and her mother said, "Oh, Mimi, she's not going back to the university. She's staying right here with Fred. Mr. Venti's got plans for him. He always wanted a son."

"I don't know why you keep saying that," said LaRhonda.

"When I get the money together I'll buy you a ring bigger than that one," said Steven in the back bedroom of a house he'd just bought at auction. He loved telling stories about the future. He moved from place to place now, couldn't see the point in renting an apartment or even a room when he owned a couple of houses and didn't care about living in a place with the kitchen cabinets in a pile in the backyard waiting to be carried off and replaced by ones he'd found at a job lot. He was really good about doing more with less. At some building site he'd found a small stall shower that had been the wrong size for the bathroom it was intended for, and bought it for ten bucks from the foreman. It was in the second bathroom of the house he was working on, and living in. We'd had sex standing up in it. It sounded a lot better than it turned out to be, but Steven seemed to like the idea. It was one of those things he could talk about after.

The other bridesmaids were two of the Holy Rollers from high school, and two girls LaRhonda had met at college and who I was pretty sure she wouldn't be seeing again. They stayed at the Ventis' house the week of the wedding, and the rooms in the children's wing were finally full. But I was the one who stayed in LaRhonda's room, and who heard her after the rehearsal dinner throwing up in her bathroom, with its metallic wallpaper and ruffled shower curtain. Her hair was in rollers for the next day, and one fell out and landed in the toilet with a plop, and I think that's what set her off. She sat back on her heels, her pink furry slippers poking out from under her nightgown, and wailed, "It was only three times and it hurt and I didn't even like it. Not one little bit."

I knelt down next to her, feeling stupid because I was probably the only bridesmaid who hadn't immediately understood the reason for getting engaged at Thanksgiving, getting married at Christmas, and quitting college. I put one arm around her shoulder, which I don't think I'd ever done in all the years we'd known one another, and then all of a sudden the weird funny feeling I'd been having for a couple of days turned into something worse, and I leaned down into the toilet and threw up, too, right on top of that pink foam roller. I'd had a lot of clams casino at the rehearsal dinner, and a couple of whiskey sours. The inside of that toilet was ugly.

"Oh, Lord, I'm sorry," I said, wiping my mouth with a piece of toilet paper. "That smell gets to you, like it's contagious." But when I looked up at LaRhonda she'd stopped crying and her mouth was open, with a little pearly drop of drool at one corner, and she was staring at me.

"Oh my God, Mimi, you, too? You're the one who is supposed to be so damn smart."

"What?"

"I figured you must have been doing something to take care of yourself, all the times you've been doing the dirty with him. And I do it three lousy times and here I am."

"I just ate a bad clam," I said, but then it happened again.

Lying in bed I stared at the ceiling, willing a bad clam onto the stainless platter with the paper doily that had been passed around before dinner. A bad clam would save my life. "You know what my mother says?" LaRhonda said from the darkness. "She says now I won't think I'm so special."

"You've only had sex with Fred three times?" I said.

"I've only had sex with Fred once."

"I didn't really care for her dress," my mother said Sunday morning when I finally got home. "That empire waist that's so popular just looks like maternity clothes to me." We were at the kitchen table and my mother was watching me carefully, to see if I showed anything on my face, but I was holding it still so I wouldn't look down at the fried eggs and bacon she'd put in front of me and get sick all over again. I kept telling myself I was hungover, which was true beyond anything I'd ever known before. Standing at the altar of the Presbyterian church, watching the peevish look on LaRhonda's face when Fred couldn't get the ring over her knuckle, trying to block out Steven's big grin as he stood two ushers down in a rented tuxedo with lapels like landing strips, I kept telling myself that I was just as smart as LaRhonda said. But I wasn't sure I believed it anymore.

We were slow-dancing to "Raindrops Keep Fallin' on My Head" at the reception when Steven whispered in my ear, "I wonder where Mr. Venti keeps his shotgun."

"They probably would have gotten married eventually anyhow."

"You think? I figured LaRhonda would have dumped him by February for some frat boy with blond hair and a rich daddy."

So had I. I wondered if the frat boy had been time one and time two, and Fred had been time three to explain away the baby. But I just said, "She has the rich daddy, so I guess that's taken care of." Then I ran for the ladies' room. It was packed the way it always was at a wedding. It's hard to throw up silently, but I thought I'd managed it until I got to the sink and one of the other bridesmaids said, "I know, right? It's that punch. It tastes like Hawaiian Punch going down but I think there's a lot of booze in it."

"Right," I said, washing my hands and hoping I was done. "I'm drinking nothing but champagne for the rest of the night."

"Don't do that," she said. "Champagne is the worst hangover ever."

"Amen, sister," said someone at one of the other sinks.

There were bottles and bottles of champagne, empties everywhere, and some of the guys were having a great time popping the corks and hitting the ceiling. "Anybody hits a chandelier, they're paying for it," Mr. Venti had yelled.

"You okay?" Steven said.

"I will be," I said.

"You got black stuff all over your eyes," he said, coming at me with a cocktail napkin that said LARHONDA AND FRED with a pair of gold bands circled above their names and a dove that looked more like a pigeon on top of the bands.

"I'll do it," I said, glad for an excuse to go back into the bathroom. LaRhonda was there, too. "I knew I'd find you in here," she said, trying to push some pieces back into the big poof of curls they'd made on her head.

"I had too much to drink," I said.

"Yeah, that's what I keep telling people, too, and then my mother laughs and starts to cry. She's going to give everybody in town something to talk about. You're next, Mimi."

"No, I'm not," I said, knowing I meant it but not what I was going to do about it. I walked out and Steven and Fred were talking, their arms around each other's shoulders, their bow ties hanging from clips off their collars, and behind them two older women danced while their husbands sat at a table with Mr. Venti. I felt a hand on my arm and it was my mother. "I'm heading home to check on your father," she said. "You okay to get yourself back? You don't look well."

"I had too much to drink," I said.

"Well, it's a wedding. I think you got a little tipsy at Ed's wedding, too."

"You're not planning a wedding like this for me, are you?"

My mother looked around and made a little bit of a face. "I always thought it made a lot more sense to spend the money on a down payment," she said. "But even so we've got years and years to think about that, Mary Margaret. Don't stay out too late."

Sometimes you don't know who in the world to ask for help and then you just run into the right person by accident, like some stranger who comes down the road when your car won't start and has jumper cables in his trunk. My lab partner, Laura, who looked like the kind of person who would someday be a Girl Scout troop leader, who someday would actually turn out to be a Girl Scout troop leader, always went to the ladies' room right after class was over because she had a long drive to the hospital where her mother was being treated for breast cancer. Three days running she found me in the stall on my knees, and on the fourth she said, "Are you expecting?"

"I think so."

"Do you want to be?"

I looked up at her and I figure it was written all over my face. It was written all over hers, too. I never asked and she never told me, never in all the time I knew her, but there was something about the way she lifted her chin and narrowed her eyes that made me know she'd been kneeling where I was and had found some way out of it. We went out to her car and she wrote something on a sheet of loose-leaf and tore it out of her binder and handed it to me.

"Are you okay for money?" she said.

"I think so," I said.

This is all I have to say about that because it's pretty much all I recall:

I took the day off work. I called in sick to school. Laura made an appointment for me so the long-distance number wouldn't show up on my mother's phone bill. She would have noticed. Before dawn I drove an hour to a grubby little bus station with a wire newspaper stand and a candy machine in one corner.

I rode for almost two hours on a dirty bus with candy wrappers on the floor in the back, which was where I was sitting. Fifth Avenues and Baby Ruths. It was early in the morning and it was a good thing I had a plastic bag in my purse, because I brought up the Cheerios I'd had for breakfast.

I fell asleep for the last ten minutes and woke when the bus went up a big loop-the-loop ramp that felt like a carnival ride in the worst way. I left the plastic bag on the floor of the bus, next to the candy wrappers. I was past caring.

I walked fourteen blocks through the city streets to an office building with an elevator that seemed to take a long time to come. I took it to the sixth floor.

The waiting room was filled with women but I can't tell you anything about them because none of us looked at each other. There were two men and they seemed to make it worse. Both of the women they were with were crying.

We all pretended to read magazines. I don't know why they had *Highlights for Children*. Maybe some women brought their kids, although I couldn't imagine why, or how the rest of us would have felt if there had been a child in the waiting room. I read "Goofus and Gallant" in *Highlights,* just the same as I always did at the dentist. Goofus chewed with his mouth open and used his hand to wipe his mouth. Gallant chewed with his mouth closed and used his napkin. I felt like I was waiting to have a tooth filled. The smell was the same as the dentist's office, too, that sharp chemical combination of whatever they used to clean the floors and whatever they used on the patients. The carpet was somewhere between tan, brown, and grubby. The way we all stared down at it, you would have thought it had the secret of life woven into the pile.

"Ruth Kostovich," one of the nurses said, and I didn't move at first. "Ruth?" she repeated, and I put down *Highlights.* The girl next to me picked it up. Somebody had already done the puzzles in pen.

The doctor was a woman. I had never seen a woman doctor before. She asked me if I had ever had an internal. When she saw the look on my face she explained about a speculum. She said it would be cold. I put my arm over my eyes. The lights were bright.

"Count backward from one hundred," the nurse said. I remember ninety-seven.

I woke up and had orange juice and an Oreo. Then I threw up into a basin. I had two Ritz crackers and fell asleep for an hour. A nurse led me to a chair in the waiting room, but there were no magazines on the table right next to me and I didn't want to try to walk across the room. I just sat and thought about nothing for a while. The nurse at the front desk said I had to wait for a friend or relative to pick me up before I could leave. When she was on the phone I slid out the door. The elevator took even longer and I was afraid the nurse would come looking for me, but there were plenty of women to keep her busy. I leaned against the wall while I waited for the elevator.

On the bus back I started to cry because I remembered the

doctor putting her hand around my ankle as she left the room and whispering, "I'm glad I was able to help you." I started to cry because I realized I was free. I was one of those people who read the papers every morning, at first because we had to for social studies, later because I just liked to do it to remind myself that there was a world outside of where I was. I already knew that a year ago there wouldn't have been any doctor, any waiting room, any anesthetic. I wondered how you found someone to do this before, and what it felt like. I was glad I didn't have to find out. Maybe Laura knew.

If anyone had asked me how I felt, I would have said, scared and relieved. Scared that someone would find out, relieved that it was over and I was done. I never for one moment thought of it as a baby, even when I was reading *Highlights for Children*. I thought of it as an anchor, dragging me down. I thought of it as my mother's disappointment like a living thing, more of a living thing, more real, than whatever had been inside of me. I thought of it as a lifetime of mornings spent listening to Steven's stories at the table, of mopping kitchen floors and folding ragged towels, of going to dinner at the diner and maybe the steak house on my birthday and looking around and thinking, No, no, no, this is not my life, this is not my life. I didn't know what my life was, or would be. I just knew it couldn't be that.

I never told anyone beforehand, especially not Steven, because he would have started making plans, a two-bedroom house with a tiny bedroom for a baby, a small ceremony with LaRhonda and Fred standing next to us. You were supposed to be so smart, Mimi, I could hear LaRhonda thinking as she stood next to me holding a bouquet. Steven would have tried to stop me. No one was going to stop me. I paid with cash from the corn can. Then I folded the whole thing up and put it in a sealed envelope in my mind, and that's where it stayed.

"How are you?" Laura said two days later as we walked into class.

"I'm fine," I said.

We had a test. I got an A. After that I never got anything but an A on anything, even statistics. And I never, in my whole life, ate an Oreo again.

Except for sex and school I lived like what Ruth called a spinster, cooking, cleaning, taking my father for hospital appointments and long drives with no destination. Somewhere nineteen-year-old girls were going to parties, but I wasn't one of them. It was like everyone and everything had moved on, and I was standing in place, shifting hay bales and making stew. Even Donald had stopped writing to me. His last letter said he'd decided to major in history, and that he had given up on the golf team because it took too much time. It could have been a dispatch from the moon, as much as it had to do with what I was doing, or not doing, or never doing. I didn't write back. What would I say? That the feed corn in the back bin got moldy and I had to shovel it out and ditch it? Every once in a while I went over to play chess with Donald's grandfather. "What do you hear from our college boy?" he would say. "He sounds good," I would say. That's how life is, I guess. You know your lines.

I went over to see LaRhonda, who was living with Fred in her old room while they looked around for a house of their own, but

I only went after her mother grabbed me outside the diner and told me how lonely LaRhonda was, all her friends back at school and no one home for another month. I guessed I was what was left.

I brought over some homemade cookies and a copy of a book about infant care, and LaRhonda's mother put the cookies on a plate and then ate three of them. I was pretty sure Mrs. Venti was over the two-hundred-pound mark, but she still favored stretch pants and a snug sweater. You could see a sharp line where her girdle ended and her real thighs began, and another one where her stomach made a donut below her bra and above her waistband. LaRhonda, on the other hand, pretty much looked like herself except for the kind of belly I'd seen before when she'd eaten half a pizza at a pajama party. From the back she didn't look pregnant at all. From the front she looked annoyed, which was normal, too.

"What do you think, Mimi? Gramma or Nana or Grandmom? I've only got a couple of months to decide." Her mother had started talking about LaRhonda's pregnancy the moment LaRhonda and Fred had gotten back from Puerto Rico on their honeymoon.

"Aren't you working tonight?" LaRhonda said to her.

When we went to LaRhonda's room it looked almost exactly the same as it had before except that the twin beds had been pushed together. They hadn't even changed the spreads. Then we went back out to the kitchen and sat at the breakfast bar. Mrs. Venti kept calling in to us from the living room, maybe because LaRhonda would barely speak to me. I was just waiting for her to pull out a sheet of paper and read me a list of my transgressions, Leviticus by way of LaRhonda Venti, or LaRhonda Nesser, which was her new name. She'd done that once when we were in middle school and she thought I was being a bad friend because I wouldn't forge an excuse note saying she'd been too sick to do the English homework. She'd written out her accusations in her diary and then read them to me right off the page.

"Fred says she keeps saying how disappointed she is in you, that you've turned your back on God's plan," Steven had said to me one day in the car. "You know what she's talking about? Which plan of God's does she mean?"

"She's crazy," I said. "She's pregnant." And I wasn't. That was what she meant. I could tell it was all she could do not to say something to me. Instead she kept folding her hands over her stomach with a sigh, shaking her head until her hoop earrings rattled. What that meant was that she wasn't buying my bad clam story before and she wasn't buying it now.

"And how are you doing?" she finally said in that snotty voice after going on for ten minutes about her bad back. But I wasn't going to talk to her about that, either. She didn't really want to hear what I had to say: that my father had been up a couple of times the night before, wandering outside and burning himself on the stove somehow, and I'd overslept and missed half of my history seminar and the professor had said, "I'd appreciate your taking attending this class as seriously as I take teaching it, Miss Miller," and I'd caught my mother the day before just sitting in her car, staring out the windshield, like she didn't know how to start the car and didn't know where she was going when she did. "You okay?" I'd said, knocking on the car window with my filthy hands, all caked with the dirt from the barn and smelling of cows. "Oh, honey, I just lost track of things for a minute there," she'd said, which coming from my mother was one of the scariest sentences I'd ever heard, right up there with "Yes, you're around three months along" from that nurse in the city.

I looked at LaRhonda and listened to her stories about her heartburn and her swollen ankles and her shoes that didn't fit anymore, hundred-dollar shoes and if her feet didn't go back to normal what was she supposed to do with them? And, as sad as my life was, I knew that I wasn't eleven years old anymore, and somewhere along the line I'd turned into a person who wasn't going to let anyone push her around. If there was a bad Mimi list I wasn't going to wait to hear it. I held on until LaRhonda finally drew breath, and then I said, "I have things to do," and shoved past her baby belly and walked out.

"You girls have a nice visit?" Mrs. Venti said as I passed through the living room, but I didn't answer.

The Langers came over the next day and I made a coconut cake and when Cissy saw it on the kitchen counter she started to sob. She was a crier for sure, but I'd never known her to cry at cake before. "Miriam, we need to talk to you and Bud," Mr. Langer said, sitting down at the kitchen table.

My mother patted Cissy on the arm. She'd started crying so hard that her nose was running, and I handed her a paper napkin. "There's no need, Cis," my mother said, and I could tell she already knew what the Langers were going to say. She was good at that, knowing but not saying. For years I thought it was pretty remarkable that I'd managed to hide from my mother what I'd done that winter, but later on it occurred to me, maybe because I knew so much about my own kids that they didn't know I knew, that my mother had known all along. There's a way you can let things happen without acknowledging them and so having to act as though you approve of them that comes in handy for a mother.

Mr. Langer looked around and my mother said, "I don't think we need to have him here. It might upset him, if he understands what's going on. He's over at the other place, watching television." The other place. In her whole life I'd never heard my mother call Ruth's house Ruth's house.

I cut the cake and put on the coffeepot. Mr. Langer and my mother passed around the cream and sugar, and then Mr. Langer cleared his throat and said, "We're selling." My mother just nodded. He went on and on, that way people do when they're saying something they feel bad about, as though the more they talk the better it will get, although it's usually the other way around. Cissy cried her way through a couple more napkins and finally took a big forkful of cake. She ate three slices out of sheer upset.

They'd sold their house to the state, put a down payment on one of the new places Ed had taken my parents to see. It had a sunporch and a patio. Cissy would have a big room to work on her dolls. Henry wasn't sure if he would still sell bait. I didn't think it was a bait shop kind of neighborhood. The town council had approved the whole development in record time, and while the paper didn't say so, and neither did the council, they'd done it because of a deal with the state to offer the houses with a lower mortgage rate to people from the valley who were willing to move fast.

Steven had driven me out there one day, and while it was mostly a mess of foundations, cinder blocks, piping, and piles of plowed snow and gravel, you could see how many houses there would be. Steven talked a lot about buying in bulk, about how much money you could make if you were ordering a hundred new toilets instead of two, but I'd started to tune out a lot of his business talk. For four weeks after I'd taken the bus to the city I wasn't supposed to have sex, and I'd kept making vague medical excuses, and he kept saying he felt like some dumb high school kid, feeling his girlfriend up in the backseat of the car. By the time I finally let him slip inside me with a big grin and a "worth waiting for, babe," two things had happened: I'd filled the prescription for birth control pills the doctor had given me, and I'd noticed how annoying he could be when we weren't both naked.

At the building site he kept saying, "Nice, very nice," about the size of the foundations and how they'd laid out the roads. But all I'd noticed was the trees. I'd hiked through the woods there a couple of times for Girl Scouts, for trailblazing and to classify leaves. The trees had been so thick that if it started to rain you barely felt a thing. They were all gone now. Thirty-five acres had been clear-cut. They'd done what developers always did, turned it into a tree desert. After the houses were built, they would put those spindly saplings along the curbs. It was like those girls in high school who took off their real eyebrows and then drew fake ones in with pencil. When I was doing my water project research I learned that clear-cutting was terrible for water maintenance. A couple days of real heavy rains, and all these people, the Langers, too, would have silt in their wells and brown water in all those new toilets. I told Steven, but he just said, "That's how they do it, babe."

"Don't be mad at me, Miriam," Cissy told my mother, wiping her eyes again. Clifton colored in the flowers on the paper napkins with crayon the way I'd done when I was a kid, but he was still too little to get them right. They didn't look like mine had. My mother said it was one of the differences between boys and girls. It seemed like there were a million of them.

My mother put her hand over Cissy's. "It's the right move, Cis," she said with a smile, and I almost dropped my coffee mug.

After the two of them drove away I put what little was left of the cake on a smaller plate. When Cissy got upset she cried first and then ate, and between her and her husband they'd managed to eat almost an entire coconut cake. Without turning around, I said to my mother, "Are you selling the farm?" Ten of the houses in the valley were already sold to the government. Two of those were empty, and the families in the rest were looking for another place to live or waiting for Winston Bally to stop by and give them a moving date.

"You can see the handwriting on the wall," Donald's grandfather told my father, but he swore he would never sell, would fight until, depending on the day, the bitter end, the moment of truth, or the last dog died. Donald's grandfather, not my father. My father said, "Fell one. One. Fell. Fell." The doctor who had said my father's speech would come back slowly now said nothing. His right side was still barely along for the ride. He liked to sit out in the cold with no coat on.

"The farm belongs to your father," my mother said. "It's never been in my name. The family always made sure of that whenever a Miller got married."

"You could get some kind of power of attorney, I bet."

"I probably could," she said. "Why don't you take what's left of that cake over to the other house? I've got laundry to do."

The morning Tom was due to get out Steven drove me to the state prison. Steven found out the date from a guy he knew whose brother worked as a parole officer. Tommy had served almost eighteen months on an assault charge. No trial, just a deal he'd told the attorney he wanted to make as fast as possible. Steven said that if he'd gone to trial he probably would have gotten a lot more. "With what he did to that guy's face, all they would have had to do was show the jury the pictures," he said.

"Don't tell my mother that," I said.

"Babe," Steven said. "Do I strike you as a stupid individual?"

Even the guys at the diner said Tommy had gotten off easy because of his military service. They'd all been willing to give him the benefit of the doubt before, but once people started to talk about selling drugs the flag wavers had gotten less certain about what a great guy Tommy was. Plus there'd been a description in the paper of the beating he'd given the other man, and it sounded like Tommy had done a thorough job. A dispute over money, the story said, and Steven said the guy had shorted Tommy on some kind of deal, although he wouldn't be more specific because he still thought he could keep me from thinking the worst of my brother. Everyone else thought the worst, though. More than once when I'd picked up a stray shift at the diner there'd been long periods of silence at the counter, where the regulars sat on stools way too tiny for their old-guy butts, their feed company hats pulled down low over sun-speckled foreheads.

The day Steven and I drove up to the prison was one of those November mornings that make you think the weather will never turn harsh, although there would surely be snow within weeks. The air was clear and fresh, chilled like lemonade, and the sky was a blue without clouds. I don't know why I remember it so well. Neither of us really wanted to be there. My course work for the second year at the community college was even tougher than the first, and Steven's business was taking off and he was complaining about losing a morning's worth of demolition. He had two guys from Poland doing a lot of the scut work now. He paid them almost nothing but he let them live in whatever house they were working on while he lived in whatever house was almost sold, or just bought. He said that back in Poland their wages and their living conditions would be much worse, and they should be grateful. They didn't act grateful, and I didn't like the way they looked at me.

Steven had bought a big Victorian house at an estate sale, with a deep half circle of a porch and built-in bookshelves and a pantry with the original oak cabinets and brass hardware. It was a great house, the first one I'd really liked, but it was a wreck, with a floor in the kitchen so soft I was afraid we were going to wind up in the basement. I'd thought he was crazy to take it on. For years it had been the neighborhood haunted house, with kids daring each other at night to run up and ring the bell and then screaming that they'd heard someone inside even though no one had lived in it for ages and the four grown kids who had inherited it had been fighting all that time about how much to sell it for. By the time Steven got to it it was in such bad shape that he'd been able to afford it. Then once he was mostly finished fixing it up two guys from Philadelphia who were looking for a place in the country offered him what he was asking, which was eight thousand dollars more than he'd thought he would get. "You can really breathe out here," one of the Philadelphia guys said, as though he was partly paying for oxygen. Steven was smart at milking that stuff. He was always putting baskets of apples and pots of mums on the front porch. He'd handed the buyers a bottle of champagne after they'd signed the contracts at the bank. He took me to the steak house that night and ordered the same kind of champagne and clinked my glass and said, "Whole new ball game, babe. Whole new ball game." I didn't like champagne. One sniff of the stuff and I was right back at LaRhonda's wedding reception, kneeling in the ladies' room.

"She's got the baby blues," Mrs. Venti told me about La-Rhonda, who had had a baby girl in June. Dee at the diner said, "An eight-pound preemie. That's what the boss says. He says he doesn't want to be called Gramps because it will make him feel old." Maybe LaRhonda had the baby blues because it was just her and her mother in the house most of the time. Her father was living more or less full-time with the diner waitress, although she didn't work at the diner anymore. She was a hostess at the Italian place Mr. Venti had opened not far from where they were building the new development. Fred was managing the McDonald's Mr. Venti had opened on the highway, and Steven said he talked at the bar about how much he wanted to go back to working construction and how his father-in-law screamed at him all the time about how bad he was at his job. "It's like he can tell when something is going wrong, and that's when he shows up," Fred told Steven, which actually was the truth. Fred didn't know that Mr. Venti had a deal with an eighteen-year-old who was working there to call him if there were problems. Also to call him if she was at home alone.

"The man has Fred's balls in his pocket," Steven said. Which hadn't stopped LaRhonda from getting pregnant when Serafina was only three months old. I thought about stopping by with a pink onesie and some advice about birth control, but with what my life was like I was not in the mood for more disapproving looks from a woman too stupid not to get pregnant twice before she was even twenty-one. My father had gone from saying random words to saying nothing at all, and the house had almost flooded twice, summer and fall. My mother and I sat on the stairs halfway up to the second floor during the second storm, eating Fritos out of the bag, watching to see if the water would start to seep under the front door, and talking about when the floors would be warped enough to need replacing. We both seemed to think the answer was never. All the times that water had gotten into the house, and it hadn't done much to it that paint and plaster couldn't repair. There had never been anything fancy enough to be ruined.

"You could never have had wall-to-wall carpeting," I'd said, sitting on the stairs.

"What?" my mother said. "Oh, that. That was just foolish."

We'd sat for a while without saying anything, which was fine with us both. My lips were puckering from all the salt in the chips. After a while the rain started to slow, so that we could tell that the water wouldn't get any higher than the next to last step to the front door. I could hear Ruth's television.

"They're watching *The Match Game*," I said.

"I think your aunt is going deaf," my mother said. "That's what happens when you're forty-five years old and do nothing but sit on your butt all day long."

"I think she turns it up for Dad. Maybe because he can't talk she thinks he can't hear."

My mother took another Frito. "We had a stroke patient come in two months ago, her whole left side was gone," she said. "She stopped by last week with zucchini bread for all the nurses. Baked six loaves herself."

"That's good zucchini bread. I had a piece. I wish we had that now."

"It's like nothing happened to her. She's got a little bit of weakness in the one leg, that's it. It's all the luck of the draw. One of the nurses says it's always worse on the right side."

"That can't be true."

She'd shrugged. At least I didn't have to worry about saving the cows from the flooding in the pasture, which I could see through the transom over the door was looking like an enormous pond. I'd sold the last of the beef cattle in July. It was sad to watch them march into the truck, their big blocky heads hung low as though they knew where they were going to wind up. I'd stopped naming them a long time ago, but still. For all my worries my father didn't even seem to notice they were gone.

I'd told Clifton the cows were going away for a while. "Where?" he said. "Delaware," I said. I don't know why, but it was the first thing that came into my mind. That, and the idea that we had become that sad thing, a farm that didn't do any farming. I'd sold our last crop of feed corn and hay, too. Our place was like my father's brain, shutting down piece by piece. Still sometimes I woke up before dawn, listening for the sound of the cows calling, then going out to the barn just to feed the cats.

Clifton hadn't minded the cows leaving as much as I thought he would. He liked to spend time with my father, watching TV in Ruth's living room. He was in all-day kindergarten now. Callie didn't like her grandmother watching him anymore, not since she found her teaching Clifton how to use a footstool to reach the teakettle and put a light under it. "She's got arthritis bad, but still," Callie said. My father and Clifton liked to watch *Captain*

*Kangaroo* on days Clifton didn't have school. He seemed a little bored by the soaps, but Ruth would make Jiffy Pop popcorn, and Clifton loved popcorn.

Callie didn't want us to tell Clifton that Tommy was coming back. Just in case, she said. "In case what?" my mother said, annoyed, but I knew what Callie meant.

I was up early to pick Tommy up, and my mother was, too, making me the kind of big breakfast I never ate, half a ham steak and a couple of pancakes. Steven came in, leaned over my shoulder, and said, "That's what I call a real breakfast." He had a knack for figuring out who wasn't buying what he was selling, and my mother was number one on the list. The Ventis had been on board from the beginning. "That's a nice-looking young man," Mrs. Venti always said, and Mr. Venti usually said, "He's going someplace." I wasn't sure, but I think Mr. Venti had invested in Steven's business, and I was pretty sure he was ticked that LaRhonda had wound up instead with Fred, who wasn't going anywhere.

My mother said, "I can make you a plate, Steve," but I pushed mine over to him and he polished it off. I got him a cup of coffee and drummed my fingers on the table while he finished it.

"You make sure your brother knows he should come right back here, Mary Margaret," my mother said, putting on her nurse's cap. They'd told the nurses years ago that they didn't have to wear their caps anymore, and a few of the younger ones even wore white pants and tunics instead of dresses. But my mother was a traditionalist. "I've got that noodle casserole for dinner, and the apple pie. I'll take care of that when I get home. You make sure your father knows he's eating dinner here. I don't give a rip what's on television. I told him Tom was coming home, but I'm not sure it registered." She sighed and put on her plaid wool car coat. "Get your brother some fresh towels and some clean clothes from your father's closet and let him take a shower.

Make him a decent cup of coffee. He probably hasn't had a decent cup of coffee for more than a year."

"Mom, it'll be fine. I know what to do. I know Tommy, remember?" Or at least I had known Tommy, a long time ago. I had this idea, of how men looked who got out of jail, all dry and wiry and tough, a boiled-down baked-hard version of a man. But Tommy had been that way even before, a guy who showed up, drunk or sober, with the whites of his eyes hatched in red and fading marks on his hands and arms, a guy who was living in ways you could only imagine and then didn't want to.

"Callie wants to wait a couple days to bring Clifton over," my mother said. "I suppose that's about right."

"I think that's a good idea," said Steven.

"I wasn't talking to you," my mother said, in a pleasant even voice that, if anything, made the insult worse. I'd heard her use that voice sometimes at the hospital when I was a kid, those times I'd wound up waiting there with a copybook on my lap when my father had had to go out on an evening fix-it call. I'd sit in the hallway with the sad families and sick people, and my mother would say something to one of them in that same pleasant even voice, something like "Now, dear, if you can't calm down I'm going to have to ask you to leave."

"We have to go," I said.

"Someday your mother is going to figure out that I'm the best thing that ever happened to her daughter," Steven said in the car.

"I think my mother thinks the best thing that will happen to her daughter is finishing college."

"Hey, have I ever done anything to mess that up? No. I'm behind you a hundred percent." He squeezed my thigh, then took my hand. "World's best boyfriend." Steven liked to talk like *The Guinness Book of Records*. World's best beer. World's best party. World's best businessman.

"I have to admit, I'm going to like hanging out with your

brother again. When he's on his game, he's the world's best guy. I hope he appreciates the effort."

The wind had picked up while we were driving, or maybe it was because we were so much farther north, but I was shivering in the car while Steven went inside to talk to the people on duty. In just a few minutes he came outside again, shaking his head.

"He's already gone," he said when he got in the car. "That thoughtless asshole got picked up more than an hour ago and left."

"Where did he go?"

"That's what I said. The stupid guard laughed and said, 'Buddy, when they leave, we don't know where they go, and we don't care.'" Steven turned the key in the ignition hard, then just sat for a minute. "I lost a whole morning's worth of work," he said.

"Where did he go?"

"I guess your mother will have to eat that whole apple pie herself," Steven said, backing out fast. "Maybe you can make her a really good cup of coffee to go with it."

"Don't be a jerk," I said.

"I'm not the jerk here," he said, riding the gas pedal, hard.

A month before I graduated from high school a woman named Gertrude Scheinman died at her house in the Catskills. The house wasn't much to look at, honestly. At some point someone showed me a picture of it and it looked like a house in Miller's Valley, with a narrow front porch and a big living room window winking out at the lawn and what seemed like the edge of a barn to one side of it. But it was the house her family had rented during the summers when she was a little girl, and after it got foreclosed, when the area was on a downward slide, she bought it. Paid cash.

You'd never know, looking at that house, that Gertie Scheinman had $2 million to give the University of Pennsylvania, to endow a scholarship for a "young woman of scientific promise who wishes to attend medical school." She gave it to Penn, not because it was where she had gone to medical school herself, but because it was the place that had rejected her. One of several. After she graduated from nursing school in 1910 and decided that the only reason she'd become a nurse was because she was female, she decided to become a doctor. She wound up studying in

Edinburgh and practicing in New York City and then semiretiring to that farmhouse in the mountains. The *semi* is because, even though she didn't have a real medical practice and was pushing eighty, women who lived in the area would come to her house to have her examine them during their pregnancies, and she would help deliver their babies in their own beds. Some were Orthodox Jewish women who couldn't have a male doctor, and some were early hippie types who wanted to do the natural thing. I don't know exactly where the $2 million came from since those women in the Catskills apparently paid mainly in jars of local honey or homemade macramé hangings. Maybe it was from Dr. Scheinman's father, who owned a big wholesale butcher firm, which she once said was how she got interested in medicine. I wondered if any of our beef cattle had wound up there. Maybe they did, and they made some money for Scheinman's, which would mean I'd come full circle, since it was the Scheinman money that paid for me to go to college, finally, not at the state university but at the University of Pennsylvania, which, my mother never got tired of telling people, was an Ivy League school.

Two years in community college, and then almost overnight I woke up to the sound of truck gears grinding outside the window of a small single room in Philadelphia. A young woman of scientific promise who wishes to attend medical school. Dr. Scheinman's niece had published a little book, a pamphlet, really, about her aunt, with a photo of the doctor on its cover, a woman with the grim look people always seemed to have in portrait photographs fifty years ago. I kept it propped on my desk all through school.

"It's the perfect opportunity for you, Mimi," Mrs. Farrell said when she showed me the letter she'd gotten as the head of the high school science department. "It pays for undergraduate and medical school studies. That's thousands and thousands of dollars' worth of tuition."

"I didn't figure on becoming a doctor," I said.

"Why not?" Mrs. Farrell said, and she had this look on her face that I knew from looking at my mother sometimes when she talked about me going to college, this look of someone who felt like they'd missed something and they wanted you to go out and get it for them. I knew if I told my mother about this scholarship I'd never hear the end of it.

"I don't know," I finally said.

I didn't even know if I could go when Mrs. Farrell first mentioned it. There was still my father to take care of. Most of the time he was with Ruth, who made sure he didn't try to fill a glass with scalding water instead of cold from the tap, that he didn't stand for hours in front of the tap trying to figure out how to turn it on or what it was for. But as soon as he walked out of Ruth's house he was on his own unless my mother or I was right there. One day I got in the shower when I thought he was all settled taking his afternoon nap in Ruth's easy chair, and there I was dripping wet and naked on the bath mat when I heard Ruth shouting, "Buddy! Buddy!" and saw him through the window wandering down the road, dragging his bum leg along the center line.

"What would it take to make you step out that door?" I said to her after I'd led him back, wearing nothing but my coat and a pair of old boots, my hair freezing into icicle strands. "Give me a clue."

"Don't get smart with me, Mimi. You and your mother go about your business ninety percent of the time while I look after him. Come have a cup of tea, Buddy. Never mind the outside." My father sat down in the easy chair with a *whoompf,* like his body was a big heavy bag and he was putting it down. That was where he died one really frigid night in February. They said he had a second stroke.

My father was slumped in the chair, his head to one side, his mouth open the way it always was when we were kids and he fell asleep watching TV. I was always afraid then that his bridge would fall out onto the floor, but he hadn't worn it since he came home from the hospital. It was in a plastic envelope in the kitchen junk drawer. I could see odd whiskers on his cheek. Sometimes there are things that you've rehearsed so many times, thought about so often, that when they happen it's like they already happened a long long time ago. My father was dead but I could tell he'd already died somewhere in my mind. I didn't even cry.

The church was full and then some for the funeral, and Mr. Venti let us have people come to the steak house for sandwiches after, and he refused to send a bill. I think, in his own way, that he liked me. He and Mrs. Venti were there, together for a change, and LaRhonda, too, although she made it clear she didn't want to be. In the church, at the lunch, by the gravestone where my father's parents were buried, I looked for Tommy, but he didn't show.

"Your brother should be ashamed of himself," said Debbie, whose big belly poked hard against her gray wool coat, but Eddie shushed her. I figured he agreed but didn't want to get my mother upset. Although my mother didn't seem very upset. She didn't cry once in public, but the night after my father died, after we'd picked out an oak coffin like we were buying a breakfront or a bureau or some other nice piece of furniture, I'd lain in bed and heard her sobbing in the kitchen. I didn't go down and sit with her. I figured if I were her I'd want to be by myself. The only other time she broke even a bit was when Callie brought Clifton to the funeral home. He was wearing a little navy blue jacket and a clip-on tie. His hair was damp, with comb marks where Callie had parted it, and my mother's voice shook as she said, "Well, don't you look nice?"

"I don't want Gramps to be dead," Clifton said, and he started to sob. The funeral home people gave him a lollipop and it didn't help much, but I wouldn't have wanted a nephew who was bought off so easily.

It made me angry at Tommy, though, angrier than him not showing up for any of the rest. He should have shown up for Clifton even if he couldn't see his way to doing it for my father. I didn't know if my mother knew, but he was still living in the area with the woman who had picked him up at the prison. Once I'd driven past a bar on Main Street and seen him getting into a truck, but by the time I'd pulled into a space and gotten out he was gone. Steven had seen him when he went to some guy's house for a drink, and he said Tommy asked about me. "I think he's embarrassed by what he's turned into," Steven said.

"What's he turned into?"

"You know, babe, he's that guy now. The guy everyone thinks is on the wrong side of things."

"Is he?"

Steven shrugged. "Who knows?" But I could tell he knew but wasn't saying.

The neighbors brought food again, some of them the same dishes they'd brought when my father first had the stroke, but there were fewer of them now, neighbors and casseroles both. Almost half the families in Miller's Valley were gone, and no one new was moving in because people couldn't see investing in a place where the government might swoop down and take what you had away. Donald's grandfather started a group called No Eminent Domain, but the group was mainly just him, and a few people who put bumper stickers on their cars to make him happy or keep him quiet. Property in the valley had never sold high, and some people thought that if the government was going to pony up a halfway decent amount they could do better somewhere else where the ground floor didn't flood every couple of years. Cissy had always had a sampler in her kitchen that said WEATHER IS GOD'S WAY OF REMINDING US WHO'S IN CHARGE. She said her mother had worked it. Once I knew about Andover I understood it better, although even as a kid it made sense to me.

My mother and I sat at the kitchen table after the funeral eating pudding cake. We were both wearing black dresses and our pumps were on the floor in the dining room. At least there hadn't been snow, and the ground wasn't so hard that they couldn't get in with the backhoe. But it was below freezing, and no one had stayed around long. I kept telling myself that maybe Tommy had showed up at the cemetery after we were all gone and the guy with the tractor was filling in. He was a guy my father knew from the VFW. I'd spotted him standing to one side of the crowd holding his red-and-black-checked trapper cap over his heart. He'd left his tractor way on the other side of the cemetery, so that what would come after we left wasn't quite so clear. That was nice of him. It was the kind of thing my father would have done.

I took a slab of pudding cake back to Ruth along with a memorial card. She was in her bedroom with the door closed. "Just leave me alone, Mimi," she said, her voice all raspy, so I did.

My mother was eating another piece of cake. "Your poor father," she said. "He must have hated how things turned out." It sounded terrible, but I knew exactly what she meant. She ate silently and poured herself some coffee.

"Now you can go to college," she said.

"Not now, Mom, all right. Not yet."

"You're going. You're going away in September. I don't want to hear any arguments, Mary Margaret. You're going."

"I'm not arguing. I just don't want to talk about it yet. Besides, who's going to look after Ruth if I'm not here?"

My mother looked wild and fierce, and she waved her fork so that crumbs of chocolate went all over. "I can look after my own sister."

"You don't."

"Don't you tell me what I can or can't do. I will. I promise you that Ruth will be fine."

"You don't even like her," I said.

She laughed, a strangled sour laugh. "You don't have to like somebody to look after them. If you're going to be a nurse you better learn that fast."

But it turned out that I wasn't going to be a nurse. I was going to be a doctor. A friend of Mrs. Farrell's was administering the scholarship, and Mrs. Farrell had sent in all the forms from my college application two years before. She sent the essay I wrote about learning to like science because of watching my father make things work in his little shed. She sent the report I wrote on Andover, and some other science projects. She never said, but I think she sent a letter explaining why I was at the community college in the first place. She told me after that it was the first year of the scholarship, and no one had really figured out how they were going to find the person who would get it, and they were relieved to have someone ready-made, who would only soak up six years of tuition instead of eight.

Mrs. Farrell came to the house one night when both of us were home, a month after my father died, and she put a letter down on the dining room table and then began to explain what was in it. The bed was gone from the living room now, and the furniture was back to normal, but the dining room table felt too big for just two people and we hadn't sat at it for a while.

When Mrs. Farrell was finished talking my mother put her face in her hands and stayed that way. After a minute or two the tears began to run from between her fingers like water coming out of the ground on either side of Miller's Creek. She wiped her face back and forth like her hands were windshield wipers, then reached across and put one hand on Mrs. Farrell's.

"I can't ever thank you enough for what you've done," she

said, and Mrs. Farrell started to cry, too, and I just sat there, amazed at the way the whole world had just tilted while we were sitting at that table. I had a plan. A stranger, a teacher, and I had a plan.

"I'm going to start buying up some properties in the city," Steven said when I told him. "That is a prime area."

"I wish I'd gotten a deal like that," said Ed, while Edward Miller Junior yelled in the background. I figured Debbie'd be asking me to babysit for him and the new baby by week two at college.

"I'm as proud as could be," said Ruth, crying. She cried a lot in those months. Anything could set her off: a divorce on the soaps, a housewife who lost everything when she picked the wrong door on one of the game shows, Clifton eating his Jiffy Pop one kernel at a time and saying, "I miss Gramps."

"Mom says she'll look after you," I said.

"I'll be fine. I've got the TV, my magazines. As long as she drops off the groceries I'll be fine."

"I've never even met a lady doctor," said Mrs. Venti, and LaRhonda sniffed. She had a patch of baby barf on her shoulder shaped like the continent of Africa. I'd met a lady doctor once, at that clinic in New York. I'd never forget her.

The first time I ever went to the movies I went with LaRhonda. Her mother took us to see *Cinderella* when we were nine or ten. We had sodas and popcorn and Junior Mints, and I threw up out the window of Mrs. Venti's Cadillac because I was embarrassed to tell her I felt sick until it was too late to do anything except roll down the window. It was a good thing that their car was the first one I'd ever been in with power windows or it might have been worse.

Just before I left for school I felt like that part of the movie when they scrub Cinderella up and turn her into a princess with an updo and a little crown and a Bibbidi-Bobbidi-Boo. My mother bought me a suitcase and new sweaters and a gold pen and pencil set and a clock radio. She bought me a red winter coat and a pair of leather gloves so thin that they were a joke for doing anything around a farm or really keeping your hands warm. It was like she was buying things for someone I would become as opposed to who I really was. It was ninety degrees out and I had an angora hat and scarf.

Eddie came and picked me up even though Debbie was annoyed that they'd had to take the baby stuff out of the wagon to make room for my things. My mother had asked him to do it, and lying in bed I tried to figure out whether it was because she didn't want Steven to take me, or whether she didn't want to do it herself because she thought the new Mimi shouldn't have a mother like her. But then I figured it was mainly because she hated to drive on the highway. She said entrance ramps made her nervous.

The waitresses at the diner had given me a set of striped sheets with a matching quilt and pillows. "Don't forget us when you're a big shot doctor," said Dee.

"If you start practicing now," I said to Ruth when we had lunch together, BLTs for a special treat, "you could be ready to come to my graduation in two years."

I don't know whether she was chewing or thinking, but after a while she said, "I wouldn't count on it."

When Eddie moved me in you could tell that he was worried. He gave me a fold-up map of the city and pointed out neighborhoods I should avoid. One of them was the neighborhood where the university was.

"This will be an adjustment, Mimi," he said, like he was sixty and I was ten. "I'm a country girl," I'd told Mrs. Farrell about why I'd be better off at State. Like a lot of other things I'd always taken for granted, it turned out it wasn't exactly true. I liked living in the city much more than I'd expected. After a couple of months I figured out that it wasn't so much trees and birds I'd always liked in the valley as it was the feeling of being alone. I guess most people think that since the city is so crowded you don't feel that way, but I did from the very beginning, maybe even more so than I had at home. Crossing the street with as many people as had been in my high school class made me feel even more alone because I didn't know any of them and none of them knew me. I hadn't crossed a street in Miller's Valley in my whole life next to someone who didn't know me, who didn't know something about my parents, something about my brothers.

"You come out here any time, Mimi," my sister-in-law liked to say. "You must be lonesome." I was, I guess, but that wasn't why Debbie was asking. She was asking because she'd popped out two babies pretty fast, one after the other, and she knew that when I walked in she could hand me one. It seemed like a lot of the girls I knew did that, had a baby and then a second baby, as though they were trying to get the whole thing over with. Or maybe not. "That second one must have been a mistake," my mother said on the phone Sunday nights, after the rates went down.

"I bet your mother thinks Kimmy was a mistake," Debbie said, trying to put frozen lasagna in the oven with one hand while she held the baby with the other. Sometimes I spent the night with little Eddie and Kimmy so Debbie could go out with her friends. Unlike Callie, she didn't offer to pay. Ed brought it up once, and Debbie said, "It's not really babysitting when it's your family, right, Mimi?" Ed didn't push it. I think he was still annoyed that I was getting a free ride at an Ivy and would have an MD after my name at the end of it. The pullout sofa in the living room of their house was uncomfortable, but no more uncomfortable than the twin bed in my dorm room.

I was lonesome, but I figured that made sense. I got to college two years after everyone in my class. They already had friends and routines. I had to study pretty much nonstop just to keep up. Being a straight A student at Miller's Valley High School and Mountain County Community College turned out to be different than being a straight A student at the University of Pennsylvania. My biochemistry professor offered me extra help with a graduate student he knew, but the grad student wanted to get paid and I didn't have much money except what I'd made in tips at the diner over the years. My father was dead, my mother was a hundred miles away, my aunt wouldn't leave the house, my best friend from grade school thought I was a sinner, and my boyfriend was busy. On paper it wasn't the best time of my life. Except for the first time in a long time, I felt like I was getting somewhere. I wasn't standing still anymore, I was moving. Now that the Scheinman scholarship meant I was going to medical school, I figured out that I'd been planning to be a nurse because it was what girls like me did. My mother was never one of those nurses who complained about the doctors, but when I listened to her talk about me becoming a doctor myself I figured out pretty quickly that I was paying her back for years of feeling like she'd come in a distant second.

"How do you feel about blood?" Debbie had asked me with a little shiver.

"Nobody really feels good about blood, Deb," my brother said, reading the sports page while little Eddie sat on his lap and tried to eat it.

"I'm fine with blood," I said.

"Ugh," Debbie said. She'd put on at least twenty pounds in the last two years. "She'd better watch the baby weight," my mother said at Thanksgiving, when Debbie had insisted on having dinner at her house for both families. The cornucopia centerpiece and the napkins covered with autumn leaves were pretty, but the turkey was kind of a disaster. Everybody drenched it in gravy, which my mother made standing at the stove, stirring like it was her job. She didn't know what to talk about with Debbie's parents. Her father asked about my courses and Ed talked about the development in Miller's Valley and Debbie talked about teething and my mother and Debbie's mother both said they put whiskey on our gums when we were babies, and Debbie said that was crazy, and that just about took care of the conversation. Ed drove the two of us back to Miller's Valley because I wanted to spend the rest of the weekend with my mother. "How hard is it to make a decent turkey?" he said, and my mother said, "Ed, a man doesn't criticize his wife to his mother, that's rule one."

"What's rule two?" I said.

"Don't sass your mother," she said. "Don't they teach that in your fancy college?" She loved saying that, too: "your fancy college."

"You're about a year from the state declaring eminent domain in the Valley, and then you're going to have to take what they give you," Ed said.

"Let's not talk business on Thanksgiving," my mother said.

"Your mother needs to sell her place soon," said Steven the next morning. "Being the last holdout in one of these deals isn't the way to go."

"Donald's grandfather will be the last holdout," I said.

"Not to be crude, but I think the state is figuring that by the time they're ready to flood the valley, that old guy will be dead and they can just take his place."

"They don't know his grandson." Maybe I didn't, either. I hadn't had a letter from Donald, a real letter, for a long time. He sent a note when my father died, but it was to all of us. He used the word *condolences*. Maybe he was a completely different person. Maybe I was, too. The guys who worked for Steven now still thought I was going to nursing school. "Love me a nurse," the plumber said. "Those damn white uniforms."

I just walked out. "Asshole," Steven said to the plumber, who was only saying what every guy I'd ever met thought.

We went out the Friday night after Thanksgiving to one of the bars on the highway. It was a big weekend, all the kids home from college. The regulars complained that there were no spots in the parking lot. Fred was on a stool near the door, watching football on the TV behind the bar.

"LaRhonda says you should come by," he said. "I think she's kind of bored."

"Right," I said.

"No, really, she is. Take it from me, she's bored out of her gourd. That's what she says every day."

"With two little kids?" I said.

"Her mom spends a lot of time taking care of the kids. That and eating. Don't tell her I said that. Your brother's here."

"What?"

Fred jerked a thumb toward a back corner of the room.

All this time, all the bad stuff, and you could still tell which booth was Tommy's because there were so many people gathered around it. If he'd had a ring you would have thought someone would be kissing it. The courtiers were the kinds of guys who were the backbone of Miller's Valley, the guys who had flamed out first year at college, the guys who thought going in the first place was a waste, the guys who didn't want the job or the life their old man had but hadn't come up with anything different yet and never would, who spent their time smoking pot and getting drunk and bitching about how they'd never gotten a fair shake, whatever that was. And the women they got pregnant and then married. Tom was still their leader, but he was a different Tom now, with half-closed eyes and hair to his shoulders. He looked like Jesus if Jesus was hungover.

I was all the way to the table before he raised his sleepy lids and saw me. His face going from slack to smile seemed to happen in slow motion, like he wasn't used to it.

"Little girl," he said. "What the hell are you doing in here?"

"It's Thanksgiving weekend. I'm off from school. I'm home with Mom."

He patted the fake leather seat next to him but I stayed standing. His hand moved in slow motion, like it was going through water. I leaned on the table and got right up in his face. It had been so long since I'd talked to him last, and I didn't know when it would happen again, so I figured I should go for it.

"Where have you been?" I said. My voice shook like I was going to cry, even though I never cry in public.

"It's a long story, kid." He smelled like bourbon and beer.

"That's what people always say when they really don't want to talk about something, or when they're dying to talk about something."

"You're a smart girl," he said. "I always knew that, that you were smart." He lit a cigarette and blew the smoke to the side so it wasn't in my face. His words were in slow motion, too, like the tape in a tape recorder whose battery was going bad. "You did good, kid. I'm happy for you. You're the American dream, right? You are. I always figured you'd be okay."

"How do you know I'm okay?"

He smiled, but his eyes didn't. "I can tell by looking," he said. A tall skinny guy came right up to the table and stood beside me. "Hey, sweetheart, what's happening?" he said, putting his hand on my back.

"My little sister," Tommy said, coming alive. He made the words sound like a hammer coming down three times, and the skinny guy backed up with his hands in the air, the way they do on TV when the sheriff pulls a gun.

"No idea, man, none, so sorry, really," he said. "I didn't mean anything, swear to God." Then he was gone. The whole crowd of guys around Tommy had disappeared, as though I'd made some sort of force field that drove them away.

"Come home," I said. "Mom will cook for you."

"Naaah," he said. "That's not a good idea."

"She misses you." I wanted to say, I miss you, I miss you so much my heart hurts, but that sounded like one of those stupid greeting card things to say. Plus when you're premed expressions like that don't work for you anymore. Broken heart, gut feeling. You're too literal, at least in the beginning, at least until you learn that a broken heart is a real thing.

"I bet she misses you, too," he said.

"Yeah, but I come home sometimes. You should, too. You owe her that much." I shouldn't have said that. The mean look Tommy had given the skinny guy came back, and his eyelids came down, and the smile was gone.

"I owe her not to have the cops show up at her house again," he said. "That's what I owe her."

"What about me?" I said, and it was like all the times I hadn't said that sentence during my whole life were there when I said it that one time.

"What about you?"

"You let me down." And now I was crying, not even trying to hide it or rein it in.

"No I didn't. Look at you. You're not down. You're up. I just left you alone. Best thing I could have done, leaving you alone."

"You could have—" But I couldn't finish. There are some sentences you just can't finish. Shouldn't finish. I don't know what I would have said anyhow.

Tommy took his time lighting another cigarette from the butt of the last one, like he didn't want to look at me, like we were done. I've never been sure, but I think as I was walking away he said, "Have a good life, corncob." But maybe I just made that up to make myself feel better or worse, I'm still not sure which.

The next morning my mother was standing at the stove and I thought about it awhile. Then I said, "I saw Tommy last night."

"Where?"

"That bar on the highway? It's called the Plugged Nickel."

She nodded and took a couple of strips of bacon out of the cast-iron frying pan. "I know the man who owns it. I don't care for you going to a place like that."

"He was asking about you."

My mother nodded.

"He seems good."

We found an osprey once behind Ruth's house when I was a kid. It's a big bird, three feet tall, with those mean little black eyes those hunting birds have. He was pressed up against the back of the house like he was hiding. He had one wing out to the side dragging in the dirt. Even if you didn't know anything about birds you could tell his wing was broken.

"Go get the long gun, Mimi," my father had said. LaRhonda put her hands over her face, then peeked from between her fingers.

Sometimes you see things that seem so not-right that you never forget them. That big bird of prey, standing on the ground, at our mercy, was like that. So was my mother when she sat down and looked at me. She looked old and beaten, like she might never get up from that chair. There was a little bit of Ruth in her eyes.

"You've always been a terrible liar, Mary Margaret," she said. "Worse even than your father was."

I can't tell you exactly when my brother disappeared. It seemed like it was near the end of my senior year in college, right after spring break. I hadn't seen him since that run-in at Thanksgiving, but Steven had talked to him at the same bar the following fall, and LaRhonda said her father had seen him at the diner right after the big snowstorm that cut off power to the valley for close to a week. She remembered because her father said he didn't want him there. LaRhonda didn't care about hurting your feelings, never had. Come to think of it, she didn't even really know when something she said would hurt your feelings. I felt sorry for her kids.

If Tom had been one of those men who had a mortgage and a car he bought on time, a wife and two kids and a boss waiting for him to sit down at his desk at nine in the morning, in other words if he'd been Ed, it would have been different. You'd go to the police and say to them, Mr. Dependable parked in the lot on Tuesday and hasn't been heard from since. But Tommy Miller wasn't Mr. Dependable, and he wasn't someone whose absence the police would worry about. He disappeared the way Aunt

Ruth had gotten housebound, or the way my father stopped talking after his stroke. He did it by inches so you couldn't figure out exactly when it started. I only really noticed myself after he missed Clifton's birthday party. That had happened before, but even when he was in jail he got some sketchy guy to drop off Tinkertoys and a card signed "Love, Daddy," although it wasn't in his handwriting. Clifton didn't know the difference.

But when I got to Callie's mom's house and there wasn't even a present things looked bad to me. I'd brought Clifton a tape recorder and a bunch of tapes because he liked to make up stories and act them out with different voices. I told him the tape recorder was from his dad, and he was traveling on business which was why he had me bring the present. Callie's boyfriend made a big fuss over the tape recorder. He was such a nice guy that I didn't even mind so much that after he married Callie he was going to move her and Clifton fifty miles away. Callie said she would still bring Clifton to see my mom, and they'd be closer to me at school so I could visit all the time.

"She deserves some happiness," my mother said. Also Clifton was coming to stay for a month in the summer. My mother had already arranged to take three weeks off work. It was like Donald all over again except with a good mother this time. Same father situation, though, although Donald had never talked about his father and Clifton talked about Tom a lot.

"When we go to the new house with Doug you'll tell my dad where I live, right, Aunt Mimi?" he said to me.

"Your dad will always know where you are, honey," I'd replied. Sometimes afterward I thought that was a dumb thing to say. Clifton couldn't even soothe himself with the notion that Tommy couldn't find him. He'd always think Tommy knew where he was but just didn't bother to show up.

By the day of Clifton's party no one had seen Tommy for a couple of months, even some of the harder guys that Steven knew from construction, the ones who were always looking for drugs and trouble. I didn't know where to begin to search for him but I had to try after my aunt Ruth called me at school and said some man had come to the house and scared her silly. "He walked right in and looked in the closets," Ruth said, her voice shaking. "He went into your mother's house, too. I said to him, You'd better not be stealing anything in there. He said, real mean, There's nothing to steal. He said Tom owes him money. A lot of money, except he used a filthy word instead." It took me a minute to figure out that he'd probably said a shitload of money. That was bad. The guy sounded like the sort who, when he said a shitload, meant it.

There was a girl in my dorm who was always offering to lend people her car. "I hardly ever use it," she liked to tell everyone, so I went to her Saturday morning and asked if I could take it for the weekend. She didn't really know me. None of them did. I studied in the library and I went to Ed's house to help look after his kids and I walked around by myself. Steven hadn't bought any houses in the city in spite of his big talk, once he found out about all the rules and regulations and permits and after some guy at a building site told him if he didn't use union plumbers he'd find his pipes ripped out overnight. But he had stayed with me a couple of times, and I could tell the girls on my floor didn't know what to make of him. The guys at school were lanky types with long hair and narrow shoulders. Steven still wore his hair short and you couldn't miss the muscles in his chest and arms. Also he had handed out business cards in the dorm hallway, just in case anyone knew someone in the market for a house in the country. Next to all the guys on barstools in Miller's Valley, talking about when their unemployment would run out and how much a pound you could get for scrap metal, he seemed like a real go-getter, but here he just seemed slick and pushy. The girl with the car was one of the ones Steven had given his card to.

"I really need a car just for the weekend," I said. "I'm a good driver. I'll change your oil if you want."

"How often are you supposed to change your oil?" she said.

"I'll just do it, okay?"

I figured I'd stay with Steven when I got to Miller's Valley. I didn't really want my mother to know I was home or I'd have to lie to her about why. I went to a couple of the bars and at one place the bartender said, "I haven't seen him in a good while and his tab is long overdue. Tell him that." Then he looked me up and down, and I knew he was wondering if I was some girl Tommy had knocked up. "I'm his sister," I said, and the guy said, "That's hard to believe," for about the millionth time in my life.

Finally I went over to the house Steven was working on. It was almost done and it didn't look like any of the workers were around. The Polish guys insisted on knocking off at four on Saturdays, but sometimes Steven would keep on spackling and painting for a couple hours after, a drop light with a 150-watt bulb hanging from a hook in the ceiling. I'd worked with him on a Saturday night more than once, although not since I'd started school. The boxy house near town was a nice little place, white paint and green shutters. The hunter green shutters were Steven's trademark, and he still told everyone when I was around about how I'd come up with the color. "It's not such a big deal," I said once, and he said, "Don't do that, babe. Don't put yourself down." How do you tell someone that you don't like being called babe, especially since he's been doing it from the first time he took your jeans off, when, let's face it, you didn't mind one single damn thing he said or did? It was just one of his routines. He called guys pal and mac. He called me babe.

Steven had a lot of routines, actually. When he brought anyone to one of the houses he was selling he put a pot of Dinty Moore stew in the oven on low heat. He said that real estate agents were always telling people they should bake cookies, but he thought stew smelled more like home than cookies, although at one house he left the stew in the oven after he turned it off and left and he'd had to air that place out for a week. He said sometimes that that's why he'd only made a thousand on it, but I thought a thousand was still a lot. He said when we were married half of it would belong to me.

He always stashed the key to a house inside the belly of a ceramic frog he kept by the back door. It looked low-rent, almost like a lawn gnome, but I'd never said anything. I put the key in the back door, but it was already open. The kitchen looked good, some kind of golden wood cabinets and a dark green Formica counter, same color as the shutters. Through the archway I could see a dining room with a wagon wheel light fixture over where a table would go. It reminded me a little of the arrangement in our house in Miller's Valley, but nicer.

I heard Steven say something from a room down the hall. It was a narrow room, maybe a baby's room for some young couple who wanted to start a family and who would be wowed by the green shutters and the gold cabinets. The floor was high-gloss hardwood, two coats of polyurethane, and Steven was lying on it with some girl with long streaky blond hair sitting on top of him, moving up and down. By the noises she was making I could tell Steven wasn't just good with me, he was good. Either that or she was a fine actress. Steven saw me standing in the doorway and his face went empty for a minute. It's a creepy feeling, walking in on someone having sex. It's even creepier when it's someone you thought was only having sex with you. I turned and went out the back door and walked around the side of the house to the little borrowed blue Volkswagen at the curb. It had a plastic flower around the radio antenna. A pink daisy. Basically that's all you needed to know about the girl who'd lent it to me.

"Whoa, babe, whoa," I heard Steven yell from inside the house, and then I heard a girl's voice say, "What?" That's what got to me as much as the sex part. The babe part. A guy who calls more than one woman babe is a guy you don't want to have any part of, even when he comes running out to the car to stop you from leaving in just a pair of jeans and bare feet. I'd turned the car on and he yanked open the passenger side door.

"Don't get in this car," I said. Behind him at the front door I could see the girl in nothing but a big T-shirt. "Who is it?" she yelled.

"His former girlfriend," I yelled back.

"Oh, Jesus Christ," said Steven. "My feet are freezing. Let me just sit in the car for a minute."

"No. I'm leaving now. I'm here looking for Tommy. Some guy came to our house and threatened my aunt. So just tell me what you know about Tommy and I will leave and you can get back to business."

"It's not what it looks like," he said. When he saw my expression he shut up about that.

"There are some rumors," Steven said, beating his hands together. It was cold for April. I was glad about that. He had goosebumps on his chest. "Somebody told me he got in with some pretty bad guys from the city. New York, not Philly."

"And?"

"And nothing. No one's seen him. Maybe he's with them. Maybe he took off because of them. Maybe's he's just laying low. He was living in that house on 502 that I tried to buy a couple years ago, remember? That little ranch with the two-car garage?"

I shook my head.

"Yeah, come on, you remember, you were there when the guy told me the roof was rotten."

"Okay, now I remember. I'll try there."

"A woman named Casey rents it. He was living with her."

"Great. Thanks." I put the car in gear. "The door?" I said.

"I'm freezing, Stevie," yelled the girl in the doorway.

"Oh, Jesus Christ. She's just some, you know, some—"

"I know. I don't care. I'm going."

He started to cry. It wasn't that big a deal. He was the kind of guy who cried at movies and birthdays and stuff like that. He enjoyed it. He thought it made him seem sensitive. But if he thought crying was going to change anything, he hadn't been paying attention all this time. I was glad we weren't indoors, though. There was one way he might possibly have gotten around me, but not out on the street with him still smelling like some lousy flowery drugstore perfume.

He leaned into the car. "Mimi," he said, pointing at me, "you're the one. You'll always be the one. You're the love of my life. Swear to God."

"If you see Tommy, call me at school. Call me right away, all right?" He nodded. His nose was dripping. He had a scratch on one shoulder.

"Otherwise don't you ever dare call me again."

"I love you," he yelled as I drove away. He meant it, too. I knew him. I knew he meant it, just like I knew he went back inside and finished what he'd started with what's-her-name. Probably more than once. Charm is like tinsel without the tree. What's tinsel without the tree? Shredded tinfoil.

I drove over to the house on 502, but no one was home, and I figured it was probably a good thing, since for the first time in my life I could imagine the feeling that made my brother want to wallop someone, and I was afraid I might wallop him for scaring me so bad if he opened the door. But I think I was mainly mad at myself. I didn't cry in the car back to school, although over the next week I did. I wasn't even sure why. I knew that I wasn't heartbroken, and I guess the fact that I wasn't made me disgusted with myself. It didn't take long before I figured out that I'd learned an important lesson, that falling into things, bad things, dumb things, things that felt good but were bad and dumb both, was the easiest thing in the world. It was a good lesson to learn when you were still young.

"I changed your oil," I said when I got back to the dorm and handed plastic flower girl her keys, but I really hadn't. I figured she'd never know the difference.

I missed the big one. I'd always thought of the storm that killed Donald's grandmother as the big one, but it turned out it wasn't even close. This one was on the evening news, the national and the local both. Eddie said there were pictures of houses he recognized with water all around them, nothing but the roofs showing, although how he could tell which house was which just by the roof I didn't know.

My mother had been at the hospital when the rain started to come down hard, and they asked her to do a double shift. Then they told her she couldn't leave because of flooding on the roads. She said afterward that she slept in a patient room and couldn't get over how uncomfortable the bed was. When she finally went back home the little barn had collapsed along with the shed my father had used as his repair shop, and both the furnace and the hot water heater were shot.

Aunt Ruth had stayed put, as always. When the flooding started to get bad Cissy Langer went over and sat with her. They went up to the attic together and took all Ruth's dolls with them. Cissy said she was glad that all her doll equipment was in her workroom at the new house, that she didn't have to keep moving it the way she once had. A waterlogged Singer sewing machine is pretty much a sewing machine that will need to be junked. I'd learned that from my father, who'd tried to repair one once. Cissy told my aunt that her doll collection was worth a pretty penny and that she couldn't afford to let it get wet. Everything else got wet because for the first time the water rose into the first floor of Ruth's house. Mr. Langer said with this storm you could get a little bit of an idea of what Miller's Valley would look like when they flooded it. That's what he said: not *if*. *When*. We knew it was *when* by that time.

I wondered if they'd gotten impatient, after all those years, the government people. I wondered whether the big one was a natural event, or whether they'd closed off the dam even more than they'd done before and let the heavy rain and Miller's Creek and the water table and gravity do the rest. But I thought about it, and then I let it go. Sometimes I thought I'd gotten a little addled about the whole thing, and that my suspicion that the water in the valley had been deliberately pushed into rising bit by bit was just one of those crazy notions that helped people make sense of the senseless world, like all the theories about who'd really killed President Kennedy or whether one of the Beatles albums told you secrets if you played the songs backward.

Ed drove up the next week and took my mother over to the new development, which was mostly finished. They were doing a good business in people who lived in low areas of the township, and women who liked shiny new better than same old.

"It looks raw," my mother said when I asked her about it. I couldn't get more out of her than that.

"She's got to be realistic," Eddie said as I held Kimmy on my hip and she chewed on a hank of my hair. My name had been her first word. Debbie didn't like that one bit, I could tell. "I have a name that's really easy to say," I said. "Clifton learned it when he was a baby, too."

"Mimi isn't any easier than Mama," Debbie had said. Which was true.

"I think Mom is ready to move," I said to Eddie. "But what about Ruth?"

"I'm tired of all that with her," Ed said.

"Which doesn't get anyone any nearer to getting her out of the house."

"She's lucky there still is a house," he said.

The big one was the storm that tipped the balance. Everyone said that afterward, although I thought they were fooling themselves and that the balance had been tipped all those years before, when Winston Bally first drove his sedan around the gravel roads of the valley. This time around, three of the houses in Miller's Valley didn't make it out in one piece. Two of them were mostly scrap wood by the time the water went down. It was a good thing no one was living in either one. One had been abandoned after its owners died and one was already owned by the state. The third one had some walls standing but it was still a teardown. That one was owned by Home Sweet Home. Eddie told me that a couple of years ago Steven had purchased three places in the valley, two that belonged to an estate with grown kids who had no interest, one that had gone into foreclosure. He'd already sold two to the state for the water project. Ed said that according to the records he'd seen, Steven had made about three thousand dollars.

"It was a smart move," he said. "You could do worse."

I didn't say anything. I wasn't going to talk to Eddie, of all people, about my love life. Steven kept sending me Hallmark cards. "Just because I'm thinking of you," they would say, with a rose edged in glitter, or "You're purrrrrrr-fect," with a photograph of a kitten. The last one I hadn't even opened, just tossed into the waste can next to my desk.

I'd missed the big one because I didn't get a chance to go back to Miller's Valley much. Every time I had two days off in a row it turned out my mother was working those days, or had something else planned. It didn't take a genius to figure out that she wanted to keep me where I was, doing what I was doing, as though to move me forward she had to give me up. I'd never seen her as happy as she'd been at my college graduation. "Magna cum laude," she said, patting my cheek in a way she hadn't done since I was a kid. "I was a summa," said Ed. "Of course you were, son," she'd said. "And I was very proud."

She gave me a white lab coat as a gift. One of the doctors at the hospital had told her the best place to buy one. Callie gave me a stethoscope, and Clifton listened to my heart with it, and the look on his face made us all laugh. "It's very noisy!" he said.

Mrs. Farrell sent me a fifty-dollar bill. "Please come back and talk to my students, Dr. Miller," she wrote. "They need the inspiration!" And I vowed I would.

My apartment was almost as small as my room at home. It was a studio with a hot plate in a little alcove and a bathroom with a shower stall so tight that I had a bruise on my hip from hitting the wall when I turned around to rinse my hair. I think I got the place because I was the only renter skinny enough to fit in that shower. It was cheap, and because of my schedule I was really only there to sleep. "If I lived here I'd spend time at our house, too," said Debbie when Ed helped bring an old bed of theirs upstairs to my place.

"She spends time at our house because you're always asking her to watch the kids," Ed said as he wrestled the mattress onto the box spring. When I listened to the two of them I kept wondering if my parents had been so annoyed with each other after

Eddie and Tommy were born. Debbie said she wanted to have two more, and Ed said she was nuts.

"They'll be fine," my mother said the one time I brought it up, when I drove to the valley for the day. "You can always tell the ones who will stick."

"How?" I said, but my mother shrugged. She just knew. Unlike Ed, she seemed to know that I was no longer with Steven. I could tell because she didn't say a word about him. I did notice there was a big fancy box of peanut brittle in her one kitchen cupboard, but I didn't know if that was an attempt, like the Hallmark cards, or just a coincidence and some patient had given it to her. I didn't ask. I guess I'm my mother's daughter. One of the things she couldn't stand about Ruth is that she had a tendency to talk about every little thing. "Silence is a virtue," my mother said sometimes. I suppose Ruth talked because she was lonely, but my mother would have made one of her mouth noises if I'd said that. Lonely. Ha.

When we talked that day in the kitchen it made an echoing sound because there wasn't much furniture in the downstairs. The big one had been big enough to soak through the couch and the easy chairs, the rugs and the throw pillows. There was no saving them. My mother had gotten two of the guys from the VFW to cart most of her furniture to the dump. Some people left their houses and just never came back. They didn't want to see what was there, all sad and sodden. After the big one people seemed to take for granted that the valley was done, and that the Valley Federal Recreation Area was happening. The government people had gone from talking about water maintenance and reservoir supply to talking about boats and swimming and waterskiing and ice skating. They'd gone from talking about taking people's houses to giving people jobs, from eminent domain to tourism. People love the sound of that word, *tourism*.

But I guess what really pushed the whole thing over the edge was that the big one killed Winston Bally. "Poetic justice," I said when I heard about it, but my mother gave me such a look. Winston Bally had been driving through the valley, making his rounds, when he blew out a tire on a dirt track that led to an old trailer where one of the oldest Janssons still lived. He walked down the track to the trailer, but Mr. Jansson wasn't home. He was already over at his nephew's house, where his niece by marriage, who he'd always liked better than his nephew anyway, was convincing him to go to the high school evacuation center, at least until the rain stopped.

When they finally found Mr. Bally's body, after the water went down, it turned out he'd had a heart attack. My mother said all you had to do was look at his color and his belly to know it had been a long time coming. But no one ever stopped talking like it was the water that killed him. Ed said the news made it sound like he was some kind of hero, like he'd given his life for Miller's Valley. Or the Valley Federal Recreation Area, more like it.

I missed it all because I was working long hours, during the day as an assistant at a research lab at the medical school and four nights a week waiting tables at an Italian restaurant. I didn't have a uniform, but the white shirt they wanted me to wear always had red sauce stains, and I wound up buying a lot of replacements. The tips were a whole lot better than they had been at the diner, and I got free meals at the end of every evening. Some days were slower than others. When it was hot outside people weren't so inclined to want penne Bolognese or clams oreganata, but I liked them anytime. There were a lot of things I'd never tasted until I left home. I tried to get my mother to try calamari, but she said she knew bait even when it was on a plate with lemon wedges and she'd just have the meatballs. Mr. Guarino, who owned the restaurant, had let my whole table eat for free after my graduation.

"Always on time, always polite, always good service," he said to my mother with his hand on one of my shoulders. I still had on my academic robe because I knew it made my mother happy to see it.

"I should hope so," said my mother as though those were the minimum requirements, which in her mind was true.

It was only a ten-minute walk from the lab to the restaurant. In the summer the city streets felt like the fields around our house, the tar all soft and spongy like wet ground under my feet. I always put on my black skirt and white shirt in the bathroom in the lab, then put my white coat over them so I wouldn't look so much like I was on my way to a waitressing job. Although the waitressing was easier and paid more than cleaning up the lab cages after the rats and mice. I was sad, that last week. Mr. Guarino was a nice man, and his nephew who tended bar and the other two waitresses had been nice to me, too. But I couldn't wait tables during med school. My adviser made it sound like I wouldn't be able to find time to sleep or eat during med school.

I was waiting to cross the street in front of the Roma Ristorante when I heard someone yelling down the block. I looked around but the sidewalk was crowded, people leaving work for home, so I kept going. I'd just stepped off the curb when I heard "Mimi!" right behind me. I turned around. It took me a minute even though I'd seen pictures over the years.

"Donald," I said. "Wow. Donald."

"Mimi," he said. "I've been calling you for the last five minutes."

"Out of the road," roared a guy in a GTO as he blew past us.

"He's right," I said.

"He didn't have to be such a jerk," Donald said as we stepped back onto the pavement.

"What are you doing here?"

"I came to find you."

"How did you even know it was me? You haven't seen me since we were thirteen."

"Your mother told me where to find you. Didn't she tell you I was coming?"

I shook my head. "You look just the same, too," Donald said. "Plus the doctor's jacket."

He was right, really. Donald and I had both been the kinds of kids who looked like adults. We had even had adult personalities. It was like we'd grown into ourselves, or at least I had. When Donald was a kid his face had looked square and heavy, like it was too big for the rest of him. Now it looked good. He was handsome. I was handsome, too, I guess. That was the kind of face I had.

"Did you go to the valley first to see your grandfather?" I said.

"I'm going after this."

"It's kind of a ghost town. They're going to flood it, finally, but don't tell your grandfather I said so. I think he's the last person who believes it won't happen."

"I don't think he really believes that. He just wants to. Your mother sounds okay with it. She sounded good when I talked to her."

"You know, she's the same. Everything else there is pretty much the same. LaRhonda is just the same, except she has kids."

"I heard. That's scary, the idea of LaRhonda being somebody's mother. I hope she's nicer to her kids than she was to us."

"She was mean to you."

"She was mean to you, too," Donald said. "You just didn't seem to mind."

"How's your mother?" I said.

Donald shrugged. "The same," he said. "My stepfather is a good guy. He and I really get along."

There was a long silence. We had exhausted everything there

was to say standing on a street corner with someone you haven't actually seen for a long time.

"Wow," I said finally. "I can't believe it's really you."

"It really is," Donald said.

I looked at my watch. Eddie and Debbie had given it to me for my graduation. It was pretty and real gold, as Debbie kept saying, but it didn't have any numbers and it was hard to read. It wasn't really a good watch for a doctor. "The band is lizard," Debbie had said, and I made a fuss, but I needed to get another one.

"I can't be late for work," I said.

"Can I take you to dinner?" Donald said.

"We can eat free after closing," I said. "If you like Italian. It's good Italian."

"I really like Italian," said Donald.

"Can you wait until ten o'clock?"

"I've been waiting almost ten years," he said, pulling at his upper lip just the way he used to, and I laughed, and then I got what he meant and looked away and then down at my watch again. If Steven had said something like that, I would have known he didn't really mean it, that it was a line, that he'd been rehearsing it, maybe even used it before. But if Donald was still anything like he'd once been, he always meant exactly what he said.

"So you're not engaged anymore," he said.

"I was never engaged."

"My grandfather said you were engaged but you weren't anymore."

"I was never engaged."

Donald nodded. "You didn't tell me what you're doing here," I said to him.

"I told you," he said. "I came to find you."

I figured it would take a week to move the stuff of a lifetime out of my mother's house. But it wasn't anywhere near that long, or that much. After the last public meeting but before the state issued its final decision, she'd started packing up little by little. She threw away a lot of things, too. Not my things, though. She'd been good about that. She'd packed up boxes of stuffed animals Tommy had won me at the county fair and old copybooks with class notes written out in pencil and even the bridesmaid dress I'd worn at LaRhonda's wedding with its dyed-to-match shoes. I put it all in the back of my car and figured I'd stop at the dump on my way to the highway. Donald and I had a decent-size apartment for a medical student and a history teacher and basketball coach at a Catholic grade school. We were in one of those mean-looking buildings they put up when I was a kid, the kind with balconies nobody ever uses that are the size of refrigerator boxes. But the place had a nice living room with a view of the city lights out the window, and a bedroom that fit more than just a bed, and a kitchen where two people could cook if we ever cooked, which we didn't because most of the time I was at the med school or the hospital, and Donald was partial to things like hoagies and cheesesteaks that he could pick up wrapped in wax paper at the deli on the corner. It was a nice apartment if you weren't too bothered by the roaches, but it didn't have room for that butt-ugly dress LaRhonda made me wear and my bio workbook from high school. Although it was kind of nice to look back at how good I'd been at bio even then. That old paperback copy of *The Group* was in there, too. My mother must have found it hidden in my closet. That one I figured I would reread.

On top of all the junk in one box was a picture that had always been on the dresser in my parents' room. My mother and my father were standing together in front of a pine tree near the end of the driveway. My father was wearing a navy blue suit and my mother was wearing a blue suit, too, but a pale blue, the color of the sky. My mother had on an orchid corsage. My father's younger brother, Ed, who had died in a car crash right after my parents got married, stood on one side of my father in a suit that looked like it was new and maybe bought on sale because it was brown and didn't fit right, all pulled open at the lapels and below the buttons. Ruth stood by my mother. She was the only one smiling. She was fifteen years old and, by anybody's lights, pretty, shiny, full of joy. My mother looked almost old enough to be her mother, although it was 1942, when any woman I saw in pictures looked old or at least adult, even in high school photographs.

"Did you put this in here by mistake?" I said.

My mother turned from packing up some pots and pans. She'd been using the same flour sifter since I was born, maybe since she'd been married. It had more dents than my father's old truck, which was going to the junkyard. "I thought you'd like to have that," she said. "You can put it right next to yours unless Donald wouldn't like it. I suppose he doesn't have one of his own parents. My recollection is that they got married in Atlantic City by some JP who used to do ceremonies in a tent at the end of a pier, right next to the roller coaster."

"He's got one of his grandparents," I said.

"I was at his grandparents' wedding, believe it or not," my mother said. "I had a pink party dress with a sash and a big bow. It had a low waist the way they did then. His grandmother's dress was kind of shapeless, really, like a nightgown. That was the style."

She was right. The dress was kind of shapeless, and both of Donald's grandparents looked so serious, like they had done something terrifying. Which I guess was about right. Although I hadn't felt that way when Donald and I got married. I hadn't felt frightened at all. We hadn't gone to a JP on a seaside pier, but there'd been just the two of us and our families at the college chapel and then dinner after at the Roma. I found a Mexican cotton wedding dress at a little hippie store near school. It was half price because it had a stain on one side that I got out by soaking it in milk, which my mother had taught me would clean off almost anything. Donald's mother was more dressed up than I was. "Well, honey, this sure is different from our wedding," said Debbie, who I recalled had complained over and over about having to keep the guest list below 250. Even if we'd invited everyone we knew there wouldn't have been 250 people. There wouldn't have been a hundred unless you counted the kids in Donald's class, who were sad that they weren't invited and who all got to try on his wedding band on Monday morning, since there was no honeymoon. LaRhonda was apparently annoyed that I hadn't asked her to be my matron of honor, but my mother told her it wasn't that kind of wedding.

"Why didn't you tell me he was coming?" I'd asked my mother after Donald showed up out of nowhere that day outside the restaurant.

"I figured it would go better if you didn't have time to think it to death," she said. "I know you, Mary Margaret."

I held the picture against my chest and looked around the old kitchen. "I don't know how you're so calm about all this," I said to my mother. "How can you stand to just leave? Your family has been here for almost two hundred years."

My mother kept taking the baking stuff out of the back of the bottom cabinets. "My family isn't here anymore. You and Ed and the kids are all down in the city. Clifton's not too far from all of you." Both of us were thinking the same thing when she said that, I bet. Both of us were thinking about where Tommy was. I had a feeling about where Tommy was, but I couldn't say it to myself, much less say it out loud to our mother. The longer he was gone, the younger he got in my mind, so that now when I thought about him, or dreamt about him, he was that high school senior with a flop of milk chocolate hair and a grin that lured even nice girls into his backseat. Maybe that's the way it always is. When I thought about my father, it wasn't as that damaged man dragging his leg into Ruth's living room. It was always in the barn at daybreak shifting hay or in the truck headed out to fix someone's machinery or in his little workroom squinting at the back of a clock radio. Sometimes I dreamt about the two of them, my father and Tom, and when I did Donald said I talked in my sleep, and he would hug me tight and kiss my hair.

I'll admit, it wasn't like it was with Steven with Donald. It was kind of like the difference between pound cake and ice cream. But I like pound cake, always have, always will. And ice cream every day just makes you sick. My mother said Steven had dropped by her new house and brought her a rosebush to plant by the door. "He still has a case on you," my mother said, "which is too bad. Although it was the best thing about that boy, that he recognized what he was getting with you."

"I don't know what I was thinking," I said.

"Oh, I know exactly what you were thinking," said my mother, taping a box shut.

"George Gresser," I said.

"Never you mind," she said, and then added, "Lesser. George Lesser."

There wasn't much more to do at her place, so she sent me over to do the final packing at Ruth's house. I dreaded it, but I couldn't tell her that. I'd seen so many people dead by that time, including the cadaver four of us had taken apart piece by piece, my first year in med school, that we'd named William Penn. But I still couldn't walk into the living room of that little house without seeing my father sitting in the chair, his head tipped to one side, his eyes filmy and fixed on something, whatever it is you see when you exhale for the last time. I'd seen a man who had had a stroke in my ER rotation and thought of my father, and another who was doing physical therapy but not with a good humor and thought of my father, and another who couldn't speak and was talking in gibberish. "Aphasia," said one of my fellow students, pleased with himself, but all I could think of was a man saying "bottle" over and over again. The problem with becoming a doctor is that you learn to think there are answers for things. But deep down inside I still believed in mysteries. I didn't know whether that was going to make me better, or worse, at my job. You learn so much science, but the best doctors I saw around me understood the human heart. I hoped I could hold on to that.

My mother hadn't bought a house in the new development, despite Ed's best efforts. "She is a stubborn woman," he said, and Debbie said, "You just figured that out?" which I have to say I didn't like one bit, although my mother was about as stubborn as a woman could be. I don't think she liked how close the development houses were to one another. Plus she said she needed a place with what she called a mother-in-law setup, which I'd first heard about from Steven a couple of years before. Up top in her new house was where she lived, a sunny living room with that wall-to-wall carpeting she'd always wanted, open to a kitchen with a breakfast bar, and then three bedrooms down the hall, one large, two small. Then if you went around to the back of the house there was another part that took up half the basement and had big glass doors to the patio and yard, which was kind of a waste because Ruth was never going to go out those doors. But Ruth had a nice light living room herself and two bedrooms.

I'd always figured that my mother would never leave the farm and the valley because it was her home, and because she wouldn't be able to get Ruth to move. But now I knew that I was more attached than she was. When she'd said, "Let them," about drowning the place where I'd lived most of my life and she'd lived all of hers, I realized that if she'd had her way she would have left long ago, and that made me realize that for most of her life she hadn't had her way about much. As for Ruth, my mother had always figured she could handle her. When I'd called her at the new house for the first time she said Ruth was already in her place downstairs. "Carrying on," she said.

"I gave her a sedative," my mother said. "How else was I going to get her out of there? I gave her a sedative and two of the boys from the ambulance squad brought her over here and hauled her in and laid her down on the bed. A brand-new bed, by the way."

"You gave her a sedative?"

"In her iced tea," my mother said as though it was the most normal thing in the world and I should have thought of it myself.

I should have thought of it myself. "What exactly did you give her? What dosage did you use?"

"Mary Margaret, I was administering sedatives when you were still in diapers. All that matters is that your aunt is in her new place, I'm in mine, and we're done with the rest. I have some packing up and cleaning out to do if you want to be useful." And so I was making myself useful.

There wasn't much packing to do at Ruth's house, either. Cissy had already carted all her dolls away, repaired and cleaned some of them, and taken them to the new place, which had a wall of bookshelves that were just the right kind of thing for doll display if you were interested in doll display. "Someday your daughter will play with these," Cissy said to me as she placed them side by side, but Ruth got that look on her face and I knew that would happen over her dead body. "They don't look the same," she said. That's what she said about everything. The stove didn't cook the same. The TV didn't work the same. "I could have let them drown you, Ruth," my mother called from the top of the stairs. "She's always been hard," Ruth muttered.

"She's right," I said. "The valley is gone."

"I miss it," Ruth said.

There wasn't much left in the old kitchen. I'd already brought Ruth her place mats, vinyl with daisies in one corner that I'd given her for Christmas, and the frying pan she used for grilled cheese. She wanted the throw pillows from her couch, which had been ruined in the big storm. My mother got new furniture for Ruth's place just the way she did for her own. While Ruth wouldn't say so, I could tell by the way she ran her hand over it that she liked the flowered pattern on the new couch. It was more her thing than the old tan couch with the scratchy upholstery that had been in her living room for twenty years.

"Just bring me a few things, Mimi," she'd said. "I need my old egg turner, and the trivet on the stove. Oh, and that picture of bluebirds I have on the bedroom wall. And the mirror from the spare room, too. I can't find my mother's marcasite brooch. If your mother hasn't taken it it might have dropped under the bed when they removed me." That was how she described it until the day she died: "they removed me." My mother wouldn't give her chapter and verse on the removal, but I got the idea from Cissy that Ruth had spent so much time yelling and screaming the first day that the near neighbors, who weren't that near, thought about calling the police.

"I never liked that brooch in the first place, which is why she got it, and why she wants a brooch when she never goes anyplace is beyond me," my mother had said. I thought the new arrangement was going to cause even more fights than the old one because sometimes Ruth could hear my mother's comments about her, and vice versa. It depended on whether the door at the top of the steps, which divided one half of the house from the other, was open.

The brooch was in the old silverware drawer, along with three forks and a bent potato peeler. It made me wonder if Ruth was developing dementia. That's another bad thing about being a medical student, although I've found it gets better once you've practiced for a while. But in the beginning you diagnose everything. "There's a name for what Ruth has," I'd told my mother once when we were on the phone, and she hung up and then called me right back and said, "Mary Margaret, if you suddenly start to act as though you've invented medical knowledge it's going to go hard for you and me."

"You should have been a doctor yourself," I'd said.

"If wishes were horses," she said, and I almost hung up on her at that point.

Cissy told me that when they'd left Andover a crew had come in and taken everything away, then bulldozed the houses and even some of the trees. But apparently Miller's Valley ran so deep, and so many of the houses were already ruins or rubble, that the water authorities said the people who were left could just walk away. Ed had tried to describe how it would work, the way they'd redirect the dam to hold more water back until it flowed down the creek bed and turned it into a river, the months it would take for the water to run hard and fast enough to reach the level they'd planned, how everyone always thought you'd flip a switch and there'd all of a sudden be forty feet of water when it actually took time. That was good, he said, because then the animals had time to get out, the deer and possums and bear and raccoon and the silent unseen bobcats and porcupine, which my father always said were there but that I'd never seen in all my life, even dead along the road. They'd have time to flee, Eddie said, and that's when I said, "I don't want to hear any of it." The water would come up and cover the houses, the barns, the fences, the old swing sets, the bales of hay, and the cornfields now lying fallow, and I didn't want to hear any of it. A couple of crews had already taken down the trees around the valley lip so that when the water got to where it was finally going to settle, the surface would be smooth for fifteen feet or so, and I didn't want to hear any of it. Below that everything else would start to rot and dissolve. It would take years and years to happen but it would happen.

I didn't want to hear any of it.

I looked around Ruth's house. It wouldn't be any great loss. When I was little I thought it was pretty big, but now that I was big I realized it was pretty little. Maybe that was what Ruth liked. It felt kind of shut in. I had everything she'd asked for, but I figured I should take one last look in the attic, where she always took shelter when the water rose. I pulled down the old wooden steps with the chain from the ceiling, and one of the treads dropped right off with a clatter. The whole place was already falling apart. The water would do its work in no time.

The things in the attic were the kinds of things you put in an attic because they really need to be thrown away but you can't bear to do it, or don't want to take the time. There were two chairs with broken cane seats, a couple of dusty milk bottles, one with dried flowers in it, and what was either a cot without legs or a stretcher. The droppings on the floor made me wonder where all the bats were going to go once the water got high enough. I figured they'd had centuries of moving from place to place when we wrecked their homes.

There was a dusty little window at one end of the attic loft, and underneath it were three suitcases, a matched set, straw-colored with a wine stripe woven in. The biggest one had a hole gnawed at one end, right by the tarnished brass corner guards. There was an old set of drapes I'd never seen before inside, and two issues of *Life* magazine. One had General Patton on the cover. The second suitcase was empty, but even without a hole you could see and smell that the mice had been living in it for a long time.

The third was one of those vanity cases that had gone out of fashion. I remembered when I was a little girl, watching an old movie with Ruth and seeing someone with one of those furs around her neck that still had its little head as she carried one of those cases off a train. Ruth said it was just big enough to hold your perfume and cosmetics and a nightie and slippers. Even then it seemed pretty useless to me.

This one had crumpled newspaper on top, and as I started to pull it out I felt something solid at the bottom. When the paper was pushed aside there was a sweet sweet smell and a cloud of dust motes that shone like tiny sequins in the pale light. I stared down for a long time at what was inside. I'd seen what was at the bottom of that case before, in the office of the obstetrician with whom I'd done my OB rotation, seen it in the ER one night, a woman from West Philadelphia who'd been out with friends and couldn't get to her own hospital in time. But it still took a minute or two for my mind to wrap itself around what my eyes were seeing, maybe because I'd never seen anything human really mummified before, the skin dark and leathery like the baby birds we'd sometimes find in the brush weeks after they'd fallen from the nest. What hair there was had come loose with the newspaper, so that it lay like bits of cotton candy over the little blunted face. It was half wrapped in a piece of fabric, a heavy yellow sateen, an old napkin or a random swatch, that was spotted brown in places. Maybe slightly less than full term, maybe just a small baby, what we'd called a neonate when we'd pulled it out of the backseat of the cab the West Philadelphia woman gave birth in.

I let the lid of the vanity case fall, some of the newspaper sticking out around its edge, and I sat down on the dirty wood floor of the attic. I was breathing hard and I put my head between my knees because I thought I might pass out. I started to open the case again, to make certain I was seeing what I thought I was seeing, but as soon as I got another whiff of that sweet smell I knew it for what it was. I sat like that for a long time, until I heard my mother downstairs.

"I'm coming down," I called.

"My goodness, you are filthy," she said, turning from the kitchen counter where she'd been fingering the marcasite brooch.

"I know."

"Don't tell me she has anything up there worth saving," my mother said.

I looked at her, trying to breathe more slowly.

"You all right, Mary Margaret? You might have had a reaction to all that dust and who knows what else up there from the squirrels and bats and whatever."

"I think I'll take a shower," I said.

"Not here you won't. There's not a towel left in the place, and the pressure's always been bad since your father put in that new pump for the well. Come over to the house. I've still got some things in the bathroom."

My hair was wet when I pulled into my mother's driveway and handed her a cardboard box from the backseat. Inside was the trivet, the egg turner, the picture, the mirror, and the brooch, all the things Ruth had asked for. "Tell Ruth I got what she wanted," I said. "Tell her everything else in the house is gone."

# Epilogue

I have to hand it to them, it was smart, the way they handled drowning the valley, smarter than I would have thought they'd be when Mr. Bally was trolling the back roads and cruising the counter at the diner. They didn't make any kind of big announcement, and they were vague with the newspapers about the timing. Then one night after dark they closed the locks on the dam and began to channel the water in, slowly at first, and then faster, harder, so that on the evening of the third day the people in town said they felt a faint tremor and thought Miller's Valley was having its first earthquake. Which I guess was true, in a way. First and last.

I was certain of exactly where the water went as it followed its path. The Miller farm had always been known to be the lowest place in the valley. The pasture went first, then our house, then the house where Ruth lived, then all the rest. I wasn't there when it happened, and my mother never talked about it, and Donald's grandfather talked about it so often that it just became one of those stories that's like wallpaper, where you don't even notice the pattern or the detail after a while. It seems like a long time ago, now. It is a long time ago, I guess, more than forty years. Or it's just yesterday. That's the way things are, at my age.

Donald and I stayed in the city for a couple of years after I graduated from medical school. A nice woman who was a hand surgeon kept telling me I should follow her into the specialty, but she also kept talking about how terrible her male colleagues and her work hours were. The women in anesthesiology and pathology were always talking about how manageable their schedules were, but I liked my patients conscious and alive. I finally figured out that I wanted to be the old-fashioned kind of doctor who gives a baby his first round of shots and then sees him through chicken pox, strep, puberty, and maybe even parenthood himself. And that was exactly what I became.

Donald's grandfather had his share of health problems, in the way old men living alone tend to do, since they don't live like humans, sure don't take care of themselves. We wound up driving north to Miller's Valley a lot to stock his refrigerator. I taped reheating instructions to the things I put in the freezer, but half the time after a month I'd see them still in there, with halos of freezer burn around the edges of the Tupperware.

"I'll feed him a couple of times a week," my mother said.

"I'll tell you, Mimi, your mother is a saint," Donald's grandfather said.

"You'd better get up here," my mother said one evening when, luckily, I'd just finished seeing my patients at the community clinic and the kids at Donald's school didn't have a game.

The heart attack Donald's grandfather had had could have been worse, and I was standing in the hallway, looking over the chart, figuring out what kind of home care we would need, when the cardiologist told Donald that it was a shame he lived so far away. "The high school is looking for a basketball coach," he said. "Your granddad told me you're the man for the job." I saw a look on Donald's face, and I realized that there was something in him that I'd never seen and that I, of all people, should have recognized. Except for his grandfather, there was no one left but me who'd really known the boy whose grandmother would sit him down at the table with a big cold glass of milk and a big wedge of warm pie and a fork on a folded paper napkin, a boy who had only been made to feel as though he was at home in one place in his whole life.

"You could take that coaching job," I said in the car on the way back to the city. The way the sentence hung in the air, it was like someone else had said it. But I guess it was me.

I like it here in Miller's Valley. When I understood that Donald wanted to come back, that he'd felt rootless all his life except for this one small spot on earth, I wasn't sure I would. It's changed now. That development Ed worked on is one of the older parts of town. Those sad little saplings are big pin oaks, and there are other, bigger, showier clumps of houses farther out. Miller's Valley is like the rest of America, a small feeble downtown with rings of suburbs, like the rings on a tree. Seventies, eighties, nineties, now.

When we first moved up from Philadelphia we rented a place right in town, but after six months the real estate agent, who had been in Tommy's class at the high school, told me she had a house she thought we might like, an old Victorian with three fireplaces and a big wraparound porch. I did like it. I'd liked it when Steven fixed it up and sold it to those two guys for a weekend house, although I didn't tell Donald that. Steven left before we came back to Miller's Valley. He'd made enough money to go somewhere in the big-money burbs farther south, but then I heard from Fred that he got overextended and lost most of what he'd made, then later on that he was climbing back up again. I'd bet on Steven bouncing back for sure, and then maybe going bust again, and so on and so forth. When we bought that old Victorian I had a cabinetmaker come in to build some bookshelves, and he had to redraw his plans because the one new wall had studs that were too far apart, two feet instead of eighteen inches. I wonder how much Steven saved on lumber with just that one small change. But that was him all over, cutting corners. I guess he was just cutting a corner that day I walked in on him and that girl, whoever she was. One day a couple of years ago I looked him up on the computer. There he was, Steven Sawicki, posed next to a convertible in the desert with a pretty blond woman in a red dress who could have been his daughter but was probably his wife, given the two little boys in polo shirts standing between them. She looked like she'd been built from spare parts in a plastic surgeon's office, and Steven looked like maybe he'd had some run-ins with that same surgeon, too, his face as smooth and unmarked as a freshly plastered wall. He runs a business in Las Vegas that rents luxury cars to tourists. You can have a Lamborghini or a Bentley for the day and roar around town pretending you're somebody you're not. "Living la Vida Loca," it says on his website. Sometimes things turn out exactly the way you imagine.

He looked happy in that picture, contented with the woman, the children, and the car, and I bet he is. He was always a glass-half-full guy, Steven. He was never mean, or dark, or hardhearted. He just wasn't ever really real. I don't regret him. I don't regret any of that, except for that one bus trip into New York City, and I only think of that every once in a while, not as something I'm sorry I did but something I had to do and wish I hadn't. He was getting me ready for something else, Steven was. I understand that now. Our daughter, Nora, had a boyfriend in high school, my Lord, you could practically feel the sex coming off the two of them, Donald was in a rage. But I knew what it was, and what was coming. Later, when she met Eric in college, and married him, I knew it would last.

When our son, Ian, met and married Devon, I knew it

wouldn't. But I smiled in the pictures, and danced at the wedding, and later I listened to him call her nasty names but I wouldn't let him do it in front of their son. I make sure my grandson knows I'm his grandmother even if his mother doesn't like me much. Everything follows patterns I've seen before.

We were happy here, Donald and I. He was one of the most beloved guys in town for years, whether the team won or lost. If he went to the hardware store to get duct tape it would be two hours before he got home, so many people stopped and talked to him, the kids he coached, their parents, his fellow teachers, the old-timers who wanted to reminisce about his grandparents. "There's a man who's found his niche," my mother said one evening when we watched him moving slowly around a potluck supper at the firehouse.

Most of my own friends are what the natives call the new people, meaning people who have been in Miller's Valley less than a hundred years. Some of them are only here on weekends. They're lawyers and bankers and doctors in the cities, Philadelphia and New York and even Washington. That's how it is with Nora. I'm happy for that much, my daughter and her husband and their little boys here most weekends and holidays. Ian lives in Ohio now and he's likely to get tenure, but still I keep hoping he'll come back, too, and at least he uses Nora's house for a month every summer while she and her family are at the beach and he's got his son, and so so do I.

All these years after she was my lab partner at the community college, Laura is still one of my closest friends, and her daughter is one of Nora's. She opened a shop on Main Street that sells nice little things. It doesn't do that well, but well enough. LaRhonda and I pretend to be friends when we see each other, but we're not, not really. Her youngest son and Ian were in Little League together, although her boy was a couple of years older. Right after the fourth baby she got a divorce, but she let Fred continue to manage the McDonald's. She seems to have given up on the Holy Roller routine, which made it easier for the two of us to get through a couple of innings in the bleachers on a hot day with small talk. Even at Little League she had on expensive sunglasses and a purse that looked like it was made out of unborn calves. One day we were sitting side by side and she said, without turning to look at me, "Who would have thought the two of us would wind up like this?"

"Like what?" I said, and she laughed, a real laugh, not mocking or sarcastic.

"You never change," she said.

I'm not sure about that. That's what Donald said when he showed up in Philadelphia, sure somehow that I was what he wanted, sure that deep inside I was still that little girl making change out of a coffee can and handing him his share of the money. Maybe everyone stays the same inside, even when their life looks nothing like what they once had, or even imagined. I don't know LaRhonda well enough now to know whether she's changed. She has a lot of money, much more than her father had. She was smart, plowing the profits from the restaurants into a development company, building houses and investing in office buildings. Steven would say she thinks big. She sent her children away to boarding school, and she said that it was because the education was better, and I have no doubt that that was true, although the high school is pretty good, plenty good enough for my kids. But it might be that LaRhonda didn't want the day-to-dayness of mothering. Or it might be that I just think that because of the girl I grew up with. Just like her own mother, she has a big house now with a whole wing for kids that's empty. Both her daughters live in California, one of her sons is in Texas, another in Denver. I see her in her Mercedes tooling around from one restaurant to another. She works longer hours than I do, managing everything she owns. She tells everybody that she's sixty, which is funny because I'll be sixty-five next birthday, and I can remember when we were both the same age. But whatever, as the kids say.

The old-timers were skeptical, when I first came back to practice medicine, especially the men. "I'm not letting Bud Miller's skinny little girl, who used to serve me eggs and hash browns, take a look at my prostate," one of them said at the diner one day, not knowing I was in a back booth. On my way to the register I tapped him on the shoulder and said, "You want to take your prostate somewhere else, Mr. Helprin, you're welcome to do it," and the whole place cracked up. But they got over it, most of them, and I have more patients than I can handle with all the new people. It's good, being a doctor in a place like this. A little girl comes in with a sore throat, and you let her listen to your heart with your stethoscope, and fifteen years later you run into her mother at the market and find out she's declared premed at the state university. A woman cries on your examining table after a miscarriage and then a year or two later she brings her first baby in for a checkup.

But the same things that make it good can make it hard, too. I told LaRhonda I was putting her daughter Serafina on the pill for her cramps and her skin, but it was really because Serafina had been having sex since she was twelve and I figured her mother would kill her if she got pregnant. I went to Mrs. Farrell's class to talk about careers in science and medicine and I looked around the room and knew which honor student had cut marks up and down her arms under her long-sleeved shirt. When a seventeen-year-old who played on the soccer team hung himself in a patch of forest above the reservoir I was maybe the only one who wasn't surprised, although I did wonder whether his mother knew more about his being gay than she let on. My son gave me a hard look after that one, and I recognized it as a look I'd given my mother over the years, a look that said, You know things but you don't do anything about them. Maybe my mother would have said the same thing to me that I wanted to say to Ian: it's a lot harder to save people than you think it is.

You know too much, doing what I do, sometimes too much for your own good. Three months after Nora left for college I looked across the kitchen table at my husband. The amber speckles in his dark brown eyes maybe made it plainer that the whites had turned yellow. He died of liver cancer the same week the daffodils finally flowered after a fierce winter. I held him up on the den sofa so he could see the flowers outside.

"All I want to look at is you, Meems," he said. No one, not even my father, not even my children, has ever loved me the way that man loved me, that's for sure. There's something satisfying in being loved that hard, maybe more than loving that hard yourself. I don't know.

Life is full of mysteries. What would have happened if Mrs. Farrell's friend hadn't told her about the scholarship? What if Steven had already sent that girl home when I showed up at that little house? Did the tiny mummy in Ruth's suitcase wind up there before or after she moved into the house behind us? If before, is that why she turned out the way she did, a mummy herself in that clapboard crypt? If after—well, that's a tougher one for me. There was only one man who spent any real time in Ruth's house, which was really his house lent out to his wife's little sister. That's the man who died there, in one of the easy chairs, who preferred being there after his stroke to being in his own home. I wonder if Ruth had always been in love with Buddy, and if Buddy loved her back. I wonder if Miriam knew. I wonder if she knew about her sister and the baby. She was a nurse, after all. I thought my mother knew everything. She didn't show a thing, when I stumbled off that drop-down ladder and back into the kitchen that day. She didn't say, Mary Margaret, what is it, although I must have looked, in her words, like death eating a cracker.

That little dried-up thing was shrouded in newspaper. I could have looked at the date on that paper. I didn't. That's another mystery to me. Did it not occur to me, or did I not want to? I had my chances. I didn't look at that newspaper when I first opened the suitcase, and I didn't look at it the next morning, when I went back to the farm for the last time. I'd been up all night, thinking about whether just before they flooded the valley the state would send in police, or inspectors, to make sure everyone was out. I pictured one of them going to the attic, opening the case, calling someone, doing those things they do when a body turns up hidden in a house.

Just after dawn I drove into the driveway. It was so quiet. People always said the valley was quiet. But I knew its background sounds, the old truck climbing the ridge, the burr of a baler, the cows, the cats. All gone now. There was the sound of crickets, and a buck cropping the grass near the road barked, coughed, and ran off when I stopped the car and got out.

I carried the vanity case down the ladder, trying not to hold it too close, which wasn't rational but I wasn't dealing with a rational thing. The cap to the well behind Ruth's house had a heavy padlock on it, and I had the key. I had my father's whole ring of keys, a heavy steel ring that he'd made himself with maybe fifty keys on it. Ones for our house and Ruth's, ones for the barns and the shed, for the basement where the Janssons kept their equipment that my father repaired and the garage where the Langers kept their mower that he worked on whenever it was spitting, keys to tractors and trucks all over the valley so that when something went sideways with a carburetor or a front-end loader he'd be ready even if no one was home. I guess you could call it a circle of trust, that ring of keys. Hard to imagine today giving one man the keys to so many different buildings and machines. None of them had been used to open anything in years. "Nothing as useless," my father used to say, "as a key that doesn't open anything anymore."

I used the key to open the padlock on the well cover. Then I opened the key ring and attached it to the leather handle of the vanity case and dropped it in. There was a splash, and then silence. The flashlight showed nothing but flat black water. I shoved the padlock back in place, hard, and listened to it close.

For years my mind skittered around what I'd found in that case like a bug after the light gets turned on. I could have asked Ruth about it when she was dying, or I could have asked my mother. I just couldn't do it. It seemed cruel somehow, to try to cast light on that sad small dried-up thing and whatever the story was behind it. But it was always there in my mind. Nothing is as it seems. There's a news flash for you.

I know from the Internet that there's a Thomas A. Miller who is a dentist in Mobile, Alabama, and a Thomas A. Miller who sells real estate in Delaware, and one who is a student at the state university right here, and one who died in 1896 and is buried in Montpelier, Vermont, and there is a picture of his tombstone. There's a Thomas A. Miller who is serving a life sentence for murder, and God forgive me, that's the one whose picture I looked for, but he was black and only eighteen. I like to think that in Texas or Maine or Oregon there's a Thomas A. Miller who maybe changed his name or just lives off the grid and who remembers me the way I remember him, young and happy. I like to think that maybe he uses a computer the same way I do and he finds Mary Margaret Miller, MD, and he says to himself, Well, corncob, you did okay. There are a lot of reasons why I didn't change my last name after I got married. That was one of them. Another was because, even before I knew I'd fly back here like a boomerang, I knew that I was the last Miller of Miller's Valley.

There's too much missing people in my life, that's for sure. I miss my mother, who died with her hand in mine when she was ninety, two years after her sister had. Ruth had a cough that wouldn't quit, and I was pretty sure that it was lung cancer, but she wouldn't go to the hospital for any of the tests or any of the treatments. I took care of her at home, and she went quietly, too. Her last word was Miriam. My mother's last word didn't really come out, was just a movement of her lips. I knew what it was, though. I could have told you what it would be all those years that she and I were sitting together, drinking tea, talking about the hospital when she was still working there and then when they rebuilt and expanded it and she volunteered at the reception desk and I was on staff. Maybe even if you'd asked that little girl listening at the heating vent what her mother's last word would be, if you could get her to the point where she could imagine something as unimaginable as her mother's death, she would have guessed that those dry lips would work themselves around the *T* and then the rest would lie on her tongue like a communion wafer before her last breath passed over the word *Tommy* like a long sad sigh.

I miss Donald and my mother, and I miss Ruth, and the Langers, and my father, I still miss my father. It's the little things that get you. I go into the toolbox to hang a new spice rack and can't find the right screwdriver, and I hear a tongue clicking in my ear and know it's Buddy Miller, saying to himself, How did I raise a girl who doesn't keep her tools handy? I miss Callie, too, who comes up for holidays and a weekend visit a couple of times a year. Clifton bought her a little house in California when he started getting steady work out there as an actor, and it was nice, with a tangerine tree in the backyard. None of us could get over that, that Callie could go out back and just pick herself a bowl of tangerines, except for Donald, who'd lived there himself. Callie said they were the best tangerines she'd ever had, but she and

Doug didn't use the house much and eventually she told Clifton to sell. The two of them just stayed with him when they went out there. When Clifton won an Emmy for that TV show he did, he held up his award and said, "This one's for you, Dad. I'm your boy." Callie thought he meant Doug, and maybe he did. But I don't think so. I spent more time watching his son be dazzled by Tommy than she did, or maybe she couldn't see it because she was still angry, for getting dazzled herself, even for a couple of nights.

I don't really miss the Miller's Valley I used to know, the one in which I grew up, my very own drowned town. It's been gone a long time now, almost as long as my brother has. They're talking about having a big celebration for the fiftieth anniversary of the recreation area when it comes around, and that'll clinch it. If something's been around fifty years, it's been around forever. Most people think it's always been there. They run fishing boats and go ice skating and sit in folding chairs and look out over the place where we all lived and it's just water to them, as far as the eye can see. I guess it's just water to me, too. I think there were a lot of reasons my mother was satisfied to see water close over the top of the valley and the farm, some that I don't like to examine too closely, but one was that she worried that I'd come flying back out of habit or duty and she wanted me to leave. But no one ever leaves the town where they grew up, not really, even if they go. When I talked to Cissy about Andover, when I was a kid, I thought her life, her past, her childhood, all of it was buried down there under the water. I didn't understand that it was above the surface, in her, the way mine is in me.

The pipe narrows at one end and opens at the other. Donald gone, and his grandfather, and my mother and father and Ruth, and LaRhonda's parents, too. But then there's Nora and Ian, and their children, and all the kids I see on the streets and in the drugstore, the kids of my kids' classmates, the grandchildren of my own. Lots of people leave here, that's for sure, but people stay, too. And some are like me. They circle back.

I never go over that way, to the recreation area. Never have, in all these years, even when the kids wanted to water-ski or swim. I let them go with someone else. I don't even drive by there. But every couple of years I have a dream. I dive down into green water and I use my arms to push myself far below the surface and when I open my eyes there are barn roofs and old fences and a chimney and a silo and sometimes I sense that Tommy's there, too, and the corn can, and my father's workbench, and a little tan vanity case floating slowly by. But I swim in the opposite direction, back toward the light, because I have to come up for air. I still need to breathe.

## ABOUT THE AUTHOR

ANNA QUINDLEN is a novelist and journalist whose work has appeared on fiction, nonfiction, and self-help bestseller lists. She is the author of eight novels: *Object Lessons, One True Thing, Black and Blue, Blessings, Rise and Shine, Every Last One, Still Life with Bread Crumbs,* and *Miller's Valley.* Her memoir, *Lots of Candles, Plenty of Cake,* published in 2012, was a number one *New York Times* bestseller. Her book *A Short Guide to a Happy Life* has sold more than a million copies. While a columnist at *The New York Times* she won the Pulitzer Prize and published two collections, *Living Out Loud* and *Thinking Out Loud.* Her *Newsweek* columns were collected in *Loud and Clear.*

AnnaQuindlen.net
Facebook.com/AnnaQuindlen
@AnnaQuindlen